PRAISE

THE TELS

"[Black] is one of those writers that we who worship this genre look for every time we pick up the novel of an author who is new to us."

"*The Tels* is SPELLBINDING! Paul Black weaves a futuristic tale with characters you will never forget. This ambitious epic is a thought-provoking and romantic story that leaves you wondering how Black dreamed up this scary sensual new world that we may one day be living in. Like "2001: A Space Odyssey" this novels tells us things about our future that feel eerily believable. You won't be able to put this novel down and when you do you'll be hoping for more. Black is a WRITER TO WATCH!"

~ *Jan Wieringa*

"The biggest complaint about science fiction is that there is always too much science and not enough fiction. In *The Tels* Paul Black brilliantly combines the two in a novel that is almost too plausible...Blending sex, government intrigue and a new reality aren't easy tasks but Black is up to it. Taking us for a ride through a world totally different from our own and yet with the emotions that aren't going to change between now and 2109...*The Tels* doesn't let go and stays with you after the last page."

~ *Leslie Rigoulot, Continental Features Syndicate*

"...a GREAT READ, full of suspense and action...."

~ *Dallas Entertainment Guide*

"...a ride through a world totally different from our own and yet with the emotions that aren't going to change between now and 2109."

"This story by Paul Black is as STRONG AND WELL WRITTEN as any of the stories of my heroes: Robert Heinlein, Isaac Asimov, Andre Norton, or Anne McCaffrey. He is one of those writers that we who worship this genre look for every time we pick up the novel of an author who is new to us...The CHARACTERS COME ALIVE for you. You feel right along with them. You can believe the decisions they make. And best of all, nothing is clear-cut and simple. The story brings us to a strong ending while leaving us with the desire for more...I recommend *The Tels* to every lover of sci-fi. Good work, Paul! Welcome to my bookshelves!"

~ *John Strange, thecityweb.com*

"The creepy thing about this book is that it reads like this all could actually be happening...I couldn't put it down!"

~ *Ann Alexander, The USA Film Festival*

"As a debut novel it's IMPRESSIVE WORK. You can totally visualize the action from start to finish...the ending takes you completely by surprise. Paul Black writes fiction with a style and edge you'd expect from a writer with a dozen books under his belt...BRAVO!"

~ *Margie Bowles, 1400 Words*

"*The Tels* is an addictive read...
manages to capture the reader from the first
ten pages... *The Tels* has it all."

"...I was totally hooked...*The Tels* is for anyone who loves a good story, with LOTS OF ACTION AND GREAT CHARACTERS."

~ *Jo Ann Holt, OC Tribune*

"*The Tels* is like no other book I've ever read. It's the first story to posture telekinetics in a way that's UNIQUE AND CHILLINGLY REAL... part *X-Files,* part cyber-thriller, it's sure to become a cult classic."

~ *Joe Goodwin, Gracie Films*

The Tels is an ADDICTIVE READ from first time novelist, Paul Black, a promising new storyteller on the sci-fi scene. He manages to capture the reader in the first ten pages. He introduces us to a set of intriguing characters in a totally believable possible future. There is a grittiness and sensuality to his writing that pours out of every word in the book. Whether it,s his description of the preparation of a good meal, the seduction of a beautiful woman, or a fight to the death, THE TELS HAS IT ALL. Even people who don,t read sci-fi will want to read this book. The action is great and would make one hell of a movie. Is Hollywood listening? Paul Black has a winner on his hands. I can hardly wait for the next installment.

~ *Cynthia A., About Towne, ITCN*

NOVEL INSTINCTS PUBLISHING
1400 Turtle Creek Blvd. Suite 140
Dallas, Texas 75207
www.novelinstincts.com

This book can be ordered on the web, at www.barnesandnoble.com or at www.amazon.com.

ISBN: 0-9726007-0-1
Library of Congress Control Number: 2003092612
Printed in the United States of America.

Cover photo: PhotoDisc / GettyOne.
Author photo by Michael Barley.

the tels

PAUL BLACK

NOVEL INSTINCTS

Acknowledgements ~ I would like to thank the following people whose help was immeasurable in the writing of this book...you know who you are and what you did: Kara, Shannon, Mary, Amy Jo, Doreen, Mike, Dennis, Tim and Tina, Jan, Scott, Susan, Jimmy and Vicki and their lovely home in Taos, Patrick, Mike and Max, Dave and Susan and their lovely home in Colorado Springs. You all were very patient, listening to my rambling, and putting up with the rough drafts and my butchered English.

To Trish, without whose support, patience and love, this book would have never been written...and besides, she came up with Jacob Whitehorse.

To William Gibson, who started it all.

With special thanks to Jay Johnson, whose help and contribution made the book better.

And finally, to Bryan, whose honest and critical assessment kept the book in check. You believed in the concept and my ability. I will be forever grateful. You're the kind of friend most people wished they had.

July 2002 ~ Dallas, TX.

FOR TRISH

~

2095

Thank you, God... 1

Jonathan felt his heart beginning to beat harder with each sudden jerk of the toggle, and the booming bass emanating from the car's MuzSat link only intensified the pounding in his chest. The Interway was clear, and Tarris piloted the car like he was raging on some biovid game, high into the bonus levels. He calmly hummed as they slipped through the hot Midwestern night.

"Well?!" Jonathan yelled over the deafening sounds of Nymphia Scooter Pie, this week's flavor for Tarris.

"Well what?" Tarris shot back and brought the music down a click.

Tarris had been Jonathan's friend ever since the "event," three years ago. He was older, cooler and could drive. And if you could drive, then in this little town you were free.

"How does it feel?"

“Oh, the car?” Tarris asked dryly.

Even Tarris’s name was cool. He was of the generation whose parents had abandoned the typical names that had permeated the culture for the last hundred and fifty years or so in favor of techno-names. Sharp-edged names. Names that melded the cultures, even the world, into a standard, much like the Internet did a century earlier. And he was Jonathan’s friend and brother figure, even, he dared think, a father figure. At least as much a father figure as a 17-year-old can be.

“The car handles as it should,” he said.

“Yeah?...” Jonathan pressed.

“Fucking right it does!” And with that, Tarris asked the car to accelerate beyond the legal Interway limit.

“How did you do that? I thought these models were unalterable.”

“Don’t worry, Jonny, just a little retroengineering trick my dad taught me.” (Jonathan hated that version of his name.) “My dad says that even after alterations, the biochip’s constructs can’t be permanent. They just regenerate and reconfigure to the factory specs and before you know it, original car. Just like it was right out of the tank.”

The car Tarris piloted was as much a car of the last century as milk that was actually milked. Or a building that was actually built. The Biolution of the mid-21st century had changed much of life. The way the world was headed in the first half of the century, who would have guessed it? The Biolution was predicted, but nobody expected it would happen this fast. And with consequences such as the event.

It was hard for Jonathan to hold back, to swallow the pain

every time the event was mentioned. Every time he thought about it. He swallowed. Hard. Thinking he could gulp down the fear. But he knew what would come next.

The tears.

He used to run. Anywhere where he could be alone. Then came the rush of memories, of faces, of a life he knew he would never have. The stolen life he would never reflect upon. The life he should have had with his mother and father. And their Hawaiian home where he used to play, three years ago.

Where he had played was now what the world called "ground zero," still dominating the news. Even if Jonathan could, he would never be able to outrun the event. In many respects, it forever changed the world. Much as, the history pads said, the atom bomb did in the mid-20th century. But what the pads left unsaid is what his grandfather called the "collateral damage." The shattered lives of thousands of relatives and friends left behind, alive.

No one saw it coming. The world's collective fear of terrorism had waned by the mid-21st century. Individualism and information had been interwoven, due in part to the Internet revolution. But the Biolution made the bandwidth issues of the late-20th and early 21st centuries a thing of the past. The world had been lulled into a false sense of security, thinking there wasn't any problem the collective intelligence networks of the G-12 couldn't find and solve. The Biochip ushered in a flood of technology that changed almost every aspect of life. Information didn't flow; it ran like a torrent. And the world, it seemed, rode along helplessly like tourists shooting rapids in a giant, guideless river raft.

The Biolution affected everything in its path. Like a monstrous

Midwestern thunderstorm, it swept across the human landscape. Even the most sacred of resources could not escape its effect. The corpulent oil industry that dominated the world since the late-19th century was irrevocably changed. Gas now could be synthetically made with biotechnology, cheaply and without end. The power of the Arab nations disappeared almost overnight and, with it, the collective grip they held on the throat of the world. This demotion in world ranking was more than their Arab pride could take. Their radical fringe elements joined forces and set out to teach the world a lesson in Arab anger. No one knew how important this lesson would be.

~

"Hey, are you crying, Jonny boy?" Tarris asked, glancing at his younger friend while piloting the vehicle through a series of sharp "S" curves.

"No! I just got crap in my eye. I need to raise this window; your driving is freaking me."

"Aw, don't worry, Jonny boy," Tarris said with that look.

Jonathan knew that look.

"Tarris is captain tonight, we're free to sail!"

"Are you riding?" Jonathan asked, though he already knew the answer. For all his strengths, Tarris had one weakness. He loved to ride. But the drugs of the latter century had evolved into a new form. A bioform. And it scared Jonathan when Tarris was riding. The phrase was true. You didn't take a drug, the drug took you. For a ride. Good or bad, you rode. And because of their biomatrix structures, each biodrug reacted differently with each individual. The effects were only somewhat predictable. That was their allure. The unknowing. The surprise inside each box. That's also why some called it Cracker Jack. Jack, for short.

"Just a little tonight...come on, it's our first time sailing this piece. I gotta have an edge, little buddy," Tarris begged. "You understand, don't you?"

Jonathan understood all too well. It wasn't the first time he had been along for a ride. Usually it went smoothly. The Tarris Jonathan knew just became more of himself. Funnier, sillier – and the girls loved this Tarris. But if it went badly, the friend he knew disappeared. The bioconstructs of the drug altered his persona, and it wasn't pretty. But tonight looked clear. Clear of the Tarris Jonathan had come to call The Mean Man.

"Hottttt damn," Tarris screamed as he, the drug, and the car all synced into perfect harmony, "let's sail toooonight!" And as his hand passed over the car's interface pad, he lightly touched the BR button, changed the ratio, caused the car to punch forward and threw Jonathan back against the seat. Tarris pushed the car to its design limits, weaving in and out of the Interway traffic, throwing the boys from side to side. The scene outside the window blurred, and the car seemed to float above the ground through the "S" curves. Tarris was piloting like it was his last ride. Jonathan couldn't tell if the cause was the altered state of the car's system or of Tarris, but whatever it was, the car reacted with pinpoint accuracy to all of his commands. After 12 miles of riding Tarris's high, Jonathan couldn't take any more.

"Tarris!" Jonathan screamed. "Tarris, please slow down!" He gripped the leather, leaving indents no biochips could reconstruct, and as he watched his friend reach the height of his ride, he began to pray. He hadn't prayed since the death of his parents. He had given up on a God he thought had abandoned him. Had abandoned man. What kind of God would allow something like the event to happen? Right now, though, he was reconsidering. If there was a God, Jonathan could have used just a little of his grace tonight.

"Now that's what I call a fucking killer ride!" the 17-year-old blared. And with that, Tarris grazed the ratio button again, and the car eased into legal speed without so much as a change in G.

"Open those eyes, little buddy," Tarris said. He piloted the car off the Interway and into the urban flow.

Jonathan looked up from his conversation with the Almighty and saw that his friend wasn't riding anymore. He couldn't tell specifically how he knew; he just knew when Tarris was coming off. Or "jerking off" as Tarris liked to put it.

"This is your captain speaking. That was one fucking killer ride, folks." Tarris burst out laughing.

"Yeah, you were the captain tonight, Tarris," Jonathan nervously agreed.

"And you...you're sitting there praying...." Tarris roared as he slapped the car's toggle to a beat only he was hearing. Neither of them saw the lights of the two-ton recycle hauler entering their road's interface space.

"SHIT, TARRIS!!"

Jonathan's heart almost exploded from his chest as he turned and realized the fate that awaited them both. In the 20-foot space between their car and the poly-bio grillwork of the hauler, Jonathan saw what was surely the end of his life. No force on earth was going to stop it.

"Motherfucker!" Tarris screamed, and his hands danced on

the protocol pad of the vehicle. But it was too late. In the chaos of the moment, Tarris had tried everything he knew, which, at 17, wasn't much. Looking past Jonathan's head to the hauler's enormous grill, all he knew now was that it was over.

While Jonathan stared at the last thing he would see in his life, he felt his fear transform. The blood rushed from his head and an intense heat took over his body. In the nanosecond before the hauler's grill impacted the window, Jonathan's vision changed to white, then to colors that twinkled, then swirled. Then it all collapsed to black.

Dead black.

~

To Jonathan, the black space seemed like purgatory. He woke to Tarris shaking his arm and an immense pain gripping not only his head, but his mind.

"Jonathan! Jonathan, wake up!" Tarris said.

Jonathan could hardly make out his friend's voice. As Tarris came into focus his face was white, but his demeanor was calm.

"Hey little guy," Tarris asked softly. "Are you all right?"

Jonathan surfaced to the moment to find himself, Tarris and the car unharmed. He pulled himself up to look out what he thought would be a shattered window of high-impact plastic only to see that the hauler was facing them about 50 feet away. Its grillwork undamaged, it just sat there, chugging like a bull ready to charge.

"What happened?" Jonathan asked through a cough, his throat dry and raw.

"Your captain saved the day! Now let's get the hell out of here!" Tarris jerked the toggle, and the car obeyed.

It was quiet inside the cabin as the car hummed along the surface of the road. Its systems were struggling with the recent input of event data that seemed to defy known physics. Both boys reflected on what could have been.

"What happened Tarris...really?"

"Well..." Tarris confessed, "I thought we were gone for sure, but the car just jerked itself about and that recycler bounced off us, sort of."

"What?..."

"Hey, who cares what happened, just that it did. Or we would be a tangle of biomatter right now, you got that, buddy? Hey, are you okay?" Tarris reached over to wipe away the little river of blood coming from Jonathan's right nostril. He was doing his big brother routine.

Jonathan jerked away. "I'm okay. I must have hit something."

"Really? I saw you when we were spinning, and you didn't hit a damn thing. In fact, you didn't even move."

It was quiet again in the cabin. Both boys just stared straight ahead. Tarris was watching the system readouts imbedded in the windshield as he piloted the car home. Jonathan's head pounded, and his clothes were drenched in sweat. He knew the captain hadn't done a damn thing to save this ship. But if Tarris hadn't saved it, who had? Or what had? Jonathan leaned back into the coolness of the leather, and only one thought managed to come into his pain-addled brain.

Thank you, God.

2109

Working the crowd... 2

"What the hell is she doing?" Jimbo asked.

"It is hard to say," his partner answered.

James McCarris, or Jimbo as his friends called him, was a Level 5 – a pretty low level for a Recruiter, but Jimbo had shown promise and the patience required of the job. His partner, on the other hand, was a Level 8. Very rare and very powerful. He was considered the best of the best. There were no other levels that a human could achieve. Of course, Levels 9 and 10 existed, but only as the last levels of the 1 through 10 Tel chart. And Level 10 was considered unattainable. Beyond the human genome. Beyond evolution. Beyond comprehension. But there were a few in the government who believed the day would come. Far off for sure. Possibly in a century or two, though, a human would go beyond the mere movement of an object, beyond the multi-grav aspects to change physical properties, most likely at the molecular level.

These were the Tels, a group of humans who had split from the pack, who had begun an evolutionary divergence from their brothers and sisters. They were headed down a new genetic path, one that would take them into another realm.

A telekinetic realm.

They were discovered in the 20th century after World War Two. Reports came out of the war of men and women who had performed extraordinary acts of strength disguised as courage. Some seemingly had moved objects without lifting a finger. After the war, the rumors continued to circulate: a child lifts a car off a dying parent, a woman stops a combine from shredding her son. These reports had always been part of the culture, but a skeptical world had dismissed them as tabloid fodder. But there were those in the governments of the superpowers who took these rumors seriously. They discovered the potential of these people. They organized branches of their governments that even their military didn't know about – so secretive, they existed in shadow. The belief was that these new humans had the potential to be the saving factor for mankind. They were the next leap. The race that would take humans to the stars.

In America, this branch was known simply as the Agency.

~

"Is she trying to move that truck? Shit, partner, she's only six." Jimbo whistled and made a clicking sound with his mouth.

His partner hated that sound. It always reconfirmed that Jimbo was from the South. *It must be,* he often thought, *genetically encoded in Southerners to make this sound after what they think is a profound statement.* To him it sounded more like Jimbo was trying to get a horse to move.

"I do not think that this little girl has the potential," Jimbo's partner said, tapping the netpad off and slipping it back into his overcoat pocket. "Her time would be better spent playing with her dolls." He turned to walk back to their car.

"Why aren't they qualifying these Potentials," Jimbo complained, "before we spend six months with them?"

"Because currently there is no other way to effectively monitor Potentials without disclosing who we are or exposing either ourselves or them to harm. We cannot just abduct them, run the biodiogs and dump them back into their lives. You know the Agency's directive as well as I do!"

Jimbo knew it. Every Tel knew it. It was the key to their existence and survival. Directive 1: Never expose the Agency, yourself or a fellow member to a Potential, until such time as a Recruiter affirms the readiness of the Potential.

"Our work here is done," Jimbo's partner said, opening the car door.

"Back to the hotel?"

"No, I am hungry. Let us stop and get some dinner, shall we?" He quietly lit a cigarette, leaned back against the seat and piloted the car into the Interway, never touching a single system's button or the toggle stick.

Jimbo had gotten used to his partner's idiosyncrasies. As a Level 8, his partner could do things most Tels couldn't. Driving a car without the physical interface all humans required, for instance. Now starting a car, even driving it, was simple and achievable for most

Level 5's. But to navigate the complex Interway, to dialog with the Interway's control systems, to smoke a cigarette, and to hold an intense conversation – that was reserved for a Level 8.

"How do you do that?" Jimbo asked enviously.

"Do what?" his partner answered. He stared out the window and let the smoke linger in the air before he mentally condensed the particles into a speck the size of a pinhead that floated gently to the car floor. "Smoke?"

"No. You know what I'm talking about..."

"You mean do what I am doing right now?"

"Yes!" Jimbo said impatiently. "It's nerve-racking. What if you miss a data input? What if your mind wanders for just a millisecond? What if something comes up in the road you aren't aware of?"

"Aware?" his partner demanded.

Jimbo knew he had crossed the line.

"What do you know of being aware?"

"Look...I..."

"That is your problem," his partner said coolly, settling back into the seat. "You are too busy looking instead of sensing."

Here comes the lesson, Jimbo thought.

"If you spent less time using your vision sense and developed your seventh sense, you would not be asking such questions.... You would already have the answer."

And he was right. It took more than the gift. It took a deep, genetic, almost instinctual sensing of your abilities. Only a few Tels had this capacity.

Oh, lucky me, I get the Dean of Telekinesis as my partner.

But Jimbo knew deep down, his partner could teach him well.

~

It was late in the evening, and the streets were void of the current of traffic that made Chicago one of the busiest cities in the world. Jimbo's partner deftly piloted the car to the curb's edge. Another Recruiter had recommended the restaurant to the senior Tel. He had said that it was...special.

"You sure this is good?" Jimbo asked. His partner fired off a look that Jimbo could swear he felt in the base of his neck. "You know, you don't have to keep demonstrating your supreme powers, oh Great One," he said, reaching to rub where he thought he felt the sensation.

"I am sorry, James," his partner answered. With that, he took his cigarette from his mouth, snuffed it out and let it fall into the recycling container at the corner. He never used his hands.

"Gotta watch that," Jimbo warned. "We're in public now."

"Yes we are, a public of which we are not a part."

"Yeah...well, let's go eat." Jimbo turned his collar up to the brisk Lake Michigan wind, and they stepped into the restaurant.

The exposed brick walls of the old renovated warehouse had captured every smell from every dish, and the cool of the street gave way to the inviting warmth from the kitchen. A young man was busy busing a table. He turned to greet the new customers with that "I'll be right with you" look.

"Smells great, I'm starved," Jimbo said. His partner said nothing and kept watching the young man.

"Welcome to Kortel's, gentlemen," the young man said,

wiping his hands on his well-stained apron. "Two for dinner?"

"Yes, please," Jimbo's partner said, removing his coat, and they were led to a small two-top by a window.

"Man, I could use a drink," Jimbo said.

"Hmmm..." his partner mused, sitting down.

Jimbo knew that tone. "What are you sensing?"

"I am not sure...someone in here..."

Jimbo leaned closer to read his partner's actions. He was in hunt mode, and his Level 8 senses were on point. Level 8's not only had the gift, but in some cases they had the sense. His partner read the menu, but he was more focused on who was triggering the "effect," as members called it. The effect was the displacement of the gravitational field created by all Tels, Potentials or Members. Some in the Agency thought Level 8's sensed an electromagnetic change much the way dogs and cats sensed the coming of an earthquake. Others believed it was genetic. An innate sensitivity to their own species. Their own kind. Whatever it was, his partner was truly intrigued by this one.

"Is the Force strong, Obi Wan?" Jimbo asked.

"What?"

"Never mind. Ancient trivia. Come on, let's order and then you can get back to hunting."

The menu was simple, but the dishes were complex. As Jimbo looked around the restaurant, he saw that everything was edge food.

"You see what I see?" he declared.

"Yes, I do." his partner said. "Want to leave?"

"No, no. I'm too damn hungry now to go looking for another place. I'll get over it."

"I thought you were against biofoods."

"Yes and no. I know it customizes the flavors to your body's chemical profile, and I do like the unique combinations, but..."

"But what?"

"It's just..."

"It is just that you are a Southern boy who likes the way foods used to taste. Like mom used to make. Am I right?"

"Very funny..."

"If you must know, I tend to concur with you."

"Well, I'll be damned," Jimbo exclaimed. "I never thought I'd see the day you would come down to my level."

"Oh, I believe we share more than you think."

"Oh really? Like what?..."

"Gentlemen," the young man interrupted, "can I start you off with a drink this evening?" He was looking distracted as he watched the workings of the restaurant.

"You bet. I'll take a beer – draft if you've got it," Jimbo said.

"Nothing for me, thank you," his partner said, carefully looking the young man up and down like a med scanner.

"Very good, I'll be back with your drink and tell you our specials then. Take a look at the appetizers tonight, gentlemen. I think you'll find we have a little something for everyone."

Jimbo waited for him to leave. "Will you loosen up, please!" he scolded. "Oh, I'm sorry, we're in hunt mode, aren't we..."

"We are not, but yes...I am." His partner continued to track the young man to the kitchen. He watched him place the order into his netpad, all the while working the crowd like he owned the place.

"It's him, isn't it?" Jimbo asked, following his partner's stare.

"I am not sure...the heat from the kitchen and the fact that I am famished makes isolating the effect difficult. I do believe, though, he might be just a 'Displacer.'"

A Displacer was Agency slang for someone who displaced the gravitational field around themselves but could no more move an object than a dog could. Level 8's usually could tell the difference between a Displacer and a true Potential.

"Maybe I could use a drink after all." Jimbo's partner trained his attention at the young man, who instantly stopped what he was doing, looked over to their table and began walking back. This time he paid no attention at all to the crowd.

"Is...there something you gentlemen need?" He had a puzzled look on his face.

"Why yes," Jimbo's partner said, "you are so perceptive. I would like a Scotch, a house blend would do, thank you. Oh, and with ice only, please."

"Very good, sir." The young man slowly turned to go, his gaze momentarily lingering on the Recruiter.

"That was totally out of protocol! Are you crazy? Fucking jerking him like that," declared Jimbo.

"Yes, yes I know..." his partner said, casually looking over the menu. "I think I will have the steak tonight. And you?"

"I'm waiting to hear the specials, or can you sense them for me?"

His partner slowly looked up over the top of his menu.

"Okay, okay...lighten up, for God's sake," Jimbo said. "You're too serious sometimes. You have to relax once in a while. You said it yourself, you can't pick up on him because you're tired and hungry. Give your Level 8 self a break now and then."

Jimbo's partner only partially listened. This Level 5 Tel, assigned to him just under a year ago, served his needs, but what he really needed was someone on his own level. Someone like his old partner. Now that Indian could hunt.

"Here you go, gentlemen," the young man interrupted, "a draft of our best beer, locally brewed, I might add. And a Scotch for you, sir." He set both drinks down and pulled out his netpad. "Tonight, we have a roasted duck, altered to your special tastes, and the fish is developed from the finest biofarms in Canada. Both come with an asparagus salad and roasted corn from an actual soil farm not too far from here. All of our foods, gentlemen, come with their genetic seals, assurance of their purity and flavor."

"I will have your filet, young man, and please prepare it the old-fashioned way. You do have an actual flame grill?" Jimbo's partner asked.

"Oh, yes sir, we do. Probably the only one in the area!"

"That is what I was told. And my friend will have?..."

"I'll have the fish," Jimbo said. "What does it simulate?"

"It will be swordfish tonight. It's especially good, if I do say so. I programmed it myself."

"Great, I'll have that!"

"Very good, I'll have your salads out in a moment." He turned and headed toward the kitchen while entering the order into his netpad.

"I don't know," Jimbo said. "He doesn't seem that special to me."

"You might be right on this one, James. Then again, he could be The Infinite Tel. We never really know at first sense, do we?"

"The Infinite Tel? Have you been drinking?" Jimbo asked. "Oh, I guess you are."

They both laughed as they leaned back and took sips from their drinks.

~

Jimbo's partner had been trained to believe there were no Tels greater than him. All Level 8's were. And this training was effective. As a young Tel entering the Agency, he had been separated from the general group. They had said he was special. Unique. And they had a reason to cull him from his peers. His level was well-suited for "certain" assignments. Only later would he find their true use for his uniqueness. But by then, it would be too late.

"Hey," Jimbo said, "when we get back to the Agency, I'm going to take a little time off. How 'bout you?"

"I do not believe I will."

"All work and no play makes for a dull Tel..."

"Yes, well, I have a certain commitment with the Agency."

"Yeah, what's up with that anyway? You're always referencing 'your commitment.'" Jimbo mockingly gestured quotations with his hands.

"Get to my level and you will understand."

"Here you go," the young man said, returning suddenly. "Only the finest in natural soil-grown salads. The dirt in this area is some of the cleanest we've ever scanned."

"Say," Jimbo inquired, "who has the bioknowledge to create these dishes? I thought this kind of food was reserved for New York or Tokyo?"

"We're asked that all the time. Actually I'm the one. This is my restaurant. I'm so sorry, I'm Jonathan Kortel. I'm principle partner and head chef. Many of the dishes here are my own personal coding." He shook Jimbo's hand, but stopped at his partner's. "Have we met before?"

"No, young man, I do not believe we have," he answered.

Jonathan hesitated. He reached to take the senior Tel's hand, and an arc of static electricity jumped between them just before their hands met. They held for a moment, each man curiously studying the other.

"Well, enjoy your salads," Jonathan said nervously. "Monis will bring you your entrees." He summoned a young, bald, street urchin of a girl to their table. He spoke quietly into her ear and rushed off to the kitchen. This time, he didn't work the crowd.

The kitchen... 3

"Jonathan, you look like you just saw a ghost!" declared Toto, the sous chef.

"Or he just saw my ex-wife!" answered Hector, the big Mexican who held reign over Kitchen Kortel.

Jonathan smiled and reverted to being an owner. "Yeah, that's real damn funny, Hector. How many tables are left? Let's hustle it up people, we've got five eight-tops and twelve four-tops, solid."

Jonathan wasn't worried, though. He and Hector went back. Their days of trial in the trendy cafe scene had given them their chops. Those early years had been rough, and to prove it, Hector boasted the burn scars no bioderm could regenerate. They developed a symbiotic relationship. One couldn't perform without the other. Jonathan knew the code and could crack it to make a dish special. But Hector had the magic to bring hydro-grown biopaste to a level that was beyond food. It was art. Tired of working the in-today, gone-tomorrow pace of big city restaurants, they decided to strike out on their own.

Jonathan had inherited talent for writing code and the delicate encryptions necessary to develop complex food algorithms from his parents. They had been independent research scientists working on the island of Hawaii's alarming loss of plant life. Yet, Jonathan didn't really need to work. The settlement from their death and the money left to him by his grandparents meant he could have slid through life. But that wasn't his way.

For his part, Hector had grown up in the streets outside the largest urban center on the planet, Mexico City. His father was a chef, as his grandfather was before him. And little Hector had been groomed to be a chef, but a chef of the new era in food. The bio era. Hector had the talent, but it was evident early on that his promise lay on the organic side, not the biotech side. He amazed even the old chefs of the city, mastering dishes that would have taken others years to learn. Eschewing the traditional route through the famous culinary school El Mercardo, Hector began at the bottom, saying if it had been good for his grandfather, it was good for him. He worked his way up through the ranks, struggled in the toughest of kitchens, and learned what it was like to create the traditional foods of his country. The old way. The original way. How can you develop foods, he would ask, in the bio form if you don't know what it's supposed to look like, smell like and, above all, taste like? To create them with your hands. To smell the chorizo under your fingernails and feel the sting of the jalapeño in your eyes. He had learned the foundation of his country's foods, and it made him proud.

Jonathan and Hector had built Kortel's into a Chicago landmark: the place to go for a food experience you could only get this side of a flight to Hong Kong or London. Their clients were loyal, and they spread the word of the two young men who had created a fusion between bio and food. But tonight, Hector sensed something wrong.

"You okay there, Jonathan?" Hector asked. "You don't look so good."

"Yeah. I just feel weird. Kinda tingly all over."

"You just need to be laid...and by my sister!" said Enrique, Hector's line chef, right hand and cousin.

The kitchen burst into laughter like a group of sailors who were riding. It was at these times Jonathan felt the techno chasm between himself and the men who turned his coding into a dining experience. Even Hector, who had shared so much with him, gave him that "you-couldn't-be-here-without-us" look. But that was rare. And as quickly as Jonathan had sensed it, Hector's deep voice returned the kitchen to business.

"Come on, *vatos*, we have art to make!" And the kitchen snapped back into its synchronized rhythm.

~

"This was a good day, eh, Jonathan?" Hector asked.

"What...yeah, it was Hector, it was..." Jonathan said distractedly while he tapped his netpad to enter the customer codes for the night's tally.

"You should get back into the kitchen. You were very good at one time," the big Mexican said softly.

Jonathan looked up pensively. He did need to get back to the essence of his craft. "Maybe I do, Hector, but who would run this place? It can't run itself, unless you got a spare hundred million lying around. Then it could, and we could just sit back at the bar and relax."

Hector laughed. The restaurant was quiet. The crew was beginning to clean up, and some of the regulars were still at the bar, waiting to be shooed out like cattle from a holding pen.

Just then a scream came from the kitchen that would drain the blood from any soul. It was Enrique. Both Hector and Jonathan knew the sound. A kitchen is a dangerous place. Hector heard his blood cousin's pain and swung around, navigating his large frame through the maze of stacked chairs and tables. Jonathan was at his heels.

"*CHINGA TU MADRE!* I'm on fucking fire, man!" Enrique screamed. The grease he was cleaning had caught fire, and the flames had jumped to the sleeve of his shirt.

Hector burst into the kitchen and reached for one of the extinguishers. Callis, the night washer, grabbed for the other one across the kitchen. By now, flames had engulfed the shirt and, with it, Enrique's upper body.

"AURGH, my face! My face!" Enrique yelled in that guttural tone instinctually recognized at the primal level. He desperately tried to escape, violently twisting in place, trapped between the antique grill and the prep island. His hands banged out an eerie sound as they flailed against the pots suspended from the ceiling.

"My cousin, I'm here!" Hector yelled. Both he and Callis raised their extinguishers in sync, their fingers dancing across the system pads to program the grease setting. They lunged toward Enrique, but instantly recoiled. The flames leaped from his body and tore away what was left of his shirt. Enrique crouched down, thinking he was now fully engulfed, while the ball of fire hung suspended in the air, roaring as it consumed the shirt. Then, like some cheap magic trick, the flames vanished in a small puff of smoke. Hector and Callis stared dumbstruck, their extinguishers at the ready. Enrique was still crouching and flailing at the phantom flames.

"Help me, motherfuckers, don't just stand there!"

"Stand up, my cousin," Hector said slowly. "You're not on fire anymore." The night washer crossed himself, said a Hail Mary and slowly backed out of the kitchen.

Enrique picked himself up and looked himself over for burned skin. "*Qué paso?*"

"I don't know," Hector said, embracing his cousin in one of his Hector hugs. "Are you all right?"

"I think my arm is burned a little." He quickly rolled his arm over to view the blisters the flames had left behind.

"Jonathan!" Hector barked. "Get the bioderm from the med kit...Jonathan?"

They all turned to see Jonathan standing like a statue at the wash station, staring blankly into the middle of the kitchen. His eyes were bright and wildly open, and his right hand was clenched as if in severe pain. A little trail of blood flowed from his right nostril.

"Jonathan?..." Hector said uncertainly, taking a step toward him.

Jonathan snapped back to the moment. He grabbed his head, his mind numb with pain, and stumbled forward, almost falling into Hector's arms.

"Oh, shit..." he groaned.

"Jonathan? Callis, get the bioderm, now!"

"Don't!" Jonathan yelled. "I'm okay. I'm okay...I'll go get it!"

Jonathan pushed away from Hector, averting his face and wiping the blood from his lip. Hector looked at Jonathan, then back to his cousin, then back to Jonathan, who was now coming around the prep station with the biomed kit.

"What the hell is going on here?" Hector demanded.

Jonathan looked up from attending to Enrique's burns. "You need to go to the hospital," he said quietly to Enrique. Hector was still standing by the wash station with his hands on his hips.

"Callis, can you take Enrique to the hospital?" Jonathan asked.

Callis just stood in the doorway in shock.

"Hector, will you tell him!" Jonathan demanded, and Hector said something only the other Mexican could understand.

Callis grabbed Enrique by the arm and led him out of the kitchen. Hector spoke to the washer, who nodded his head and disappeared out the back door.

After years of working with these men, Jonathan had learned a little Spanish. But what Hector had said escaped him. "What was that all about?"

"Nothing, Jonathan, nothing..."

"Nothing my ass. What did you say to him?"

"I said 'quit acting like you've seen the devil, you Catholic shit, and take him to the hospital.'"

"The devil?"

"Yes, the devil!"

"I...I..."

"I'm not the devil?" Hector offered.

"Yes, I'm definitely not the devil!" Jonathan slumped on the stool by the prep station. "But I don't know what I am," he said under his breath.

"Jonathan, what are you saying?"

"I don't know, Hector....What was that?"

"How should I know! An act of God? A miracle? Why, what do you think?"

It was hard for Jonathan to speak about it. All his life he had experienced these little "episodes." These *magic* tricks. The pencil in third grade. The book thrown at his mom. The recycle truck with Tarris. The elevator ride with the girl in New York.

"It can't be me," Jonathan said in anguish. Anger filled his eyes as he held back the deep realization of what was happening. "This is not me, goddamn it!"

A glass jar filled with their finest soil-grown herbs exploded on the prep shelf. Hector jumped as the glass shards ricocheted about the kitchen. Jonathan never looked up. His mind was too focused.

Hector put his hand on his friend's shoulder. "Jonathan, it's impossible. You're not some freak, man. Enrique just threw the shirt off in his struggle, and it burned up before our eyes. I've seen this kind of shit on the TVids."

Jonathan continued to stare.

"I told that asshole Gonzalez not to pressure those jars too tight," Hector said. He glared back toward the shelf. "Shit, I'll get him to clean this up in the morning. Let's go get a drink, partner."

~

It was past two in the morning when Hector and Jonathan pulled up to the bar, having said nothing to each other the whole way over. The argon sign flashed "Blind Monkey." They walked to the front door, which was padded with riveted red vinyl and, as Jonathan reached, swung out to meet him. Hector didn't notice. Jonathan just smiled. They pushed though the crowd of street smack, tech workers, market jockeys and young riders. They squeezed to the bar and secured a space amongst the night dead.

"Oban," Hector said. "And I'll take a Tequila Fuck, Caesar."

Caesar grinned. He knew their drinks, because they were his regulars, kind of celebs in their business.

"Tough day, boys?" he asked, wiping a clean glass for the Scotch.

Jonathan said nothing and continued to stare into the mirror behind the bar.

"I'll say," Hector answered. "How's business been?"

"Fucking crazy," Caesar said. "It's this weather. Brings them in every time."

"I love it!" Hector yelled, and he threw back his tequila. "Jonathan, come on. You haven't said two words. Have your drink and let's forget about it."

"Guess you're right. Sorry, Hector. What am I thinking?" Jonathan laughed and sipped his Scotch. He studied his reflection in the mirror. He knew what he was thinking.

He was a freak.

One week later... 4

"Good morning, gentlemen."

The Unit Director's in a good mood, thought Jimbo.

"So our little girl wasn't who we thought?" he asked them.

"No, I do not think she had the potential," Jimbo's partner said, casually looking out the window.

"Well," replied the director, opening a new file pad, "it's better to be cautious and right than expeditious and wrong."

"Yes, sir," Jimbo chimed. Both Level 8's just looked at him.

"Let's forget about her for the moment, shall we? We have something else to discuss." He spun the file pad around to face the two Recruiters.

Jimbo was pissed. He needed a break and was tired of being hostage to his partner's "commitment" to the Agency.

"We have a special case for you boys. This is Jonathan

Kortel." The file pad's screen displayed a vid of Jonathan going about his business: working with a customer, buying supplies at the markets, entering his home. A gravitational flux level was displayed that tracked to the vid like a time code.

Jimbo whistled. "Man, this boy's grav flux is off the chart. Say!" he said. He leaned closer to the vid screen. "This is the guy from the restaurant we were at." He slapped his partner's shoulder.

"Yes he is," the Unit Director said. His eyes narrowed at the senior Tel. "You had a sensing there, didn't you?"

"Yes, Stewart, I did."

"And your report says this was a different sensing than for the usual Potential.

"Yes..."

"What does your gut say?"

The Unit Director preferred this phrase, even though the gut was hardly the organ that did the sensing. Jimbo's partner hated it.

"My gut says we need to try one of Mr. Kortel's specials again. He is quite a chef. My meal was excellent. And yours, James?"

"Yeah, fine...but sir, I didn't get a feel for this guy being all that special."

His partner cracked a grin.

"And why was that, Jim?" the Unit Director asked.

Jimbo froze for a second. "Just a feeling...sir."

"Excellent, Jim. Keep working on your Sense. We're going to get you to a Level 6, I know it," he said mockingly. "Now take this and study it. I want you two in the field by the end of the week. That will be all."

Both Recruiters rose from their chairs.

"Please stay..." he directed Jimbo's partner.

"I'll see you at the terminal, James," his partner said. Jimbo nodded and closed the door on the way out.

The Unit Director gestured for him to sit back down.

"What do you think...what do you really think?" he asked the senior Tel.

"I think, Stewart, we have a Potential here." His disinformation was calculated, because he had left out just a little bit of data in his report. He had sensed Jonathan right from the start. Usually his seventh sense would pick up the "effect." But as soon as he had entered the restaurant, it wasn't just his seventh sense that felt the pulse; it was more like his entire being reacted to a sudden shift – a shift that was deep, rich and different. Almost on a genetic level. Not like anything he had ever felt or sensed before. This wasn't the usual electromagnetic field displacements of the typical Potential. This was...harmonic.

Like music.

"So you don't think we have something special here? Look at his readings, like his Field Flux. My God, look at his APT Waves!" The Unit Director spun the file pad around mentally.

The senior Tel snapped the lid of the file pad shut. He raised it until it was level with the Unit Director's face and moved it against his nose, pressing him back against his chair.

"No, I do not think we do," he said, hands still folded. "But if you insist, Stewart, I will take this child you have assigned me, and we will discover what is really going on in Chicago."

"Good," the Unit Director said in a nasal voice. "Now get going!"

The senior Tel slowly rose from his seat, lit a cigarette and calmly strolled out of the room. When the door clicked shut, the file pad dropped into the Unit Director's lap.

Liquid Courage... 5

More than two weeks had passed since the incident in the kitchen. Callis had resigned, but this was *no problema*, since there were plenty of other desperate men and women who needed Hector's pity. Even though the U.S. and Mexico had merged years ago, the Rio Grande might just as well be an ocean for those without status. The social and economic imbalances that had widened the gulf between the two countries was predicted to disappear with the creation of the super nation. Instead, things remained the same as they had for centuries. The Biolution did not reach the third world, much less the second, as fast as it had engulfed the first. By the time biotechnology had reached the interior of Mexico, the former United States was decades ahead. Hector wanted to close the gap, one person at a time.

The kitchen had begun to treat Jonathan differently, and

Hector had noticed. It wasn't that they feared him. It wasn't even that they believed the rumor that he had floated while eating the flames with his mind. No, it was that there had always been a bond between the bioprogrammer and his army. Now, the troops were worried that their general was changing, and they didn't understand how or why.

The night had begun as a typical night. The four-top by the fireplace complained about the service. The sous chef almost cut off his finger. The biofridges were at 60 percent limit. The new hostess had overbooked the eight o'clock hour, and the city food inspector was entertaining his girlfriend without noticing his wife in booth number five.

"Jonathan, you know it's Enrique's birthday today?" Hector quizzed while he put the finish on the last Saffron Salmon for the night.

"Oh shit," Jonathan said, embarrassed. "That's right. What's going on after close?"

Hector's broad smile said it all. "What else? Liquid, my friend...Liquid!"

~

Liquid Courage was the place for out-of-town conventioneers to play, the hot-wired salesman to close the deal, or anyone who had the available cash to entertain the sexiest women the city could offer. Part Vegas show club, part sex bar and part oasis to the rich; to play the Liquid life took money, lots of money, because its girls were pros. Every military boy riding or bachelor saying farewell to his freedom paid homage at its doors. And that was just to get in. Once inside, true players went straight for The Den. The Den was the gate to empyrean. If you had the cash, you lived your dreams.

Usually Enrique and the boys stayed on the main floor, where the circus of sin was choreographed and monitored. But tonight, the crew of Kitchen Kortel wanted a deeper drink of the Liquid life.

"To The Den, *cabrones*!" Enrique raised his fist and the troops followed.

Jonathan hung back, soaking in the energy of the main floor. Dancers were spinning or hanging, and the whole place undulated to the intense bass rhythms of the latest chart risers from Africa, Cuba and the Pacific Rim. Liquid Courage was like a circus gone horribly wrong. It occupied the space between reality and fantasy. Beautiful women hung in the air, their bodies floating, and nothing more than crystal sequins covered what the imagination already had seen. The floor dancers intertwined themselves around men and women who where either riding or drunk. Everyone's chip cards had already been swiped at the door, so freedom ruled.

"Gentlemen, do we have reservations?" the Den's doorman yelled over TransDust, a recent German import from the Euroclub scene.

"Yes, we do. It's under Kortel!" Enrique screamed back, as VIPs with dancers slid past them through the door.

The doorman studied his netpad and snapped it shut. "First timers," he cooed at the Den's bouncer, whose sex was up for debate. They kissed and coolly looked at Enrique, whose attention was captured by their ever-changing, living tattoos.

"Welcome to the Den, gentlemen. Anari is waiting. She will show you to your table." His pale hand passed over the door's small antique lion head knocker. A hot beam of light streamed from the knocker to the knob, and the door slowly swung open.

Inside the Den, the music changed. The hard-driving sounds of TransDust fell away as Anari closed the door. The Den was carved out of what appeared to be solid rock, which even felt cool and damp to the touch. But it couldn't have been. They were 40 stories above the ground.

"Gentlemen, pleassse," Anari said. She hung on the "S" to reveal a wicked smile. Her small Asian frame was wrapped in what appeared to be traditional Japanese silks, but as she moved the silks reconstituted to leave open areas of mesh shaped as animals. A tiger gave away a glimpse of her neck, an elephant her inner thigh, and a snake, her dark nipples. Biofabric. Living, programmable cloth that could reform its shape at the whim of the wearer. "Custom" was the word for retail. If you couldn't change for the customer, let the product do it for you.

"Here you are, gentlemen." She directed them to a large booth just off the Den's main stage. Jonathan slipped her his chipcard.

"Thank you, but no. Everything in the Den was taken care of when you entered Liquid Courage." She raised a plastic eyebrow and gently placed the chipcard back into Jonathan's hand.

"Tara will be right over to get your orders...enjoyyy." And again she hung on the "Y" as a crane transformed into a water buffalo and exposed a perfect set of breasts. Jonathan put his card away while she and her "porno kimono" disappeared into the recesses of the Den.

"Now that's service. Could she come work for us?" Toto asked.

Jonathan smiled. The Den had a deep rhythmic hum. The music laid like a thick blanket over the muffled conversations, and it was hard to make out where one ended and the other began. Oriental businessmen drank their sake while skinny topless Asian girls massaged their necks or whatever else their yen could buy. Jonathan could see that the Den was for the elite. The booths were a virtual library of the city's who's who. Carlos Souza, known for his aggressive soccer style, was holding court with four bioenhanced blondes who acted delighted to see him yet scanned the Den for their next victims. Mega-businessman Custus Carter was deep in conversation with a redhead with electric blue skin, who occasionally came up for air. Carrie Straw, a TVid news reader and underground bisexual, was still in her on-air makeup (not that she would stand out here). And Mayhem, former rock netstar turned sleazy netporn producer, was sporting his signature vintage kilt, crushed straw cowboy hat and sim-eel boots. He was busy riding the curve with his main girl chained to what was once his best asset.

How did I miss all this? Jonathan asked himself.

"Gentlemen, you're dry," Tara, a pretty little he/she announced, flipping open his/her netpad as he/she approached their booth. "Wait, I know what men like you need.... You are men?"

They looked at each other and nodded.

"A Bucket of Sin!" he/she sang.

"Well, all right!" yelled Enrique." It is my birthday, god-damn it!"

"I see..." purred Tara. He/she reached over and grabbed his crotch. "You are a man." The men from Kitchen Kortel burst into howls and took turns reaching for Enrique's crotch, only to be batted desperately away.

On the stage, a lone dancer slowly swayed to the rough beat of Desperate Sense, a group that had been ahead of their time but never received much netplay. *What an odd choice for dance music*, Jonathan thought. The girl wrapped herself around the pole, pulled her legs up and locked her ankles together. She leaned back as casually as if she were sinking into her favorite chair and hung there upside down, alone, while Desperate Sense moaned its electric lament. She shifted her gaze to stare at Jonathan with that "I caught you" look and smiled softly, which caused her cheeks to push her eyes almost shut. She righted herself and swung down, ending perfectly in time with the song. Collecting her things from the stage, she stood up to unveil a tall, lean frame with proportional breasts and muscular legs. She rotated her shoulders back, looked about the room and slowly walked to the bar. Something about her gait intrigued Jonathan. It was predacious, almost sexual – like a cat stalking its prey.

When she reached the bar, a tall man in a sharply cut suit wrapped his arm around her waist and spoke into her ear. She pulled herself around him to face Jonathan's booth, but kept her face buried in the man's neck. The presentation of the Bucket of Sin distracted him for a moment. He grabbed his glass and turned back to find the dancer still listening to her mark, but looking right at him. Her curly blonde hair fell over her eyes like a wispy veil. She kissed the man's neck, her eyes never leaving Jonathan's. Suddenly self-aware, he quickly jerked his attention back to the table, which was deep into its third birthday toast. Girls were circling like ravenous vultures. He raised his glass to toast when he felt someone nestle beside him in the booth. It was the dancer. She didn't say a word, but motioned for him to finish.

"To Enrique," he declared. "One lucky *chinga el madre*!"

He felt her lean to his ear. "It's *chinga tu madre*," she

whispered, and then squeezed his arm almost affectionately.

He turned while sipping his drink, brushing up against her curls and coming face to face with her. She didn't pull back. She held her gaze. Jonathan was transfixed by her blue eyes. Blue eyes that she was born with, as far as he could tell. In fact, there didn't appear to be anything bioenhanced about her at all.

"Hello..." she started.

"Sorry...Hello. I'm Jonathan. And you are?..."

"I'm Nicki." She smiled, and her upper lip curled to expose a little gum above her teeth. She quickly corrected it and introduced a new smile. A model's fake smile, but pretty nonetheless. "This is my club smile..." she said, posing.

"I think I prefer the real smile," Jonathan said.

Taken aback, her smile disappeared and slowly returned as it first appeared. "Really? I don't look too gummy?" She laughed and cleared her throat with a small cough. She took a drag from her cigarette.

Pity, Jonathan thought, *so young, so pretty, and she's already going to need bioregeneration for her lungs.*

She blew her smoke up out of the booth. "First time?" she asked.

"To the Den, yes, but not to Liquid."

"Oh, great..."

"Your music, what an unusual selection."

"Desperate Sense? I love them. They were so far out front." She lit another cigarette. "You don't mind, do you?"

"No," Jonathan lied.

"I know it's a nasty habit, but I figure I can always get regen'd."

The glow of the lighter filled her face, and Jonathan saw for the first time how pretty she really was. A natural beauty. Not created at the hands of a biosurgeon.

"Let's down another Bucket!" she declared to the table, and the men cheered in approval.

"So how long have you been dancing?" Jonathan asked.

"You mean here, or total?"

"Total..."

"About five years..."

"How old are you...if I may ask?"

"How old are you?" she snapped back.

"Twenty-nine."

"Twenty-one," she whispered.

"You've been dancing since you were sixteen?"

"Shhh...I don't usually tell people that just because of that reaction."

"No, it's okay. I don't have any agenda. Just surprised."

"Are you from here?"

"No, I was born..." (*here it comes*, Jonathan thought) "...in Hawaii."

"Really..." she said, her mind already skipping past this small talk she had heard a million times before. Then it hit her, and she slowly turned to meet his look. She put out her cigarette and slid closer to him. She tilted her head as seriousness filled her face. Her eyes asked if he was all right, and he read them. She never said a word.

"I'm okay, really." But he wasn't. It was a general fact that Jonathan and the millions of survivors of the "event" would receive the world's grief till the generations were gone.

~

The event happened on a beautiful spring day in the islands of Hawaii in 2092. The islands woke up and went through their workday morning routine. Then at precisely noon, one million Hawaiians, tourists and military personnel (not to mention all animal, plant and aquatic life within a 300-mile radius) were vaporized. Or, more accurately, debiolized. This was the new term that became the word of the moment, probably of the century. Most people still clung to the old term, vaporized. They just couldn't wrap their minds around the idea that a bomb didn't blast. That there was no mushroom cloud, no rain of fire, no vaporizing of anything. Like an ice cream sundae on a hot afternoon, the congealing of matter that was once the Hawaiian Islands horrified the world and stumped scientists. They didn't really know what the people experienced. All matter simply began reforming. Or, as the TVids news analysts termed it, merging. Jonathan often wondered if the terrorists really knew what they were doing, or, worse yet, what they were creating. Even today, after years of analysis by the world's best scientific minds, everything on the islands (including his parents) was part of a giant biological sundae in the middle of the Pacific Ocean. A sundae that was still melting.

~

"I...I'm sorry..." she said and gently touched his knee.

He looked down at her hand and felt something he hadn't felt in a long time. Compassion.

"Hey," she said, changing the moment, "wanna dance?"

From so close, Jonathan could see that her makeup was soft, not harsh like the other dancers. "Yes, I'd like that," he answered.

She took his hand and slowly pulled him from the booth. The men of Kitchen Kortel all "ooohed" as they left. She led him past other dark booths, filled with desperate patrons and hungry girls, to the last bar, which was dormant. It was used only for those parties where status was your invitation. On the way, he watched her stride with her shoulders pulled tight. The small of her lower back and the tops of her legs met in the most perfect ass Jonathan had ever seen. She looked back. Her face was serious, and her eyes were slits. But she wasn't smiling this time. She was a pro, and she meant business. She placed him in a large over-stuffed wingback and pushed him against the wall. Gently spreading his legs with her feet, she picked up right with the music. She first pulled her top over her head, letting her breasts bounce lightly with the beat. Then she turned and slid off her skirt, her soft skin an inch from Jonathan's chin. Spinning around she leaned over him, letting her hair fall over his head and face. She licked his ear and pressed her whole body against him. Jonathan didn't look at her breasts or any other part of her, as most marks do. He didn't grab or grope like the frat boys riding high on Jack. He delicately traced the curves of her body, with his focus on one thing.

Her crystal blue eyes.

A handful of times in her thousands of dances, a mark had played it cool. But even they were nothing compared to this one. Something in this one unnerved her, but intrigued her, too. He seemed into her, not her body. As she danced, she pressed and rubbed in sync to his touches. It was like they were dancing together, if that were possible for a stripper and her mark. The music stopped with their faces almost touching. They held for a moment, and then she leaned in and kissed him on the mouth, breaking her first rule (not to mention five of the city's).

Jonathan kissed back, and when he did, he felt a strange energy course through his body. She squeezed his hand.

"Hey you..." he whispered.

She slowly opened her eyes. He could sense that she had felt it, too. She smiled, but not the model smile. Just a small smile. The woman, not the dancer, was looking back.

"That was..." she replied, parting her lips just slightly as if to say something, yet holding back.

"Wonderful," Jonathan finished.

"Yes," she said. "Yes it was....What's your last name?"

"Kortel. And yours?" he asked softly.

"Tamara...Tamara Connor," she said, breaking the second of her rules.

They both waited, wondering.

"Well!" she said, going professional on him. "Welcome..." she leaned close to his face and whispered, "...to the Den, Mr. Kortel." She lightly kissed him again.

The music started up again.

~

When they returned to the booth, the men of Kitchen Kortel were in full swing. The music was pumping out harsh techno trash direct from the streets of Tel Aviv, and there were empty silver buckets strewn over the table. Half-naked girls were sprawled, standing or dancing, and the men were feeling no pain.

"I need to go freshen up," Tamara said. She let her hand fall from his.

"See you in a sec?" Jonathan asked.

"Yeahhh..." She held onto the "H" like she had just created that response custom for him.

Jonathan fell into the booth almost on top of Hector, who was halfway to the floor with a German/Latino fusion girl who couldn't stop giggling.

"God help me, don't tell my wife!" he pleaded to Jonathan.

"Don't worry," Jonathan assured. "What goes on here..." and the men answered in chorus, "...stays here!" Their roar of laughter shook the Den.

A sec turned into minutes. Jonathan looked around, but Tamara was gone. He slammed the last of his drink, got up to leave and continued to glance about the Den.

"Give her up, Jonathan," Hector said, barely conscious. "Take it from me, I know these type." And he did.

Jonathan shrugged at Hector, high-fived his men, at least those who could still raise their arms, and walked toward the Den's exit. The door opened without his request, and on the other side the doorman now worked a long line of young, drunk quarry. Jonathan scanned the club one last time for Tamara. The main floor was wall-to-wall press-the-flesh. As he neared the exit, he felt a hand slip a card into his front pants pocket.

"Call me," Tamara whispered, breaking her last and most important rule.

Tamara Connor... 6

"Today?!" Jimbo yelled as he washed the three-hour flight off his face. His partner emerged from the stall.

"What is your hurry, James? We are going to take our time with this one."

"At least he has a profession we can enjoy. Remember that hydro-service guy? God, that place stank. Three months to find he's nothing but a fucking Uri Gellar."

The two Recruiters left the airport and headed toward Jonathan's apartment.

"Did you pack the new gravscanner?" his partner asked as they entered the Interway.

"Yeah, and the Agency said to be careful with it. It's still a beta model."

"Excellent. We should be able to define his field ratio quite accurately now."

They slipped through the city, again reviewing Jonathan's preliminary data, searching for the footprint of the gift. All good Recruiters knew the drill. A Potential must be investigated thoroughly. Set-up begins by establishing a base. Jimbo had chosen a small hotel a block from Jonathan's loft. From there, they could monitor him almost without leaving the base. Biotechnology had created a cluster of equipment so sensitive it made surveillance virtually indetectable. But his partner preferred a different method. The old-fashioned way.

He called it hunting.

~

"It is the hunt, James, that makes recruiting interesting."

"I have to agree with you, partner." Jimbo said. He emptied the equipment case. "Don't get me wrong. I love this proprietary high-tech gear we get to play with. But the hunt is the best part. Especially when a Potential has the gift."

"That is an extraordinary moment, is it not?" his partner said. He methodically began transferring his clothes from suitcase to closet.

"The look on their faces when they discover what they really are...it's..."

"Rewarding, James?" his partner finished.

"Yeah, rewarding. I remember when they first told me. It was like a weight was lifted off my shoulders. And you know what else? For the first time, you feel like you've found your family. I know it's weird, but growing up, you have a sense that you're not really a part of the rest of the population. Know what I mean?"

"Exactly," his partner said, stopping the routine of setting up base. "They never understand, do they?"

They were the friends and family all Tels left behind. Tels would be "disconnected" from their families, according to the situation. The Agency had fingers throughout the information net, so that just about any disconnection could be backed up with the appropriate cover. Or, if the subject was a child, the arrogance of the Agency dictated that he or she just disappeared, only to find their holofaces on the side of milk containers. And in appropriate situations, the Agency could even fake a person's death. All in the name of the greater good. Once the gravity of their situation had sunk in, most new Potentials never looked back. Why should they? They weren't human; they were a new species. Humanlike, but not like them.

The Agency became your family.

"How about you? How did they disconnect you?" Jimbo asked.

"I was different," his partner reflected.

Forty years ago, Jimbo's partner had been singled out, like all Level 8 Potentials were. The Agency conducted tests that could calculate the current and potential level of any Tel. His partner was the highest ever recorded. Of course this information was restricted, even within the Agency. A Tel who displayed such a high-level potential was culled from the group to begin a different path than others in their class. And one as high as his partner was special, indeed.

The world was a dangerous place in 2061. The Biolution was beginning, the third world felt cheated, and the key to the Arab cartel's power was threatened. The Agency saw a need for a special corps of men and women who could exercise their power for the security of the world. It was their duty to protect their human cousins from themselves. And if that meant that certain situations demanded difficult solutions, then the Agency had the answer. The perfect weapon for an imperfect world. It was kept secret from most in the Agency and hidden from other branches of government, but in an emergency these squads would be dispatched, always in twos. A foreign dignitary's brain hemorrhages at a state function. He collapses and dies before he hits the floor. A diplomat has a seizure at the signing of a weapons treaty. Simple. Clean. Perfect. Jimbo's partner had been one of the best.

"I was disconnected at a young age, James. My mother and father were poor. To them...I was killed in an accident."

"Oh...I'm sorry," Jimbo said, turning his attention back to the equipment.

"No need, James. They were better off because of it. I would have been too much for them to understand. My father was just a farmer." At that, his partner slowly closed his suitcase. "Well," he said, straightening his tie. "Let us go pay a visit to Kortel's fine dining. Shall we?"

~

Jonathan reviewed the room from the kitchen. The two guys in black coats at the front door looked very familiar. He flipped Tamara's card through his fingers, reflecting on what Hector had said. It was slow, and they were going to lose some money tonight.

"Hector, can you close by yourself tonight?" Jonathan asked

over his shoulder.

"Yes, yes...go and get it out of your system, my friend," Hector answered.

Jonathan turned around to see the big Mexican shaking his knife at him. Enrique sang a made-up Liquid Courage song under his breath.

Hector walked over. "Jonathan, she's just a stripper...probably got a kid..."

"...or two!" Enrique chimed in.

"Shut the fuck up!" Hector snapped.

"It's Mr. Shut the Fuck Up to you!" Enrique laughed.

"Yeah, yeah, whatever. Jonathan, seriously, do you really want to get involved with a girl like this? Take it from me, my friend, there're two types of dancers – ones that are fucked up and ones that are more fucked up. You with me?"

"I know, don't worry. I just want to have a little fun, that's all. I'll see ya in the morning." He slapped Hector in the chest with the back of his hand and headed out.

~

When Jonathan entered Liquid Courage it was oddly slow, but he had never been there before two in the morning. The main floor was sparsely filled with an odd juxtaposition of military and business types. He made his way to the Den, only to find the vampiresque doorman was nowhere around. He parked himself at the back bar and ordered a drink.

"Slow tonight?" he questioned the bar back. The kid turned to display a novel assortment of rings that interlocked through piercings in his head. He sounded like a wind chime when he spoke.

"Yeah, for a Tuesday, I guess. It'll pick up in an hour." He tossed the glass he had been cleaning over his head and caught it behind his back.

Jonathan was just getting settled when a finger dragged lightly across the back of his shoulders. He twisted around to find Tamara next to him. Her hair was straight and her makeup harsh. She wore a sexy evening dress cut to her navel, and the spiked dog collar added an odd 20th-century touch. Her hand came to rest on his.

"Hey, you..." she said.

"Hey," he replied. "Nice hair."

"You like?"

"Yes," he lied.

"So, what brings you to Club Liquid?" She smiled, and the harshness of her makeup softened.

He leaned closer and smiled back. "What do you think?"

"To see little ol' me?" she asked in her best Southern twang, putting her finger to her chin.

"Yes," he said seriously, slowly losing his smile.

Her smile shrank as well, and she adopted his demeanor like a mirror. Matching his seriousness, she tilted her head and slowly parted her lips. She pulled his hands up with hers and held them tight to her chest. "I was hoping you'd come back, Jonathan." She tugged him off the chair, towards the Den. With a wave of her hand over the knocker, she sent the beam of light dancing, and the door swung open. There was no one in the Den tonight.

"Anari sweetie, number 12?" she inquired.

Anari spread her arms and bowed, her ninja outfit hugging

her small frame. "The Den is yours," she said, her mask muffling her voice.

Tamara led Jonathan by the hand deep into the Den to number 12. As they slid into the booth, Anari ninjaed through the room, landing by the table as they settled in. "A Crasher for Nicki and a Oban for Jonathan?" Her eyes darted between the two of them.

"Yes," Tamara answered, and Anari left the table.

"How did she know?" Jonathan asked.

"Your profile data is in the system. I'm sure she checked it on her netpad. She's the best. I should know." She raised one eyebrow and giggled.

"I don't want to know," Jonathan said, gesturing.

"Oh, I bet you'd watch." She poked him in the ribs with her finger.

"Hey, cool it, you." He groaned, and she poked him again. He grabbed her finger on the third strike, stopping it dead, and began to twist it.

"Owww..." she squealed.

He pulled her closer. They froze for a moment to take each other in.

"A Crasher for madame," Anari said, suddenly appearing. "And a Scotch with ice for the gentleman. Hiieee!" She ninja kicked her way back to the bar, battling an enemy only she could see.

"Jonathan...what an old name..." Tamara said softly.

"My parents were traditionalists, I think." Jonathan said, still holding onto her finger.

"I like it. It's Biblical. That's rare these days."

He let go of her finger and spread his hand. She answered

his request and interlaced her fingers with his, never dropping her attention from him. She could tell that the mention of his parents triggered a stream of unwelcome memories. In his face, she saw the pain of the loss come forward, and she could tell that the wounds were deep. She squeezed his hand tighter.

"Does it hurt...still?" she quietly asked.

"I'd be a liar if I said it doesn't. Hell, it's still on the news almost every damn night."

"Oh, baby..."

She dropped her dancer's wall and touched his face. He turned away, but she brought his face around. Her tender feelings pushed through even the harsh makeup. They sat there quietly as she stroked his face and head. He closed his eyes and leaned into her touch. He felt a lump rising in his throat. A tear began to form at the edge of his eye. His instinct was to tighten up and man-out on her, but the moment felt so right. She felt so right. It had been a long time.

He let the tear fall.

She pretended not to notice.

Just then, the door of the Den burst open, and four fat fake cowboys strode inside, dusting themselves off like they had just brought a herd into Chicago. With a girl on each arm, they piled into the first booth they saw. Jonathan turned away and wiped the tear as if he were simply straightening his hair. The two of them sat up and sipped their drinks.

"So," he said, changing the mood. "What do you do for..." He stopped. Tamara was standing up, and he hadn't noticed that the music had started.

She put her finger to his lips and whispered in his ear. "Shhh,

Mr. Kortel. I want you, right now." Her arms crossed her chest, pushing her breasts up and together. Her hands grabbed the sides of her dress and slowly slid it up and over her head. All she wore was a triangle of crystal sequins between her legs. They refracted a small spotlight that was aimed into the booth and sent red, blue and green bits of light to dance across the walls.

Now her makeup makes sense, Jonathan thought.

Her look was serious. Her hips swayed to the rhythm of the song, gradually coming closer and closer until they were grinding him into the back of the booth. She grabbed his hands and led them to her breasts. He pulled back – partly out of club protocol and partly out of fear. She held her grip. Tamara wanted him, and he felt it.

"It's okay, lover," she whispered.

Jonathan looked up at her. His hands followed her thighs to her waist. He pulled her close and gently kissed her breasts to the pace of the slow Latin beat. Then he bit down on one of her nipples, which hardened in his mouth. Her head dropped back and a soft moan escaped.

"Oh, God..." she sighed as she fell forward and kissed the top of his head. Jonathan bit harder. His fingers dug into her skin. She pulled away and kneeled between his legs. Tamara ran her chin down the front of his chest and across his stomach and stopped with her mouth pressing on the firmness in his pants.

It was her turn to bite down.

~

As the eighth song faded, Tamara lifted her head off his chest. She wasn't bothering to dance anymore. They sat in the booth just holding each other, having done about as much as they could without risking major jail time, not to mention a heavy fine.

"What...was..." She stopped herself.

"What, baby?..."

"What was that?" she asked seriously. She really wanted to know, because in all her years as a dancer she had never felt a connection like she had felt tonight.

Jonathan pulled her away and held her there. He knew from her eyes that they weren't "dancer" and "mark" anymore. They were more. Much more. In their passion, he had felt the same strange energy run through his body that he had felt before. She began to speak, but he motioned her to stop. He raised his hand, placed it on her heart, closed his eyes and imagined a ball of white light moving from his own heart, down his arm, through his hand and into her chest.

She jerked a little at the moment he imagined it entering.

He opened his eyes to find her trembling, his hand still at her heart. Her eyes were closed tight. A tear was crawling down her cheek.

"Shhh, it's all right," he whispered.

She fell onto his chest, and he held her tight. He didn't care what Hector said. He didn't care what his men would think. All he knew was that they had a connection he couldn't explain, and he wanted to be with her. Even if it was just for the night, he needed her like a drug addict needs his ride. She was his drug. And he was becoming addicted.

~

"Our specials tonight are roasted squid, bioenhanced for a

true deep sea flavor. And..." the waitress flipped open her netpad, "...turkey? Guaranteed...to bring back...the memories of Thanksgiving." She looked up from her pad and shrugged.

"Are you new here, young lady?" Jimbo's partner quizzed.

"Yes sir, I'm sorry. I don't know the system yet. And to tell you the truth," she bent down to confide, "I'm a little nervous, this place being so famous and all."

"It is all right dear, you are doing fine. I will have the turkey."

"And I'll take the squid!" Jimbo announced. His partner looked up, surprised.

"I'm branching out, you said so yourself."

"Good, James, good," the senior Tel said, glancing about. He hailed a passing waiter. "Is Jonathan Kortel in tonight?"

"He was, sir, but he left early," the young waiter said. "May I tell him who was inquiring?"

"No, no, I am just a big fan of his programming."

"We all are, sir. He and Hector are the best."

"Yes, Hector...is he in?"

"Yes, he is. Would you like me to go ask if he has a moment?"

"That would be splendid, thank you." The waiter nodded in approval and hurried off to the kitchen.

"Taking a big risk here, boss," Jimbo warned.

"Sometimes, James, we have to take risks. The reward with this one will be substantial."

Hector, his large frame wrapped in his blood and biopaste-stained apron, sauntered through the restaurant like an Incan emperor. Usually Jonathan met with fans, but tonight, it was Hector's turn to tap his fifteen minutes.

"Gentlemen, welcome to Kortel's!" he bellowed. "I hope you find everything perfect?"

"We do indeed, sir," the senior Tel said, taking control. "This is our second time here."

"Are you in town for business or pleasure?"

"Business."

"Well, we love our loyal customers. What are we having?"

"The specials."

"Ah, good, the turkey is my programming tonight."

The senior Tel shifted in his seat. "And Mr. Kortel, is he off tonight?"

"Yes, he left early. He had a date." Hector chuckled.

"Really, the TVids say he is quite the bachelor catch. But he seems a workaholic..."

"Yes, we rib him for that. All work and no play, you know. But it's paid off." Hector spanned the room with his arms.

"Yes, your restaurant has quite the reputation. Tell me..." (Jimbo watched as his partner lifted one eyebrow, signaling he was about to demonstrate what a Level 8 could really do) "...where would one go if they were on a date?"

"Well...that's really not for me to sa..." Hector stammered. A small drop of sweat traversed his sideburn.

"I am sorry, what was that?" his partner asked, leaning closer.

Jimbo cringed as he watched the senior Tel exercise his level by surgically displacing the air pressure around Hector's head, pinpointing the exact area in the brain where the minimal amount of grav touch would deliver the maximum amount of effect.

"He's seeing someone at Liquid Courage..." Hector's voice

trailed off, and he stared blankly into space.

"Oh, that is so wonderful to hear. It is good to see him getting out." The senior Tel released the grav pressure slowly so that Hector wouldn't jerk when the connection was severed.

Hector reached for his forehead, rubbing at the newly implanted pain.

"Are you all right?" the senior Tel inquired.

"Oh yes, this is a tough business. It's just been a long day. If you'll excuse me, I need to get back to the kitchen. Good night, gentlemen." He turned and slowly walked back to the kitchen.

Jimbo glared in contempt as his partner turned his attention to the menu.

"James, I just might have a dessert tonight," the senior Tel announced.

Jimbo just kept glaring.

~

"I have to go," Tamara whispered.

"What time is it?" Jonathan asked, checking his watch. "Shit, it's four in the morning!"

The Den had emptied, though neither of them noticed the wax and wane of patrons between eleven o'clock to three. They had withdrawn to the cocoon they had created for themselves. If they had crossed the line, they didn't care. The Den had become their sanctuary, and Anari was their gatekeeper. She slowly approached the booth.

"Last call, you two," Anari cautiously said.

"We're done, Anari," Jonathan said smiling.

"You both look well done, if you ask me."

"And no one did, sweetie," Tamara replied, stretching.

Jonathan began to reach for his chipcard.

"Don't worry, Jonathan," Anari said. "This has been compliments of Liquid Courage." She motioned to the Den's front door, where a man in a tailored, polybio European suit stood. His back was unusually straight, almost military in stature, and his drink reflected the lights from the club.

"Hey, isn't that the guy you were with the first night we met?" Jonathan asked Tamara. "You two were at the bar."

"Yeah, that's Joshua. He owns Club Courage." The man raised his glass to them, turned and left the Den.

"Well...I..." Jonathan began.

"Need to do nothing," she finished. "He has more money than God. If he wants to treat, let him. It's rare. Take it as a compliment, baby. I know him. He doesn't give them out very often." She kissed him on the cheek. "Let me walk you out."

"Why don't we..." he began, but she silenced him with a finger.

"I need you too, lover," she whispered. "But I can't tonight. I have to get up early. I have an important meeting."

"Cancel it," he urged.

"Believe me, I would...oh, I would so much." She pulled him close and kissed him. "But I can't, I just can't."

Jonathan held her away, searching her face for the real reason. For the first time that night, Tamara didn't meet his eyes. She knew what was coming. She had been here so often she had become dead to its consequence.

Jonathan lifted her chin, forcing her to acknowledge his look.

He slowly smiled. "What's his name...or is it her name?"

Tamara looked up. "Nicole."

"And she's?..."

"Four."

He immediately read her anguish. "Tamara," he said, fumbling for the right words. "I'm not like that. I love children...really."

"Oh yeah," she said, toughening. "If you only knew how often I've heard that!" She turned away.

"Tamara!" He pulled her around, bringing her tight to his face. "Look at me. Listen very carefully...I don't lie. And I'm not going to run judgment on you, Tamara," he whispered. "I'm not like other guys you've met before."

Tamara studied his face. His sincerity cut through her cynicism deep into her heart. Why would a guy like this care about her? She reached up and touched his face.

No, she thought, *you're not like anyone I've met before.*

Hunting... 7

"I take back everything I said earlier, hunting is boring. Give me the biotech shit any day!"

"They told me you were patient," his partner said through the haze of another of his custom Vietnamese cigarettes.

"I am. But it's four thirty in the morning! Hey, here's our boy."

They watched Jonathan and Tamara step to the street. The car jockeys were doing wind sprints to meet the demand pouring out of the building.

"She's hot!" Jimbo exclaimed. "Looks like our boy likes the strippers. Man, I can see why." He dialed up the vision reception of the field optics, standard issue for the Agency.

Jonathan kissed Tamara good night and shut the door of her car. She pulled away from the curb, then jerked to a stop. Jonathan went to her window.

"What are they saying?" asked Jimbo's partner.

Jimbo clicked the lens to Language Enhance drive.

"I can't get them. There's way too much interference...she's saying something about lunch...tomorrow...Blind Monkey...and...oh." Jimbo removed his eyes from the field optics.

"Well?" his partner pressed.

"None of our business, partner."

"It is our business, James."

Jimbo turned and faced him sternly. "It's none of our fucking business."

The senior Tel studied his young associate for a moment. "Perhaps you are right. Follow her home."

"Her?"

"Yes, I believe we might be seeing a lot of Jonathan there."

~

Mornings in a restaurant such as Kortel's are dysfunctionally chaotic, at best. Given the day, Hector could have five delivery men arguing about their orders, a waiter needing to be bailed out of jail, a serviceman checking the biopacks on the hydroponics, which had held the week's shrimp specials now spoiling in static water tanks that died at 2:30 that morning because the new bar back had never run a biosterilizer, or twelve cases of Chilean Merlot missing, even though they were counted at close last night. On this particular day the grill, which is the hallmark of the kitchen, refused to light no matter what Enrique tried. *Where the hell is Jonathan?*

"Has anyone seen our lover boy?" Hector asked.

Everyone looked up, their expressions more blank than the

salmon biopaste from Canada.

"Has he even called?" Hector was desperate.

"No!" Enrique yelled over the laser drill's deafening sound.

"Is that fixed, yet?" Hector yelled.

"Almost!" Enrique crawled farther into the grill's small opening.

"I'm gonna kill..." Hector's netphone rang.

"Hector."

"Jonathan, where the hell are you?" Hector asked savagely.

"Hey, look, I'm sorry. I need a favor. I'm going to take a few days off, and before I get the lecture, just let me have it my way this time, okay?"

Hector hesitated. "Is she that special, my friend?"

"I...I don't know Hector. But I do know I need to play this out. Call it stupid, call it whatever you want, but there's something going on...it's hard to put into words. I'm not even sure what I'm doing. This might be a total disaster, but if I don't see where it goes, I'll never forgive myself. This one isn't open for debate, partner. You understand?"

"Jonathan, you know what I think? I think you need this. Go to her. Be with her. Fall in love with her if you want. You worked hard to build this restaurant, we worked hard, and you deserve the time. Take it, my friend. She is pretty. I can't blame you in the least. Hell, I'm envious. Shit, Jonathan, go fuck her or love her or give yourself to her. But when you come back, I want one hundred percent of you. Now go, before I change my fucking mind."

"Thanks, Hector, I'll see you soon."

Hector disconnected and stared at his netphone for a

moment. "Hell, I am losing my fucking mind....Okay you *vatos*, get this kitchen cooking. We have three hours before we open!" The big Mexican watched as the men of Kitchen Kortel slammed into gear. He loved his partner like a brother, which made the nagging feeling of trouble even more intense. Hector turned his attention to his crew. They were prepping the kitchen like army ants. Not once did they question when their general would return.

A test... 8

Jonathan leaned back against the headboard of his bed. The morning sun cascaded into the room with a clean light that made the metal surfaces glow yellow and gold.

The high loft ceilings contained cobwebs that predated the Biolution. On his side of town, artists and musicians filled the bodegas, not the pseudorich transworlders who flocked to the North Side like cranes to an oasis. He sat there wondering what was to come, what his next move should be. His dating history had been the typical list of social queens seeking "Mrs." degrees and bar chicks thinking sex was their ticket to happiness. Occasionally the errant nice girl came along, but there was never that special something, that strange energy.

Sipping his own specially programmed blend, Jonathan slipped to the window and looked down. The day had begun for the rest of Chicago, but not for him. He was still back in the booth, with her. As he watched the alluvion of the streets, he felt as if he were observing his own situation from above. He had nothing in common with her. He tried to imagine their future, if there was one. What would they talk about? What would they do? Did he really want to become an instant daddy? The loft's AI brought him back to the present.

"Jonathan, it's eleven o'clock. You should prepare for your lunch appointment."

"Thank you, Max. Do I have any netmail?"

"Yes, seven messages. Two from your lawyer. One from Tobby. One from the city inspection department. One from Dining magazine. Two from Terikia."

"God, what does she want?" he said under his breath. Terikia had been the last, and probably weirdest, one of all, and that had been almost ten months ago. "Max," he asked, stepping into the hydroshower, "what's the weather this week?"

"Today will be partly cloudy with a 10 percent chance of rain. The high will be 82 and the low will be 69. For tomorrow and the rest of the five-day extended forecast, expect continued sunny skies, highs in the lower 80s, lows in the high 60s. A cool front is approaching from the east..."

"Thank you, Max. How's the juice and milk?" he said over the rush of air and recycled water.

"They are within acceptable ranges. Would you like them chilled?"

"No, I was just wondering if we needed to get some new ones."

"The bread is at limit. The bioeggpaste is at half-life. The lettuce brick is acceptable. The hydrofruit is at..."

"Got it! Got it! Thank you, Max. Just do a rundown and order what we need. You know the drill."

"Yes, Jonathan. Will there be anything else?"

"Yeah, can you fast-forward me to tonight with Tamara?"

"Excuse me, sir?"

"Nothing. Thank you, Max."

Emerging from the hydroshower, Jonathan grabbed a towel. He still loved towels, even though no one used them anymore. He loved the way they felt against his body. The Biolution had changed so much of the contemporary home, and towels, along with toasters, ovens, refrigerators and about a thousand other labor-saving devices invented in the 20th century, gave way to the new generation of technology. Bioliving enhanced every facet of the home and had Martha Stewart's descendants rolling in their graves.

Jonathan examined himself in the mirror. He was in good shape; he should be for as much as he worked out. As with all males, his self-doubt and insecurities could be temporarily masked with a little attention to muscle tone and contemporary dermal care. He dressed casually in a pair of comfortable jeans, ergosandals and a light simwool sweater. He left the loft in the care of itself.

~

The Blind Monkey was jumping as usual for a midweek business crowd. Jonathan knew the staff, having frequented their bar after closing his kitchen. Deaka was working the front door, and he knew she wouldn't give him any grief. She smiled at him as he approached.

"Hey, Deaka."

"Hi, Jonathan. What brings you here in the middle of the day?"

"I'm meeting someone. She's kinda tall, curly blonde hair..."

"Has a kid with her?" She snapped her gum.

Jonathan hesitated. "Maybe..."

"Booth five, by the window." She pointed her netpad in the direction of the booth.

"Thanks." Jonathan began to walk past her, but Deaka slammed the netpad into his chest and stopped him in midstride.

"She's a knockout, Jonathan, but are you ready to become a daddy?" A broad, thin smile spread across Deaka's face.

"Fuck you, Deaka."

"You tried." Her gum snapped like an antique .38 going off.

Jonathan saw Tamara sitting on the sunlit side of the booth, but he couldn't see little Nicole.

"Morning," he said, bending to kiss her.

"Hi, baby." She returned the kiss. Her hair was curly again, and her makeup was barely noticeable. She wore a man's collared shirt, old baggy pleated pants and work boots any construction guy would kill for. Jonathan couldn't decide whether it was a statement against being half-naked and having to perform as the perfect female or whether she just didn't care.

She reached across the table and took his hands. For a second they just sat there, letting the reality of what they were doing soak in. They were together – outside the club.

"Well?" he asked.

"Well what?" she replied.

"Where's Nicole?"

She smiled and poked her head under the booth. "Hey, silly,

come up and meet someone."

A little head covered by curls appeared over the top of the table. Tamara brushed them back to reveal the face of a cherub who smiled at Jonathan, her eyes squinting shut. She was a perfect reproduction of her mother. Jonathan felt his heart go to the little girl, and, in an instant, he saw Tamara as a child. His eyes went back and forth between the two of them. Tamara's expression had changed. She knew exactly what he was thinking. His look gave it all away. She affectionately squeezed his hands.

"Hello, Mr. Kortel," the little voice said.

"Hello there," he said, clearing his throat. "I've heard a lot about you."

She giggled and disappeared back under the table.

"Shy one, isn't she?" Jonathan said.

"Not really," Tamara answered, slowly looking up at him, "when you get to know her."

"I hope I will," he replied.

~

They ordered sandwiches, and Nicole played with her horses under the booth. They talked about everything. Tamara had a tough life, being raised right in the city. Her father and mother had been small-time dealers in ride. Those were the early years, when the biodrugs were in their infancy. They had done time for it but had cleaned up their act some years back. Tamara had lived with her grandparents for awhile but later had become fairly close to her parents, especially her mom. Nicole was the product of a teen pregnancy that Tamara stubbornly wanted to see through. She had married the father, but that had lasted all of a month. She was wild, but she wasn't stupid. At 16 she had tested out of school with almost straight A's. She ran away from home, leaving Nicole in the care of her grandparents, and headed for Nevada.

"Why Nevada?" Jonathan asked.

Tamara leaned back and folded her arms tightly across her chest.

"Hey, that's okay. Your life is your life," he said.

"The Ranch..." she blurted.

The booth went silent.

Jonathan knew what that name meant. For more than 160 years, 12 owners, 3,821 girls and 73 million condoms had kept the Chicken Ranch the oldest working brothel in New America. Jonathan just looked at her. Half pity, half curiosity. He reached over and gathered her hands into his.

"For how long?" he asked.

"Not long. About a year." She stared blankly out the window.

"Was it..." he began.

"You know," she interrupted, staring out to the street. "You make great money for basically sitting around reading vidbooks. And it's very clean. Man, you wouldn't believe the tests...every other day." Her voice trailed off. She checked to see that Nicole wasn't listening.

"You know, I've done them all," she said quietly. "Young ones, dumb ones....You know who treats you the best? The old guys. They're real nice. Heck, you don't even have sex with them. They just want to talk. Three thousand dollars for 30 minutes of conversation about their dead wives." Her eyes remained blank.

They finished their meals. Jonathan didn't know what to say. He could see Tamara was distracted, mentally out in a past that still clearly impacted her life.

"Mommy, can we go?" Nicole said from below, tugging on Tamara's pant leg.

"Sure, baby. It's time." She gathered up her child and began to climb out of the booth. "I'm sorry," she said to Jonathan. Her mood changed as she hiked Nicole onto her hip. "I'm taking Nicole over to her grandmother's for the weekend. Meet me back at my place in about 40 minutes. Let's just go do something this afternoon....I don't care, maybe to the museum."

"It was good meeting you, Nicole," Jonathan said. "I hope I'll see you soon." He reached over and wiped away a little run that was coming out of Nicole's nose. She giggled and quickly buried her face into Tamara's neck. Tamara smiled, because no guy she knew would ever have done that.

She leaned over and kissed him on the cheek.

~

"Man, she's had it rough," Jimbo said, pulling the biomicro-transceiver out of his ear. The two Recruiters watched as Jonathan, Tamara and Nicole walked past their booth and out of the Blind Monkey. "Kortel doesn't have to worry about the competition. This sandwich is rank."

"I think we need a little test, James," his partner mused.

"Really?" Jimbo asked. He turned his attention to the window, where he could see Jonathan, Tamara and Nicole as they waited at the corner for the signal to change.

"James," his partner instructed, "I want you to watch those people." He pointed to a group of tourists crowded behind Tamara at the corner. "If they begin to pass her, hold them back." He looked at him seriously. "You *can* do this? It is in your level parameters?"

Jimbo nodded "yes" knowing that this was going to be a serious test, and it was neither the time nor the place for mistakes. Jonathan was about to undergo a severe test of GDRD – Gravitational Distortion Reflex Displacement. It was a standard test all Recruiters put their Potentials through, although this time Jimbo felt it was going to be "an extreme condition setup," which typically was reserved for tough cases and never used on the first test.

Jimbo sensed his partner was about to change the rules.

Tamara, holding Nicole in her arms, was talking with Jonathan, while down the street, a quarter-ton kit cab sped toward them, weaving in and out of traffic like a drunken linebacker heading toward their intersection.

"Be tight with your imaging, James, I may need you," his partner warned. The senior Tel began to focus a grav field for the kit cab.

Tamara struggled with Nicole's fussiness, and the tourists behind her grew impatient. The signal shifted. Tamara was first to step off the curb – possibly into oblivion.

"Steady, James, steady...watch them. They are about to move!" his partner said.

Twenty feet from the corner, the kit cab entered the imaging threshold for both Tels. The senior Tel converged the fields and pushed and displaced the kit cab into Tamara and Nicole's path. One of the tourists had already shoved his way around to Tamara's left side.

"James, that one," he said, pointing. "Watch that one for God's sake!"

The cab's pilot, trying desperately to overcome the unseen force that had taken over his cab, engaged the brake units. Their high-pitched squeal sent a pedestrian diving to the sidewalk. A woman screamed. A man anticipated the horror of the scene about to unfold and yelled out to God. Jimbo jerked the tourist circumnavigating Tamara back like a dog being yanked by its leash. He held the six others frozen in their steps. His partner, pushing against the tremendous force of the kit cab's technology, strained his level to its limits. Tamara looked to her right and saw the cab violently swerve in their direction. A scream so loud that the vessels in her vocal cords began to microhemorrhage erupted from her throat.

Jonathan jumped to the right of Tamara and Nicole, futilely trying to shield them with his body, as if he, alone, could absorb the impact from the quarter-ton vehicle. He was partially right. The thought of losing someone he so desperately wanted was the exact formula to trigger the "effect." To Jonathan, the scene went to white, then to colors that twinkled, then swirled. Then something different appeared.

Music.

Harmonic tones filled his mind, and he didn't black out as before. The whole scene slowly entered his consciousness frame by frame. Through the windshield of the kit cab, he could count every beat of the driver's heart in the vein that throbbed on his forehead. The man tore at the wheel, trying to turn away. Jonathan heard himself scream, "NO!" but never felt the sound in his throat. In that moment, the kit cab jerked away from them and back into traffic, throwing the pilot against the door window. His hands left the wheel and slapped him in the face. The cab swerved once, twice, then crashed into the side of a recycle hauler. The force of the impact lifted the cab's back end into the air.

In the time it took for a nerve to fire, the GDRD test was over.

People rushed to the kit cab pilot's aid. The tourists ran across the street. Jonathan stood motionless, halfway turned toward where the cab had been, yet still hugging Tamara and Nicole. Tamara clutched her child and trembled uncontrollably. Nicole was screaming, her face awash in tears and mucus.

Unlike any previous experience he had with the effect, this time Jonathan's eyes were open and his mind was focused. He knew what he had done, and he began to realize that his life was forever changed. A large trail of blood flowed from his nose to the edge of his mouth.

~

"Hmmm," the senior Tel said, casually observing the chaos of the accident engulf the corner. "This Potential is very strong, James."

James McCarris was sweating profusely. He slammed his palm down on the table and slapped at his coffee cup, sending it flying into the booth next to them. He stormed out of the Blind Monkey and charged down the sidewalk to get as far away as possible from the "accident" that had just happened at the corner. His partner scrambled after him. As Jimbo turned down an alley, his partner seized his shoulder. Jimbo, a big Southern man, quickly turned and brushed off the grip like dandruff. He grabbed a handful of coat and shirt and slammed his partner against the wet brick wall.

"You are one twisted motherfucker," he growled. He pressed his face within inches of his partner's. "If you ever put me in a situation like..."

Suddenly, Jimbo grabbed at his throat. Coughing for the air that should have been in his lungs, he dropped to one knee. His partner straightened up, adjusted his shirt and tie, and lit a cigarette.

"If I ever what, James?" he said contemptibly, holding Jimbo in a breathing limbo, letting in just enough air to keep him conscious. "Put you in a situation to where you get to test your level? Or where you get to truly see where we stand on the evolutionary scale?" He circled his struggling partner, seemingly uninterested in his agony. He blew three perfect little smoke rings. "James, the problem with you is you have not accepted your lot in life. You are a Tel. We are not like them! They are, as a species, over. Done! FINISHED!"

He bent down to meet Jimbo's contorted face. "James, please...look at me. I know it hurts, but it is for your own education. I cannot teach you if you are blinded by self-righteousness." He released his telekinetic grip at Jimbo's throat. "Now, let us go and work together on this case." He began walking away, leaving Jimbo struggling to his feet.

~

"Jonathan!" Tamara screamed. "Nicki!" She pulled the child close to her chest. Jonathan looked about, hoping no one had picked up what had just happened.

"It's okay, it's okay. We're fine. Come on. Let's get out of here!" He rushed them across the street toward the garage where they had parked. His thoughts were a torrent of images from his past. All the little clues: the pencil, the book, the tree, the hauler, the countless little "oddities"...the fire in the kitchen. It all came together. But to what? His mind raced as he gathered them into Tamara's car.

Tamara had calmed to the point where she began to get mad. "What the hell was that cabby doing?" she demanded.

"Just thank God he swerved in time," Jonathan lied. "Here, take Nicole to her grandmother's and meet me at my place."

Tamara stopped locking Nicole into her safety seat and looked back at Jonathan, framed in the car window.

"It's okay, baby," he gently said to her. "I want you to stay...with me tonight. Is that all right?"

Tamara tilted her head and intently studied Jonathan's face. She saw the seriousness in his eyes. Taking his hand, she smiled and silently nodded yes.

Who am I... 9

Jonathan watched Tamara inch her way past the accident, which had now become a circus of EMS's and city police. He walked toward the No. 6 L-Tram Station in a daze, not really sure what to do next. What was he supposed to do with this ability? Run the restaurant? Become a superhero and fight crime? *What the hell is going on,* he wondered. He began to question his whole understanding of the world and his place in it. Were there others like him? How would he know? Overwhelmed, he looked beyond the tall, century-old glass-skinned building that had made Chicago so famous and into the afternoon sky. "Where are you now?" he asked God.

Back down the sidewalk, a recycle can was strapped to a street sign. Jonathan spotted it. He focused his attention on the can, closed his eyes and imagined a ball of white energy leaping from the middle of his forehead and striking the can.

Nothing.

He tried again.

Again, nothing.

Frustrated, he remembered the music that had entered his mind just before he had moved the cab. He closed his eyes, focused his body energy, created the ball and listened for the music.

Nothing. Again.

"How the hell does this work?" he questioned under his breath.

Then it occurred to him that each episode happened under some sort of duress. *There must be a trigger,* he thought, *a common thread through all these events.*

Suddenly, a high-pitched screech caught Jonathan's attention. He looked across the street and saw an older woman vault out of the path of a WorldEx van. The woman had moved with all the speed and grace of a girl half her age. She also told the WorldEx driver where he could make his next delivery.

Then it hit him. Adrenaline.

Evolution's genetic leftover. Instinctual instructions blueprinted onto our genetic mapping that helped us survive the dawn of our existence. The cool, thick feeling all humans get when confronted with a stressful situation. Fight or flight.

Jonathan closed his eyes, focused his body energy, created the ball, listened for the music and tried to create an image that would trigger an adrenaline flow. He thought of Tamara being killed by the kit cab.

Like an instinctual trigger, his mind clicked, and he felt the blood drain from his face as adrenaline began to fill his system.

Random musical tones rushed into his mind. His vision shifted from swirling colors to white. Then, as if he had kicked it with his foot, the can tore from the sign pole, its contents ejected into the street. A Channel 6 TVid truck swerved out of the way, its driver swearing at the can like it could actually hear.

A metallic taste filled Jonathan's mouth. He slowly opened his eyes and stared at the can as it came to a rest in the middle of the street. The warm afternoon sun highlighted the people rushing about. He was now resolved to the cold, hard reality that he was not like these people. He was something else – something off the evolutionary chart.

Way off.

He felt, at the same time, both empowered and scared. And he also felt something that had been with him since the death of his parents. An empty feeling of separation. But this time it was different. In the faces of the people walking past, he searched for some signs of himself, of his own humanity. But for the first time in his life, Jonathan Kortel felt disconnected from the world. Set apart in a sea of humanity.

He was, he felt, truly and totally alone.

Touched me... 10

"James, it looks like our Mr. Kortel has discovered his true nature," his partner said, removing the biomicrotransceiver from his ear and folding the field optics back into its case. The senior Tel lit another cigarette and watched from across the street as his Potential slowly walked away from the recycle can and headed toward the L-Tram Station.

Jimbo was silent.

"Please, James, get over what happened back there," his partner ordered. "This kind of behavior is not going to help us in this case."

"How do you want me to react? You nearly goddamn choked me to death!"

"James I am sorry for that, but sometimes a little pressure can make a bigger impression than words."

"Impression alright," Jimbo said, "on my fucking windpipe!"

"James, you may not realize this, but I believe you have potential to be a great Recruiter. You did well earlier. Now lifting that tourist off the street may have been a bit extreme, but nonetheless, we did accomplish the test, and with no interventions."

An "intervention" was Agency slang for inadvertently exposing their real nature to outsiders. Jimbo's partner had never had an intervention in any of his cases, and he was going to keep it that way.

"In fact," his partner continued, "I think people believe that was a real accident back there. Your focus was good, your threshold field was contained, and your GFV was," he flipped open his netpad, "solid and stable. That is what being a professional is all about. You did very well, James."

Jimbo just smiled at his verbal pat on the head.

~

Jonathan unlocked the door to his loft and slowly stepped in. He glanced about the room, confronted by the evidence of a life he had come to enjoy. It all seemed so foreign to him now. He looked down at a pencil on the counter, and it instantly flew to his outstretched hand.

"Shit..." he sighed. He didn't even need to prep. He just asked it to come, and it did. He tried the sofa. It didn't budge. A vase. It slowly rose, hovered, and then crashed to the floor, shattering into hundreds of fragments.

"Damn..." he said sadly. It had been a gift from Hector. "...Guess I'd better get the hang of this." He tried various objects, probing the limits of his new ability, and began to find that certain sizes and weights he could move with no preparation, while others he couldn't. If he prepared, though, he could move big, heavy items with very little effort.

"Jonathan?"

"Yes, Max?"

"What are you doing?"

"Playing around..."

"Oh, very good. I will add this to my database. While you were out, you had three net messages from..."

"Max?"

"Yes, Jonathan?"

"Go off line for a while, please."

"Very good, sir."

Silence filled the loft.

He stood in the middle of the floor as the late afternoon light crept toward the wall. His eyes were closed. His mind was empty. He was listening to the universe. If he were truly the only one, he decided, then he was the first of a new breed of human. He breathed in and exhaled, raised his arms and held them out from his sides. He let his head fall back.

"Oh, God," he started, "show me what I need. This is going to be too big for me. I'm just a..."

The door tone hummed. Max was off line.

It hummed again.

"Max!"

"Sir, a Miss Tamara Connor is here to see you."

"Please," he smiled, "send her up. Thank you," he said under his breath, looking up.

~

When Jonathan opened the door to his loft, Tamara just stood there. She brushed her hair from her face. He looked at her oddly.

"What?" she asked.

He continued to look.

"I'm not in my heels, silly."

Jonathan blushed, having just realized her actual height.

"Nice place," she said. Her voice carried no hint of the near-death experience they had just been through. Jonathan watched her walk into the room. Nothing could change that walk. Even through her baggy clothes, it was as obvious as her beauty.

"Tamara," he said, "stand still for a moment."

She stopped and pulled her shoulders around. The late golden light from the large west windows washed over her. Her eyes focused on him almost like an animal's.

"God, you're beautiful," he said.

Tamara smiled, lowered her head and walked slowly toward him. He gathered her into his arms. She tilted her head and, as her curls fell away, Jonathan saw again the woman, not the dancer. Her eyes told him she wanted nothing else but to be with him that night. He kissed her gently and felt that same strange energy run from the base of his neck through his body. Then he kissed her a second time and, as he did, placed his hand to her heart. This time, though, he had control over his telekinetic delivery.

He felt her gasp against his lips.

"Oh God, baby...I need you," she said into his ear, holding his hand at her chest.

"I need you, too," he said. "I don't know why, but I do."

"Be careful," she whispered. "My world is a lot different than yours."

He pulled back to read her face. Brushing her hair aside, he didn't look at her, he looked into her.

"Tamara," he said, "I know."

~

The moonlight poured into the loft like milk as they made love. Tamara let go, and, for the first time in her life, she felt close to someone without the fear. She hardly knew this man, yet she felt closer to him than she ever had to anyone else. They both knew their connection seemed deeper. Truer. Like old souls. Jonathan made love to her as though these were his last days on earth. And as he held her in his arms, he had a sense that, after today, they might be.

~

"Tamara Connor. Tamara Connor. You have a netcall."

The loft was quiet.

"Excuse me, Tamara, you have a netcall."

"What?..." Tamara asked, blearily looking about the dark room and coughing lightly.

"It's Max, baby," Jonathan groaned. "Yeah, Max, what's up?"

"I'm sorry to wake the both of you, but Miss Connor has a netcall."

"Put it through. And no visual," Jonathan ordered.

"Mommy?..." the small voice asked.

"Nicki honey," Tamara replied. "It's four in the morning...what's the matter?"

"I can't sleep."

"It's okay, little one, now go see grandma and crawl into bed with her. Take Teddy Boo with you."

"Okay, mommy. Night-night."

"Good night, sweetie." Max disconnected the line as Tamara fell back against the pillows.

"You don't mind me giving her your code, do you?...Jonathan?"

She turned to find her lover breathing quietly, hugging his pillow. The moonlight rippled over him as she ran her finger down the curves of his back. She lay there in the calm of the loft and looked at him, wondering if they would last.

"You've touched me like no one else has," she said softly. And she pulled the covers over herself and let the tears silently fall to the pillow.

Infant... 11

Jimbo reclined against the headboard of the hotel bed and studied the netpad's data stream. Jonathan Kortel's telekinetic profile was scary. The GDRD test with the kit cab collected an immense amount of raw data, which revealed that Jonathan was at least a Level 8. His Gravity Field Flux ratios, ATP waves, Electromagnetic Displacement Grid readings, Wave Convergence Threshold and 20 other parameters were all at or near peak levels. The test also set a new tone in the approach the Recruiters would take with this particular Potential.

His partner was visibly disturbed by something he found in the data.

"What is it?" Jimbo asked.

His partner didn't look up. He sat there at the cramped hotel table, exhaustively picking apart Jonathan's data like a vulture on a dead carcass. Cigarette butts were piled in the ashtray, a reminder that his studies had not yielded the information he was desperate to find.

"Damn!" his partner exclaimed.

Jimbo, having never heard his partner swear before, looked up to see his partner's netpad floating about a foot off the hotel table. It held steady, then began to vibrate, building speed until it looked like a small flat blur, which is when it exploded. Parts radiated out in an almost perfect sphere, but they flew no farther than the circumference of a basketball. The pieces hung suspended where they were like some sort of horrendously difficult three-dimensional game. Finally they fell, bouncing and splintering about the tabletop.

His partner was seriously pissed.

"You alright there?" Jimbo asked.

"Yes," he said, still staring at the space the netpad had formerly occupied.

In the 22 years the senior Tel had been a Recruiter, he had reviewed more data on more Potentials than anyone in the Agency. He was known to have a keen sense of seeing clues to a Potential's promise in the data. And something within the terraquads of data on Jonathan Kortel clearly had him worried.

He snuffed out the last of his cigarette. "James, there is something here..."

"Or was here," Jimbo corrected.

"...that disturbs me. Mr. Kortel appears to be a Level 8. But look at his Field Threshold and his Imaging Threshold."

Jimbo flipped his netpad open and scanned down to the two charts.

"And?..." Jimbo questioned.

"Look at the peak levels in the FT and IT."

"Yeah?..."

"Now, see the tiny spike, right before the main MOT spike?"

"MOT?" Jimbo repeated, confused.

"Moment of Truth? James, really, you have heard that before?"

Jimbo remained silent, searching the spikes for what his partner had already found.

"I don't see it," he said with frustration.

"That little spike, James. I've never seen that before in all my years as a Recruiter."

"You used a contraction!" Jimbo was stunned.

"Excuse me?"

"You used a fucking contraction. Shit, you are worried."

The room fell silent.

His partner kept staring.

~

The rest of the afternoon was quiet. Jimbo had fallen asleep while his partner continued to assay the results of the GDRD test. Jonathan Kortel appeared to be a Level 8, but the two spikes in his FT and IT charts said differently. He had shown an intense ability to tighten his Imaging Threshold almost to the width of a needle. And his Field Threshold was immense – at least twice the normal range. These two key bits of data pointed to only one thing: Jonathan Kortel was in the embryonic stages of developing to a Level 9. This was not good. There were only ten Level 8's in the world, and the appearance of a

Level 9 changed the playing field altogether. As the highest testing Tel ever, Jimbo's partner felt something else from the data. Something he had never felt in his life.

Fear.

The introduction of a Level 9 would change the telekinetic world forever. Eights had set the standard for more than 70 years. Since the first discovery of a Level 8 in 2030, the Tel world had a standard that created balance and stability. If Jonathan Kortel was truly an infant Level 9, then the Tel Chart might require adjustment. Testing would be refined. Level assignments would shift. And the senior Tel's status would diminish. Jonathan Kortel could be the Gabriel, trumpeting a new era for mankind. At the moment, though, the senior Tel felt Jonathan was more like an infant wielding a charged Light-Force bioweapon. If his calculations were accurate, the curve for Jonathan's growth was beginning to increase...and at an alarming rate. In a matter of days, he could achieve NTB.

"No Turning Back" was Agency-speak for the instant a Tel crossed the divide between awareness and acceptance. Most often, once a Tel accepted his or her condition, the LR, or Learn Rate, skyrocketed. There were no more emotional walls, no mental confusion – just a clear and present resolve to grow, develop and master their ability. Once Jonathan "crossed," the senior Tel feared he might not be able to control him. Having a live-wire Level 9 loose in the world would be a dangerous situation, and one the senior Tel was determined to avoid.

He watched the moon rise.

He smoked another cigarette.

~

Jonathan woke to the sound of rain hitting the metal roof. He rolled over looking for his lover.

"Hey, Tam?..." he quietly said, grabbing at the empty pillow.

He listened to the rain.

"Tamara?...Max!"

"Yes, sir?"

"Is Tamara in the loft?"

"No, sir. She left this morning at 8:37. She did leave you a message, however."

"Play it...please," Jonathan said cautiously.

Max engaged the message.

"Morning, baby..." her voice was somber and cool. "...Don't take this wrong. I...I really...last night was wonderful. It was so intense. We're so intense. You're the first guy that I've felt..." she hesitated, "...close to in a long time, maybe ever. When you touch me, it's almost too much. My feelings are...weird. I'm so drawn to you, it's like innate. I feel like we've known each other a long time....You know what I mean? Hey, look, I guess I'm freaking here just a little. It's not you....It's me. It's a little scary, sort of, I mean the intensity and all." She paused for a moment; the dead space killed Jonathan. "Baby, my life is so different from yours. Look at what I do. And there's Nicki. I can't hope that you'll learn to like her, even...love her. I can't ask that of you. Oh, Jonathan, I'm sorry....Bear with me for just a bit. I need some space. This is all too fast....I can't believe that I could..." her voice trailed off to a whisper. "...Umm, hey, I'm working tonight. Please come by. We'll talk. Take care, lover."

Max ended the message.

Jonathan was numb. His heart was collapsing from its own weight. He was beyond crying. The message cut right through him. He looked at a bowl filled with fruit, and it exploded, spraying yellow and green shards about the room. He slumped to the edge of the bed and cupped his head in his hands. The glass decanter given as the award for the Best New Chef in Chicago imploded, releasing its 30-year-old Scotch over the side table. The frame holding the only image he had of his parents shattered, slicing the photo into pieces. Oblivious to the destruction happening around him, he could think only of her.

Empty and alone, he stepped into the bathroom and glared at himself in the mirror. He drew back his fist, but the mirror shattered before he could throw the punch. Max asked repeatedly what was wrong. Jonathan's only reply was to switch him off at the system panel on the way to the hydroshower. He stood there frozen, with the air and water pulsing against his body. He brought his hands to his face to wipe away the previous night, but all he could do was smell their passion. Like a metaphor, she was right there at his fingertips.

MOT... 12

Anari sat at the bar resting her chin in her hand. Her bioshifting hair extension moved about her head to form intricate geometric shapes: first a multidimensional knot, then a ponytail in the shape of a real pony. She was bored out of her mind. The Den was empty, and the rent on her apartment was past due. Liquid Courage was suffering for a Saturday night. Gone were the BioUrologist Conventioneers who, for the last week, had swarmed over the city like drunken polyestered locusts. Gone, too, was their small contingent of lesbian doctors who had taken a liking to the club's "relaxed" policies on what could and couldn't be touched.

Anari wanted some action tonight. "Tebby, this isn't going to be good for me," she said with a yawn, her hair now in the shape of the Eiffel Tower. The young bar back laughed, and his rings clinked together in a sick tonal rhythm. On the main floor, a handful of military boys were betting who could slam the most Napalm Drops. At a four-top were the Too Blacks, slick, inner-city biodrug street repers suited up in their badest all-rain biogear just laughin' and slappin'. Except for the one or two horny husbands at the one-tops, club Liquid was dead.

Tamara was prepping in the locker room. She stared blankly into the mirror as the makeup artist sprayed the finishing highlights onto an intense palette of eye shadow. Tamara was there, but not there. Her mind was torn between the life she had and the life that Jonathan Kortel represented. He was 10 years older – not that that's bad, but she was still young and pretty wild for a single mother. She could not stop feeling the wonderful energy that had passed between them. Like a sexual hangover, it lingered in her system. She had never felt anything like it before, but its presence had both happy and scary overtones. Other dancers had always told her to find an older guy. They would be less put off by a single mom, they had said, than a guy her own age. But Tamara wanted someone real. Age was not as much an issue as the person. Her next move had never been far from her mind. Getting out of the professional sex trade had always been part of the plan, but how was another story. She had gone to a city college for a time and excelled in art. Art history and drawing were her favorite subjects, but what she could do with a degree in art history was up for debate in the 22nd century. As Blade put the final line on her eyelids, Tamara gazed at the eyes in the mirror. They look tired. After five years as a professional dancer, prostitute, student and single mother, Tamara's soul was beginning to show wear.

"Now, there we go!" Blade said smugly. "That's hot, if I do say so."

Being sexy for another fucked-up, drunk businessman was the last thing Tamara wanted to be doing. She leaned forward and intently studied the person looking back at her from the mirror.

"Honey, is it not what you wanted?" Blade asked, surprised.

Tamara didn't answer. "You're lying to yourself again," she said to her reflection. She closed her eyes and raised her hand to her heart. All she could feel was him.

~

Tamara had asked the VJ to track from her slow stuff. She wasn't in the spirit for any electro-funk from the African coast. It was 9:15, and Liquid was only at two stages. She came out as she had a million times before. There could have been two or two hundred marks; with the lights hitting her eyes for the first time, it all looked black to her. She slid over the stage floor and out to the edge that jutted into the crowd (if there had been one). A businessman on his VIDphone looked up in mid-conversation and gave her a thumbs-up. Tamara wanted to wretch. She bent over, her ass facing the Too Blacks, reached between her spread legs and slid her fingers from the center of her ass to the top of her thong. She straightened and glanced over her shoulder at the biodrug lords with the look she had been giving since she was 16.

"Okay, you fuckers," Tamara said under her breath, and she started to dance as seductively as she could. The four-top repers came alive, banging their Buckets of Sin with their fists. Their gold jewelry reflected the stage lights, which had swung over to highlight their table. One got up and approached the main stage. Tamara danced over. She side-stepped right in front of him, then at the perfect moment in the song bent over backwards. Her legs spread wide apart, her back arched off the floor, she lay there humping the air. She slid her fingers up her crotch, past her breasts to the tip of her tongue.

The mark smiled at her and revealed his name in a perfect natural gold upper setting. "MR. COOL SHIT" was definitely a player.

He slipped out a Liquid five-C note as she crawled catlike towards him. She rubbed herself against him and purred in his ear.

"Say, baby," Mr. Cool Shit said, sliding her the note, "I'll see you at the next stage." He pinched her clitoris through her simmesh thong. Tamara didn't jump. She was a pro, but on the main floor, especially main stage, certain touching was way out of the zone. She smiled sex right back at him.

Tamara finished her set with her best pole work. Not one Liquid dollar. She picked up her things like an automaton, jumped off stage and sauntered to stage two. As she passed the drug lords, Mr. Cool Shit smiled his name. She never took off her "come fuck me look" all the way to stage two. His gaze tracked her like a poacher.

The next girl on the main stage requested EuroTech dance crap. Tamara jammed to its beat like she was riding on Z Dust. Mr. Cool Shit rose from his table, high-fiving his brothers. He straightened his French biothread tie, pulled his cuffs out of his suit sleeves and approached stage two as if he owned Tamara. She read his look. She changed her dance to ensure he would tip and tip big. Mr. Cool Shit pulled out a wad of Liquid five hundreds as big as his fist.

Tamara pulled her thong down to the top of what little pubic hair she hadn't removed. Liquid was dead, and she needed the cash. Mr. Cool Shit laughed and licked his lips.

"Baby, I know that's right," he laughed as she bent down to greet him.

"Having a good time?" she purred.

"Damn straight." He slid two five-C notes into the front of her thong. They were so crisp they almost cut her skin.

"Yeah, baby..." she whispered into his ear, then licked it. With the taste of his poly-layered hair gel on her tongue, she stood and bent backwards, reaching for the floor. Mr. Cool Shit thought he'd test the standards of Liquid Courage. Her legs were spread, and her crotch was in his face. As soon as her hands touched the floor, Mr. Cool Shit pulled her thong aside and pressed his tongue into the gap. Startled, Tamara dropped to her back, leaving Mr. Cool Shit smiling his name and licking the air.

She kicked him across the face.

The force of the blow surprised even Tamara. Mr. Cool Shit's head snapped back so fast that his Czech-made Micro-Night Shades flew halfway to the main stage. He quickly pulled his head around and grabbed her ankle, his nails digging into her skin. He wasn't smiling his name any longer.

She kicked him again.

He slowly brought his head back and grinned. His name now was MR. COOL HIT. He spat blood and his "S" tooth onto the stage. "You fucking bitch whore!" he yelled. He jerked her forward by her ankle. His lieutenants jumped to their feet.

She kicked him for the last time.

"Oh, you gonna fucking pay, bitch!" He threw open his suit coat and reached into it.

The VJ stopped the music. The club went silent. The dancer

on the main stage crouched down on her 12-inch heels in the middle of the stage. She buried her face in her knees knowing too well what would come next.

Mr. Cool Hit pulled out a hand-held Light-Force bioweapon – not the standard issue for young drug lords climbing the corporate ladder out of the inner city. It was very light and very hard to get.

Its polycarbon and titanium housing reflected in Tamara's eyes. She didn't need to see the weapon to know that this reper was about to cap this little white girl's ass. In fear, she recoiled, slamming her forehead into the stage pole. Whether from pain or from her anticipated death, she shut her eyes tight and tears streamed down her cheeks. The light from the weapon's discharge filled her vision with white.

A girl screamed behind her.

She waited for the pain.

~

After a second, Tamara's mind recovered from her own death. The club remained silent. Nothing had happened. Still clutching the pole, she could taste blood running down her forehead into the corner of her mouth. She slowly opened her eyes and turned in the direction of the light blast.

There, two inches from her face, the end of the bioweapon beam floated motionless in the air. It was silent and glowed a brilliant white. It was as thin as a needle and protruded from the muzzle about three feet, which likewise was still in the hand of Mr. Cool Hit. His coat was flung open, suspended in midflap. His bloodied spittle was frozen in the air just in front of his open mouth, which appeared ready to finish a sentence. Even his stance was halted in midstep, his left foot four inches off the floor. The whole scene resembled a bad holoposter from some black Euro-action vid.

Tamara was shaking. Her legs buckled, and she crumpled to the base of the pole. The few people in the club were also standing motionless, but it was by their own choice. Mr Cool Hit's brothers, though, had fallen back into their chairs, stunned.

There was a scream at the rear of the club, near the back bar.

"Tamara!"

Fear had gripped Tamara so tightly, she could hardly make out the voice.

"Tamara!" Anari screamed again. "Look!"

Tamara followed the direction of the scream. There, next to Anari, was Jonathan. His head was tilted back, and his eyes were closed. Arms outstretched, his fists were clenched as tightly as his teeth. Blood poured from his ears, his nose and his eyes. His chest arched like he had been shot in the back, and he was floating.

Anari's hands were at her mouth as if she were about to gag. She looked back and forth between Jonathan and Tamara.

"Tamara, look! Look at him!" she screamed, pointing.

Tamara, and the whole of Liquid Courage, couldn't take their eyes from Jonathan. An admixture of blood and sweat dripped from him onto the floor three inches beneath his feet. No one moved. There was a gasp from one of the dancers.

Tamara carefully avoided the suspended Light-Force beam, climbed down from the stage and ran to her lover. Stopping short of him, the reality of the moment hit her hard.

Anari reached out to touch him. She jerked back.

"Oh my God, he's burning up!" she whispered.

Tamara cautiously approached. "Baby," she pleaded, her shock giving way to the need of the moment, "talk to me, please. Can you hear me?" She was beginning to cry.

"Are you all right?" Jonathan said hoarsely.

"Oh God, yes, yes baby, I am," she whispered to him, now only inches from his face.

His eyes opened, and his head fell forward. He caved to the floor, supporting himself on hands and knees, spitting blood onto Tamara's shoes. Simultaneously, the Light-Force bioweapon completed its discharge, and the wall mirror behind stage two debiolized into a gooey puddle. Mr. Cool Hit, released from Jonathan's telekinetic grip, finished his lunge toward the edge of the stage: "...ucking whore!"

Four standard Light-Force street handguns appeared from behind each bar, their high-pitched whines indicating that they would be fully charged in less than a second.

"Drop the weapon, motherfucker, or you'll end up like the mirror!"

Mr. Cool Hit smarted out. His bioweapon hit the carpet without a sound.

Tamara knelt beside Jonathan. "Jonathan. Oh baby, what did you..."

"I couldn't see you die!" Jonathan cried. He tried to stand but was too exhausted. His spit out blood again.

Tamara touched his back. It was burning hot. He looked at her for the first time. Tears and blood created a web of small rivers over his face.

"Oh, Tamara," he reached up for her. "I had to stop it...I need you so much..." his voice faded.

Tamara gathered him into her arms and held him close. He was shaking. "I need you too, lover," she whispered into his ear. She squeezed him tightly, and he coughed blood down her back.

~

James McCarris was leaning forward on his elbows at a table just off the second stage. He was shocked at what he had just seen. His hands shook so badly that there was more of his drink on the table than in his glass. "Did you see that!? Did you fucking see that!?" he said in disbelief.

His partner didn't respond. He was also visibly shaken by what he had just witnessed. Never in all his years had he seen someone like this. *Jonathan's Learn Rate curve,* he conjectured, *was off the planet.*

"Is that possible!? Can he really do that!?" There was fear in Jimbo's voice. "What the fuck is going on here!?"

His partner couldn't talk. His mind was too busy calculating the parameters of what he was seeing. His netpad readings were running wild. Faster than he could scan, his mind had come to the realization of who, or what, he was confronting. Jonathan Kortel was something new, and his netpad couldn't define him.

"Sir..." Jimbo whispered in the dead silence of the club, "...he's faster than light! He's faster than fucking light....He created a grav field that froze a Light-Force beam dead in its tracks....That can't be..." His voice trailed off. As Jimbo stared at the Light-Force beam suspended in air, the intensity of the situation tore at his mind.

"Oh God..." he quietly uttered.

"That," his partner finally answered, "is what I believe we are dealing with here."

He snapped his netpad shut.

With no interventions... 13

Jonathan surveyed the club, wiping the sweat and blood from his face. He felt about a dozen people staring at him. Tamara was holding him up. “I’ve got to get out of here,” he coughed.

“Jonathan, you’re hurt...” Tamara pleaded.

“Jonathan, listen to her,” Anari said. “You are seriously fucked up. You’re bleeding all over the place.”

She was right. The blood wouldn’t stop flowing from his nose, and he could taste it in his throat.

“I can’t stay, don’t you get it?!” he said, voice rising. “Look at what I just did! What the hell am I?!” He was now seriously freaking. He pushed Tamara off of him and stumbled backwards into the buffet table. Jerking about, he searched for the exit.

“Baby, don’t. Please, let me help you!” Tamara cried.

Without a hand laid on them, small tables and chairs flew

out of Jonathan's way as he stumbled toward the front of the club, coughing and spitting blood.

"Jonathan," Tamara screamed, "please don't go...please..."

Jonathan stopped, crumbling against a pillar, sending its hydro-grown plant crashing to the floor. He turned to see his love standing there, her shoulders slumped and arms to her sides. She was sobbing. Jonathan had never seen anyone look so helpless. She raised her eyes to him. Her makeup had melted into a nightmarish look.

"...I...I...think I love you," she said softly, not believing what she heard herself say.

Jonathan looked to her, then to the exit, and back to her. He knew he couldn't stay. Soon Liquid Courage would be a full-out media show of city police, VID trucks and young-gun reporters. And that was the last thing he could face. "I can't," he groaned. "I'm sorry, baby." Jonathan picked himself up and ran out into the lobby.

Tamara dropped to her knees.

~

The two Recruiters sat at their table and struggled with the input streaming into their senses. The laws of physics were supposed to define the property and nature of all matter. Tonight, though, the laws of physics at Club Courage were from another universe. Jonathan was definitely a Level 9, possibly heading toward Level 10, and he had just stumbled out of Liquid Courage into a very dangerous world.

That, Jimbo thought, *was some serious shit.*

"James, we have a containment issue here," the senior Tel declared.

"No shit, Hawkins!" Jimbo mocked.

"Shut this place down, James. Kill the power at the main grid for this floor and give me a grav field burst, from there to there." His sweeping gesture covered the whole of the main room. He looked at his colleague for the first time. "And James, I do not need to tell you the seriousness of this containment, do I?"

"No sir," Jimbo said soberly.

The two Tels, shifting gears into professional mode, slowly rose unnoticed from their chairs. This was the moment when all their training would be brought to bear. Jimbo did as he was told. All the doors slammed shut and locked. The lights in the club went out. A slow murmur began to build until it gave way to yells and panic.

"I am sorry, James," his partner said coldly through the blackness and confusion, "but some people are going to be hurt."

The senior Tel quietly went into telekinetic phase, whereupon silence fell over Liquid Courage for a second time that evening.

~

Not long before this, Anari had been consoling her best friend, who was kneeling on the floor. "Come on, sweetie, he'll be okay. He's not going to leave you," she lied.

Anari gathered Tamara and led her back to the Den. There wasn't a soul around. The two of them drew comfort from the thick granite and Teflon walls as they fell into a booth near the back. Tamara was visibly stunned. Appearing like she had just heard the news of a child's death, Tamara stared blankly forward. The events of the night played again and again in her head. She dug deep for the street toughness that had always served her well, but she couldn't seem to find it. To realize love and lose it all at the same time had taken its toll on the 21-year-old.

Then the lights went out in the Den.

"What the fuck?..." Anari said under her breath. Anari was a "streetie." Her sixth sense kicked in, and she read the moment. "Come on!" she ordered and yanked Tamara out of the booth. Anari used her netpad light to guide them haltingly to the back of the Den. She waved her keycard at the exit door's system pad. No response. She tried again. Nothing.

"Shit!" Anari exclaimed. "In here!" They ran toward the biopaste locker near the kitchen. Anari grabbed the handle and yanked the door open. It hissed as it swung, blasting them with the sweet smell of the world's finest hydroponic-biopaste. They tumbled in, and Anari kicked the door shut. They leaned against the cool, 12-inch-thick lead wall. The usual hum of the biotanks was gone, and the pitch blackness concealed the size of the room.

Tamara reached through the darkness and took Anari's hand.

"Thanks, Anari," Tamara finally said.

"*No problema,* chicky."

They sat there quietly, waiting for the next chapter in an already strange night.

~

"James, the lights, please."

The low industrial hum of electricity returned to the club as the bar lights and stage spots grew back to full illumination. The two Tels stood like generals after a battle. The drug lord and his lieutenants, the businessman on the VIDphone, the four-top of military boys, the Liquid workers and freelance dancers: all were strewn about the club, unconscious. Some had fallen right where they stood. Others had landed in not-so-comfortable ways.

The senior Tel was clearly exhausted.

"You all right?" Jimbo asked, surveying the telekinetic carnage.

"Yes, James, just a little tired. Could you please see if anyone is seriously hurt." He collapsed into his chair.

Jimbo went from person to person, checking pulses and taking readings from his netpad. A petite Latina dancer had landed with her leg underneath her hip. It was fractured in three places.

"This looks bad, boss."

"Will she live?"

"Oh yeah, but she may not dance again." Jimbo moved on to the next victim, keeping a running tally. One broken wrist. Two cracked ribs. One guy was bleeding severely from the ears and nose. "Sir..."

"Yes, James," his partner answered, already knowing what Jimbo was going to say.

"I think we lost one here."

"What do the med readings say, goddamn it!"

"He's dead, sir."

His partner went silent and rubbed his forehead. "Okay, James, let's finish up," he finally said.

The senior Tel brushed back his salt-and-pepper hair. Assignments like this didn't help the aging process. He looked around at his handiwork. "James, they look so...fragile."

Jimbo finished his scans. If Jonathan Kortel was truly heading for Level 9 status, the Recruiters needed to act fast. The exponential rise in his LR was unnerving at best. No data had ever been recorded on a Level 9, much less a Level 10, and Level 10's were thought to be impossible to achieve. It appeared to the Recruiters that the impossible was possible.

"We're missing Tamara and the Asian," Jimbo said. "You want me to go find them?"

"No, James, we will deal with that containment issue later." He wiped the sweat from his brow. "For now, our concentration should be on finishing here and moving on to Jonathan."

To Jimbo, for the first time his partner looked his age. His hair was wet with sweat, his skin was pale, and he actually looked frail sitting in the club's oversized chair.

The senior Tel lifted his eyes to Jimbo with all the seriousness of his years. "This should appear, James, as an electrobiomicroburst. The building has enough net linkhubs. If we destroy the one on this floor, it could inflict this type of damage quite easily."

"What will they remember?" Jimbo asked.

"Well, I can tell you what they will definitely not remember. They will not remember the last 24 hours. And some may have severe motor-function challenges for the next week or two." His voice grew tired, and he looked in the direction of the bar back lying in a pool of his own blood.

"I am very sorry for that young man. This was not his affair."

"Let's go find the linkhub, sir," Jimbo suggested. "We haven't much time. Kortel's loose, and we're not getting any closer to him."

His partner nodded in agreement.

~

The blackness of the biopaste locker was calming, and, for Anari, a little calm was needed to regroup. Without warning, the low lights of the room came on. The soft drone of the biotank motors revved up, and their tiny bubbling sound resumed. Anari checked out Tamara.

"You look like shit, girlie!"

Tamara smiled, cracking the now dried makeup mask she was sporting. "Don't worry. I feel like shit, too."

Tamara's head pounded from the emotion of the night. She let it fall back against the wall and closed her eyes. At that moment, all she could think of was life without Jonathan. She had to get it together if she was going to salvage what was left of her life with him. "Let's go!" Tamara barked, her own street sense finally appearing.

They left the locker and headed back into the club. What they found was more surreal than what they had left. They cautiously checked the unconscious people.

"What happened here?" Anari asked, picking up and dropping the limp wrist of the night manager.

"Oh no!" screamed Tamara. "It's Tebby...I think he's...dead."

Anari ran to her side.

They stared down at the young bar back. One side of his face rested in a pool of deep red blood that was slowly fanning out. His eyes were open, his rings were silent, and he looked strangely peaceful.

"He was a cool dude," Anari said.

A groan came from the main stage.

They ran up to stage number one, where the lights were still trained on the dancer awakening from her telekinetic sleep. She sat up and crossed her legs, rubbing her face.

"Oh, man...god, what the hell am I doing here?" she asked gruffly.

Puzzled, Tamara glanced at Anari, then back to the dancer. "Where do you think you should be?" Tamara asked.

"I was at home, making some breakfast, which I never do..." she grabbed her head in pain. "Oh shit...what the fuck is going on?" She looked around the club confused. Someone groaned at a two-top, and a cough came from the bar. Tamara and Anari watched as one by one, Liquid Courage began to wake up.

"She doesn't remember a thing," Tamara whispered to Anari.

"Yeah, like not a thing since yesterday. This is getting just a little weird."

Suddenly an explosion shook the building near the elevators. The force threw Tamara and Anari to their hands and knees. The piercing tone of the fire alarm system stung their ears. Emergency lights flooded the club, and the bitter taste of fire retardant began to fill the room.

"Let's get the hell out of here! This place is gonna be crawling with fire and police in about five minutes!" Tamara yelled over the hiss of retardant mist. They scrambled back toward the Den, and Anari noticed the young bar back on her way past. She realized that things would never be quite the same in the land of Liquid Courage.

To see a friend... 14

"Lights, Max."

The loft's lights grew in intensity. Jonathan's earlier telekinetic rampage was still in evidence. He had no time to waste. His ability was outpacing his control over it. He quickly began to pack.

"Will you be leaving for a time, sir?"

"Yes, Max, but I don't know for how long."

"Very good. I will notify the..."

"No! Max, that's all right. Don't change any of the loft's protocols."

"Yes, sir. Where are you going, sir?"

Jonathan stopped packing and looked out the large windows. The sun was beginning to rise over the city. "I'm going to see a dear friend."

"Why, sir?"

Taken aback by the intuitive question of his loft's AI, Jonathan hesitated for a second. "I can't tell you."

"Very good, sir. Will there be anything else?"

"You still have Tamara Connor's voice print in memory?"

"Yes, sir."

"Then the message I'm about to leave is for her ears only. Use her voice print as the only access to the message. Understood?"

"Perfectly, sir. Shall I encrypt it so no one can access it?"

"Yes, Max, that will be fine. Oh, and Max?"

"Yes, sir?"

"I want to amend my will. Please adjust it so that upon my death, my personal wealth – not the business holdings – is put in a trust for a Nicole Connor, at such time as she comes of age...blah, blah, blah. You know what to do. Access your legal database. It should all be in there. You still have her voice print and net address information?"

"Yes, sir. I will need your retina scan for authorization."

"I know. And make it accessible by her mother, Tamara Connor. Her net address is the same as Nicole's."

"Yes, sir."

"And Max, if any report of my death comes across the net in the next few days or weeks..." his voice trailed off.

"Sir?"

"Hell, just let Tamara know, will you please?"

"Very good, sir."

"Are you ready for my message?"

"Yes, sir."

~

While Jonathan dictated, he paced the room, solemnly reviewing the items that had been destroyed. So many years of memories, and it was all about to change. He picked up his gear bag and turned to go.

"Sir?"

"Yeah, Max?"

"Good luck."

Jonathan stopped. He thought he heard a trace of sadness in the AI's voice output.

"You can go off line now, Max, until you recognize the voice print of Hector, Tamara or Nicole."

Jonathan walked out the front door, headed for the one man who might know what was happening to him. Someone he could trust.

The message... 15

It was 3 a.m. when the Recruiters entered Jonathan's loft.

"Lights, please."

There was no response.

"Lights, please, Max," Jimbo repeated.

They waited.

"He's off line," Jimbo said.

"He is using a voice print ID matrix," his partner said, working his netpad. "No matter." The loft's basic functions came to life. He lit another cigarette and took a long drag. "What do you sense, James?"

Jimbo was studying the loft. As he walked about the living room, his hands grazed over certain items: a photo of Jonathan and Hector deep-sea fishing, a small Mexican mask, an old book by an 18th century author with the inscription: To Jonathan, love Dad.

"Moby Dick..." Jimbo said under his breath.

"What, James?"

"Melville, Herman Melville. Moby Dick. I haven't seen this since I was a kid."

"One of the greatest works of human literature, James."

"Yeah, I loved this book." Jimbo studied the inscription.

"What are you sensing?" his partner questioned. "What is your seventh sense saying about Jonathan Kortel?"

Jimbo continued to touch and sense the essence of the man they were hunting. Like an old Southern bloodhound, he let his seventh sense take over his actions. When Potentials deny their abilities, they often run, and usually to someone close, such as a brother or sister. But Jonathan Kortel had no family. The Recruiters would have to rely on simple detective work to find their Potential, and Jonathan Kortel would be a difficult hunt.

His partner casually smoked as he watched his young associate track Jonathan's telekinetic "scent."

"It looks like he's in emotional pain," Jimbo announced.

"Oh, how is that?"

"Look at all this broken stuff. This is a clean, neat, put-together kind of guy. These trashed items are typical of a Potential struggling with his new ability."

"But..." his partner probed.

"But something's off. Most of these are very personal items. Potentials typically don't 'test out' on their personal stuff. They test out on things they can do without, junk, typically. He was distraught, probably over the dancer. Look here, this photo and this piece of art. And here, the Melville book. Why would he tear it apart?"

"Because?..." his partner quizzed.

"Because he's probably in love with her, and he's denying that. And he's in conflict with his new ability."

"And he is out there, somewhere, mentally unstable." His partner pointed to the large windows. "James, if our Jonathan Kortel is really developing into a Level 9, then the key to finding him will be Miss Connor."

"Max, play back..." Jimbo ordered.

"Oh, do not bother, James. Max is off line, and that is simple enough to correct, but I am sure Jonathan, being the excellent programmer that he is, has encrypted Max." He flipped open his netpad and began the hacking sequence to bring Max back on line. "Max?" he asked.

"Gentlemen, your presence is unauthorized. I will have to notify building security."

"Don't bother, Max." Jimbo said, still mulling through the loft. "They're off line to you."

"Max," the senior Tel asked, "where did Jonathan go?"

"I am unable to answer your request, sir."

"Yeah, yeah, we already knew you'd say that, too," Jimbo yelled from the back bedroom.

His partner was busy hacking into Max's matrix, downloading any of Jonathan's data that he could access into his netpad. "He has left her a message that is voice ID'd for her ears only, James, and these encryption codes are difficult." Frustrated, he snapped the netpad shut. "He is a damn good programmer."

"What about the other chef, Hector?" Jimbo asked.

"Possible. Go ahead and set up a VIDTrans there...and there," the senior Tel ordered, indicating a spot across the room. "I am sure Miss Connor will show up and retrieve his message. And when she does, Max's matrix will be exposed for our entry. We might get something, we might not. It is hard to say. But I do know this, she will lead us to him. I have a good feeling about her."

Jimbo's partner returned Max to his default settings while Jimbo set up the VIDTrans. Despite all their sophisticated equipment, they had failed to beat Jonathan's code. He had programmed Max's bioconstruct to be almost impossible for any hacker to breach without damage to the entire core matrix.

In the middle of the living room, Jimbo's partner stood gazing at the city through the loft's large windows. He was compressing his smoke into tiny little particle balls and letting them drop to the carpet, which he often did when his mind was working overtime.

"How you gonna play this one, boss?" Jimbo asked.

"James, if Jonathan is a Level 9, then we must be very careful not to...what is the word?"

"Spook him?"

"Yes...spook him. He will soon become very strong, stronger than I can control. So we have to befriend him, get him to trust us and trust the Agency. Pressure will not work on this one, James. Believe me. He is independent. And do you know what the most volatile factor is in this whole equation?" Morning light was beginning to stream into the loft. He blew a perfect smoke ring, letting it hang in front of him before compressing it into a little cube that floated into his outstretched hand. He slowly curled his fingers over the cube. "He might be in love, James. And that scares me the most."

Jimbo examined the system's panel to shut off the lights. "Say

Max," he said impulsively, "why are you named Max?"

"I am named after Jonathan's brother."

"We have no record of him having a brother," the senior Tel quipped.

"He died in childbirth, July 22, 2080, in Honolulu, Oahu, in the Hawaiian Islands."

The Tels exchanged a glance.

The senior Tel finished his cigarette, and they began to leave, but Jimbo stopped and stepped back into the loft. He walked toward the table and stretched out his hand. The book from Jonathan's father quietly flew into it. Jimbo turned it lovingly, caressing its soft leather cover.

"Call me Ishmael..." he said under his breath, pocketing the book in his coat.

~

Tamara woke to Anari standing on her head in the middle of the apartment. She was breathing softly in and out.

"Good morning, sunshine," Anari said, too cheery for the time of day.

"Morning," Tamara said, rubbing the sleep out of her eyes. "What are you doing?"

"My yoga," she answered. Anari fell over, spun around and ended up in full lotus position, with one finger to a nostril.

Tamara lit a cigarette and fell back against the bed.

Anari's apartment was a tiny 1-1 on the city's south side. Tamara had crashed there because, after dropping Nicole off at her grandmother's, she had been in no shape to deal with the late-night pilot crazies of the Interway. Anari was part Korean, part black and part anyone's guess. Having been found in a newspaper recycle bin at the end of Korea's last war with itself, she had been kicked from foster home to foster home. Her last and longest-lasting family was from the city. When she turned 18, she split and began a career in the late-night club scene. Doing everything from waitressing to dancing, she landed at Liquid Courage through a friend who knew Joshua. Her apartment was sparsely furnished with a professional's attention to design.

Tamara closed her eyes and emptied her mind.

Anari screamed at the top of her lungs.

"What the hell are you doing?" Tamara said, covering her ears.

"Primal screaming."

"Primal whating?"

"Screaming. You should try it. It helps you get in touch with your real self. It's an old technique from 20th century pop psychology. I think it came out of that weird California thing...PEST, yeah, I think that's what it was called. I found it in an old book." She took a sip from her hydro-root celery tea.

Tamara gathered the blankets around her, clutching them for their innate security. She looked out the window and tried not to think of the events of last night. It was hard, though. The realization of what her lover was, of what he did (if she really knew), was almost too much to comprehend. She and Anari had said nothing on the ride back to her apartment. There had been no need. Anari had known Tamara for a long time and could read her like a netpad.

Anari handed her a cup of tea. "Hey, chicky, don't worry," she consoled.

"Don't worry?" Tamara took a long drag off her cigarette. "You did see what I saw last night, didn't you?" She sipped the tea and winced at its bitterness.

"I did!" Anari said. "But what did he do? If he did stop that Light-Force the reper was using, how? Some brain thing? I mean, come on, is Jonathan some gov experiment? How well do you know this guy, Tam?"

Tamara pulled in her knees tightly and began to rock. The end of her cigarette touched the blanket, which began to hiss from the burn.

"Oh fucking shit!" Tamara batted wildly at the little burning threads that floated up from the blanket. "Anari, I'm so sorry, I'll get you a new one, really."

"Tam, don't worry...come on, it's just a blanket." Anari walked over and sat next to her. "Everything's going to be all right."

"Anari, that was telekinesis. Jonathan must be telekinetic, and if he can stop a weapon that powerful, he must be equally powerful..." She kept staring and rocking, unable to bring herself to finish the thought.

"What if he's, you know...not human?" Anari asked.

"You mean an alien? No, no way."

"No, I mean, a *different* human. Something from evolution, you know."

"He might be." Tamara closed her eyes. If her lover was more than human, then what did that make him? She put her hand to her heart and remembered the energy that flowed between them, the intense heat and tingling that filled her chest when he touched her. She had fallen in love with a man who could stop a weapon as powerful as a Light-Force, and she had no idea where he was.

One person might know, though.

"Max..." she said under her breath.

"What, Tam?"

"Come on, get dressed." Tamara said, toughing up. "We're heading out."

"Where?" Anari asked.

"To see a friend."

~

Tamara and Anari cautiously approached the door to Jonathan's loft.

"Are you sure he's not here?" Anari asked.

"I've called at least twenty times," Tamara said.

"Okay then. I'm following you, chicky,"

Tamara put out her cigarette.

"Max, it's me, Tamara Connor."

There was a long pause.

"Max, it's..."

"Good afternoon, Tamara." And the door unlatched.

The lights slowly came on as they entered.

"How are you today, Miss Connor? Who is your friend?"

"Max, this is Anari, and I'm fine, thanks."

They looked around the loft. Stepping through broken art and glass, Tamara was clearly disturbed.

"This place is trashed," Anari said.

"Yeah, and this isn't how he would have left it."

"Jonathan destroyed the items you see," Max interrupted.

"Why, Max?" Tamara asked.

"These are the physical, telekinetic results of the emotional duress he experienced after hearing your message."

"What did you say, girl?" Anari asked.

Tamara just stared.

"Girl?"

"I told him how I felt...then, I mean. Okay, I was freaked a little..." She lit up another cigarette.

"Well, by the looks of this place, you hurt him pretty bad."

Tamara scanned the room. Some, if not all, of Jonathan's favorite things were destroyed. He had told her about the mask that Hector had brought back to him. And the book his dad had given him as a child.

"Hey, where's the book?" Tamara said. She went to the table where Jonathan had kept it. "The book's gone. That's really strange."

"What book's that?" Anari asked.

"Moby Dick. It was real special to him. It was one of the only things he had from his father."

"Moby who? What is it, porn?"

Tamara shot Anari a look. "No. It's a classic."

"Tamara, there is a message for you," Max said.

"Really..." Tamara said slowly. "Please play it."

"Hey, you," Jonathan's holoimage appeared in the middle of the loft. He looked tired and his voice was rough. "I hope you're alone. But if not, well, it doesn't matter. Hi, Anari, if that's you." Anari smiled and looked over to Tamara. "Hey, baby, listen. What happened tonight was kind of an epiphany for me. All my life I've known that I was different in some way...I just couldn't put my finger on it. But some things have happened recently, and they've all culminated at the club with that reper pulling Light out on you." Jonathan's voice began to shake a little. "When he drew, I was talking to Anari. You need to thank her, baby, she really saved your life. She punched my arm so hard....It's still sore, girl, if you're in the room. Anyway, look, ah...I couldn't see you die in front of my eyes. I think I would have lost it right there. I've come to need you. You're like a drug to me, baby." Jonathan laughed and then coughed hard for a few seconds. "Sorry, I'm still feeling pretty bad. That last...hell, I don't even know what to call it. Episode...ah...telekinetic display? Whatever, it took it out of me. But you know, lover," his voice went soft, "I would have died to save you." He coughed again. "You looked so...helpless standing there. And when you told me you loved me, well...Hey, cover your ears, Anari, okay?...Tamara, listen carefully. I know we don't know each other, really, but what I do know has hit me deep. I'm not leaving you...like your message, I need a little space, too. This is a weird thing that's happening to me, and I have to get it together in order to deal with it. Do you understand? Please do. I'll be back, believe me. I need you too much. I would tell you where I'm going, but I have a feeling the less people know the better. Don't take offense to that, baby. I think it's for your own safety." He paused for a moment and folded his arms tightly across his chest. "Look, you should know that if news of my death comes down the net, Max has been instructed to contact you..."

Tamara closed her eyes.

"Oh hell, look, if I die, I'm giving Nicole most of my money. It's for both of you. Take care of her. Get her a great education. I don't have anyone, baby, you know that. The government would take most of it. I want you to have it." His voice cracked. "And baby,

I wasn't asleep the other night...you've touched me too...I have to go now. Take care and be safe." Jonathan's holoimage disappeared.

Tamara stood motionless in the loft.

A little tear hung in the corner of Anari's eye. She saw that her friend had picked up a photo of Jonathan as a little boy. Anari could feel her pain without even asking. Tamara was about the only true friend Anari had, and it tore her up to see her this way.

"Hey, Tam...I..."

Tamara motioned for her to stop. She couldn't turn away from the photo of the young boy who had grown up to move mountains with his mind.

Tarris... 16

As the Airbus began its initial vert-descent into Albuquerque, Jonathan finished his drink. It was early evening, and the world always looked perfect from 58,000 feet. He had declined the use of the AB 800's workout room. Still fatigued from his telekinetic world premiere at the club the previous night, he chose the comfort of the plane's second-level sleeper stations. The blood had stopped flowing, and the pain in his mind had been fairly nominal considering he had just defied the speed of light. The plane's Rolls-Royce bioturbines emitted a low droning sound as the pilot corrected for turbulence over the Sangre de Cristo front range.

The last time Jonathan had seen Tarris was not long after the accident. Tarris had always been a wild child, and his drug habit had become a problem. He had been Jonathan's best friend until he left for college. He was always the one who could help him get straight on anything from complex quantum math to girls. He was the brother Jonathan had never had.

"Good evening, ladies and gentlemen. This is your first officer speaking. It looks like a beautiful evening in Albuquerque; the winds are calm, and there's a temperature of 82 degrees. We should be touching down in about 17 minutes. Flight attendants, please prepare the cabins for our initial vert-descent into New Mexico."

Tarris was a programming genius. He had taught Jonathan much of what made him the programmer he was today, and he was always flattered that Jonathan would reference him in interviews and articles. But Tarris's passion was gaming. He had developed the first holovid interface that didn't require the usual protocols that slowed uplink time off the net. He had worked for BioGame Industries, a huge Pacific Rim conglomerate that had its hands into everything from vertslots to holoporn. The gaming division was its brain trust, and Tarris was its golden child – at least until the time Tarris went for a midnight "century run" with the L.A. Ducati club. Jonathan had warned Tarris about riding and biking a long time ago. Tarris loved his drugs, and he loved his Ducati. But late one night about 10 years ago, he had mixed the two – and mixed them bad.

"Sir, please stow your VIDscreen, we'll be descending shortly. Thank you."

It had been a tough night for Tarris and his team. Marketing was putting on the pressure for a Christmas release date, but the complex programming for Stealth War, the new game for kids 13 and up, was too stubborn to comply. After months of testing, the game's download time was still too long. Marketing had made it clear that download time was the key to success in the Game category. And nobody knew the critical nature of download better than Tarris. Frustrated, he dismissed his team for the night and returned the netcall he had received from the Ducati Club of Los Angles. It was one call, he later would tell Jonathan, he wished he had never returned.

"Ah, ladies and gentlemen, this is your first officer again. We've been told by Albuquerque tower that we're going to experience some chop on our final vert-descent into the airport, so we're gonna ask that you return to your seats."

Tarris had met up with the club just outside L.A. *A run in the hills,* he had thought, *was just the thing to get the old brain clear again.* And a little recreational drug ride wouldn't hurt, either. He started the Ducati SS2300 and clicked it into its night-ride setting. Rolling into the Interway, he would tell Jonathan later, he felt his drug ride was going to be weird, but he didn't turn back.

As the pack wound its way through the California night, Tarris grew more and more uneasy with the drug he had taken. The usual effects of mild euphoria and enhanced senses had been replaced by paranoiac tension and a slight loss of motor skill. The Ducati SS was a smooth and solid bike, but it was still an aggressive machine, and you didn't jerk around with 600 pounds of biotechnology. Tarris began to lean into a typical Interway curve, and the new guy next to him looked over and pointed to his bike. Nothing unusual, except it was night, and they were redlining at 255 mph. For a fellow rider to divert his attention on a curve at that speed, something must definitely be wrong. Tarris braked. First mistake. In his fog of confusion, he used the front braking system. The biosport bike's onboard computer would have read the situation and applied the rear braking system at that speed and angle of attack, but Tarris, being the wild child, had disengaged the safety protocols. Second mistake. He said it made for a more authentic ride. Even with his self-inflating foam impact suit, the last thing Tarris remembered after that was coming out of post-op at L.A. County General.

~

The plane's vertical descent was flawless, and its touchdown hardly noticeable. Jonathan unbuckled, grabbed his gear and made his way to the exit. In the terminal, he pushed through throngs of teenage bioboarders, ski bums and Texas families struggling with vacation gear. Since the Biolution, a season with no snow was an impossibility, which made New Mexico the new Mecca for those who loved the slopes. It was June, and the season was still at full tilt.

The drive to Taos was always relaxing, and it was just what Jonathan needed. The sun was setting as the car slipped in and out of the dark shadows of the mountains. New Mexico was still relatively unspoiled, and he could see why Tarris had made his home here.

It was late when Jonathan came into Taos. What had been a small artist colony and vacation spot in the late 20th century had turned into a tourist's nightmare of Indian casinos, bioshirt shops and half-price ski outlets after the Biolution. Jonathan couldn't believe Tarris would have settled in a place like this. But his directions took him out of town toward Tres Piedras, population: 75.

It took another hour through the stark land before Jonathan saw renewed signs of human activity. He went around what little town there was and down a narrow gravel road. He drove through two sharp curves, past the shell of a burned-out antique propeller passenger plane, its tail section buried halfway into the side of a hill, and over a steep embankment. Jonathan stepped out of his car and looked over a compound of various metal-roofed buildings draped with black solar panels that reflected the dark night sky of New Mexico. Old tires and glass bottles filled some of the walls, and a dog barked off in the distance.

The dry night air had cooled quickly, and it felt good on Jonathan's face. Fresh. Crisp. Real.

He began the walk down the small hill to the compound. An antique rifle shot rang out, kicking up dirt at Jonathan's feet. Its sound echoed through the hills.

"Who the fuck are you?" a voice called out from nowhere discernable.

"Tarris?"

"Jonathan? Jonathan fucking Kortel?"

The door to the middle building burst open, flooding a small area of the ground with light. Tarris rolled out into it.

"What the hell are you doing here?" Tarris asked as Jonathan came down the hill into the compound.

"I needed a drink!" He bent down and hugged his boyhood friend.

"You could have fucking called!"

"Yeah, well, I'm off-line for a time. I'll tell you all about it."

"I want to hear! Must be pretty important to bring you all the way out here. Or is it *she's* pretty important?" Tarris laughed.

"Is that a new chair?" Jonathan said, changing the subject.

"Yeah, it's the best. It's almost like fucking walking," Tarris said, rolling his eyes. "No, really, this thing is state-of-the-art. Check this out man, I designed it myself." Tarris rolled back a few feet and engaged the chair's system. Its biomedtronic technology made a soft hissing sound while lifting his body to a standing position. The chair's biopoly carbon tubing reformed into a support frame that molded against the back of his legs. The two small multiwheelbase platforms attached to his feet separated and became bootlike pads. The chair's back also shifted and wrapped partly around Tarris's midsection to provide support for his lower back. Throughout Tarris's legs and hips, implants controlled by an on-board computer matrix provided the interface connection for his brain to dialogue with his legs.

Tarris "walked" over to Jonathan. "Now," he said, his arms outstretched, "give your big brother a real hug."

~

Tarris poured Jonathan another Scotch. Light from a small lamp reflected off of Tarris's face. Jonathan could see that, for 33, his friend was looking older than his years. He had been beaten down. Whether by the accident or his harsh New Mexican environment was hard to say, but Jonathan could tell that the wild child of his boyhood had tamed a bit.

"Sounds like she's pretty special to you," Tarris said, sipping foam from the surface of his fresh margarita. He knew his friend, and he sensed Jonathan had revealed just the tip of the iceberg that really was bothering him.

"Yeah, she is..." Jonathan's voice wandered.

"Buddy, what is it?" Tarris said passionately. "It's me. Tarris. I know everything about you."

"No, you don't. There's more, Tarris...a lot more."

Jonathan talked for more than two hours. He told Tarris everything: the history of inexplicable experiences throughout his life, the kitchen fire and, finally, the Light-Force episode at Liquid Courage. Tarris sat motionless in his chair, quietly absorbing the anguish of his friend and sipping his margarita.

Jonathan ended his monologue by downing the last of his Scotch and watching the dying fire. The piñon smell was comforting, reminding him of the restaurant and the men of Kitchen Kortel. He finally looked over to Tarris, who had not taken his gaze from him.

"Am I a freak, Tarris?" Jonathan asked in a low voice.

His friend paused and focused on his margarita. Finally, he said, "Let me show you something, Jonathan." He scooted over to a bookshelf to the left of the fireplace, and rolling back, flipped through a large textbook. Finding the place, he handed it to Jonathan. "Here, buddy, read this."

Tarris rolled to another part of the house and started rummaging through a closet. Jonathan could hear him pulling boxes apart and swearing under his breath.

"Ohhh, it's gravity displacement. I wondered how it worked." Jonathan yelled over the commotion Tarris was making, "Where did you get this book?"

"It's from grad school. An old psych teacher had it, and he

gave it to me. It goes into all sorts of paranormal shit. Here we go!" Tarris exclaimed, and he came rolling back down the hallway. He came up to the table brushing the dust off the book he had retrieved, but suddenly he stopped and stared at Jonathan reading.

"This is so interesting, do you really think I have..." Jonathan said, interrupting himself when he saw the smile on his friend's face.

"What?...What is it Tarris?"

"Do something."

"Well, I..."

"Come on, shit. We're out in the middle of nowhere. It's me, Tarris."

Jonathan smiled, put the book down and leaned forward on the table.

"So, you want to see something?" The buzz from the Scotch had kicked in.

Tarris nodded, still smiling.

Jonathan didn't move a muscle or close his eyes. He just kept looking at his friend. A moment passed.

Tarris lost his smile. "Hey, you're not bullshitting me..." Just then he rose off the brick floor in his chair. Tarris began to laugh. "Holy shit, Jonny! This is fucking out of control!" He continued to rise until he hit his head on one of the room's *vigas*. "Okay, okay, bring me down!" Jonathan slowly lowered him to the floor, and Tarris motored back to the table as fast as his chair would take him. "What's it like?" Tarris asked.

"Well, that sort of stuff's not too tough anymore. I think I'm growing in ability. I've noticed that it gains strength each day. It's like it becomes more familiar, more comfortable to me. Like it's instinctual."

"Yeah, but man, you stopped a Light-Force weapon! That's damn fast, buddy. That's faster than light."

"Yeah, I know. That's one I can't explain. Yet." Jonathan reflectively jingled the ice cubes in his glass.

"I know how you did it. It was the extreme adrenaline rush you got from the fear of seeing your girl get killed by that reper." Tarris leaned within inches of Jonathan's face; his breath stank of tequila. "Love is a powerful thing. I should know." And he winked.

"Really?" Jonathan asked.

Tarris leaned back and smiled.

"Tarris, are you holding out on me? Who is she? What's her name?"

"Georgia. She'll be here later. She works the blackjack tables at The Diamond Horseshoe in Taos." He raised an eyebrow. "And you should see her in her uniform, mmm, shit, she is one fine woman, Jonathan." Tarris slammed his margarita and belched.

"Oh...here." Tarris threw Jonathan the other book. It landed in a dust cloud on his lap. "This might give you some more insight. Good night, buddy." He started to leave, but stopped and looked back. "Hey, Jonathan," he said with care in his eyes. "I'm glad you're here."

"Me too."

Tarris continued down the hall to the back of the house. Jonathan spun the book around to read its cover: Ten Things the Government Doesn't Want You to Know.

He flipped through chapters on aliens, the Challenger Explosion and the Kennedy assassinations, but one titled "The Tels" coldly grabbed his attention. It described a theory of a shadowy government agency staffed by men and women at various levels of telekinetic power. The Tel chart was explained, and the Agency's long history, starting in the early 1950s all the way to the present, was detailed as if it really existed. Jonathan finished and checked his watch. Two in the morning. He was tired. It had been a long trip, and the Scotch was tugging him toward the bed. As he looked around Tarris's home, he thought of Tamara and his message. "I miss you..." he said in the quiet of the living room. The fire crackled down to a pile of glowing, orange embers. He glanced down at the book. "Wouldn't that be the shits if you guys were real." He fell asleep as the fire died out.

~

Jonathan woke up to the scent of coffee brewing on a real flame stove. He looked around to find he was still in the chair, but he had been wrapped in a warm, natural wool Navaho blanket. Someone in the kitchen was humming a tune he couldn't quite make out.

"Good morning," she said.

"Good morning...Georgia?" Jonathan asked.

"Yes, I'm sure Tarris has told you all about me," she said over the whine of the blender.

"No, not really. We didn't get to it last night," Jonathan said, unwrapping himself from his Navaho cocoon. In the kitchen he found a tall girl with straight, black, shoulder-length hair prepping a breakfast shake in a blender. She wore blue jeans, sandals and a loose-fitting natural cotton shirt unbuttoned deep into her cleavage. She grinned at the sight of him. Her lips were thin, and her smile was broad, and when she really smiled, her lower lip curled down to give a glimpse of how she appeared as a little girl. But what struck Jonathan the most were her eyes – dark eyes, almost as black as her hair.

"Here you go. This ought to take the edge off." She offered him some coffee in a huge ceramic mug. Steam wafted above it as she handed it to him.

"Thanks, this smells great." Jonathan walked to an enormous window in the dining room. It seemed a frame for the mountains to the east, a giant painting continuously changing with sunlight and seasons.

"This is our favorite view," Georgia said, wiping fruit juice from her hands and joining him to share the view.

"How long have you been with Tarris?"

"Oh, about a year. We met at a bar in Taos."

"That's great that you're so..." he stopped, suddenly realizing he had set himself up.

"What," she said, smiling at catching him, "that a woman like me can love a paraplegic?"

"Well, no...I didn't mean it that way."

"It's okay," she laughed. "Tarris can be very persuasive when he wants to be. And besides," she leaned over, as if confiding a secret, "don't let that chair fool you. Not everything is off line below the belt with Tarris." She smiled broadly again and returned to the kitchen.

Jonathan turned back to the view, embarrassed that his first conversation with her was a little awkward.

"Tarris told me a lot about you," she said.

Jonathan choked on the coffee in his mouth.

She looked up from the sink. "Don't worry, Mr. Telekinetic, your secret is safe with us."

"Oh, great, so you know, too."

"Hey," she stopped prepping and turned to face him. "Don't worry. I'm very open to this kind of thing. So is Tarris. You're safe here with us. Stay as long as you want. Here, let me refill you." She came over and took his mug. When their hands touched, an energy passed between them almost like a static discharge.

"Oh!" she said, almost dropping the mug. "I hate this dry air sometimes. The static can build up so much. Watch it with Tarris and that darn chair. It can almost stop your heart." She took his cup back to the kitchen to refill it.

"So, you've met Georgia. Wasn't I right?" Tarris beamed as he motored his way from the back porch to Georgia. She bent down and gave him a long, passionate kiss. "God, I love this girl!" He slapped her butt as she passed him with her shake on the way to the hall. Tarris winked at Jonathan. "Is that fine or what?"

Jonathan watched her for a second before turning back to the mountains. "Do you think the Agency really exists?" he asked Tarris, who was now standing up with his chair and making some toast.

With all the skill of a gymnast, Tarris went from countertop to cabinet, "walking" almost without effort. One of his foot pads caught in the grout of the tiled floor. "Goddamn this floor. I'm going to change it out when the residuals come in from my next game. What did you ask? Oh, the Agency, right. I don't know for sure. But if you ask some folks out here, they'll tell you it does."

"If they're so secret," Jonathan asked, looking over to the kitchen, "how do you get in touch with them?"

"I wouldn't worry about that; they'll probably get in touch with you." Tarris pointed the knife he was using at Jonathan to emphasize that last word.

Jonathan recoiled – both at the knife and at the thought that he was possibly being watched. It unnerved him, and Tarris could tell.

"Hey, Jonathan, if they do exist, at least you're not alone. Maybe they can teach you how to harness your abilities. Put it to good use for mankind and all that kinda stuff." He crunched down on his toast and leaned against the counter like he still had use of his legs.

"Well, one thing's for sure," Jonathan said. "My life has changed forever."

"I'll tell you what," Tarris responded, as he joined Jonathan at the window, "I know that story, buddy."

Contact... 17

Doc Martin's was a Taos institution. Even with its 21st century urban transformation, Taos still had little pieces of history. Doc Martin's was the place for a drink with friends and a great meal for less than four hundred bucks, and it had been that way for nearly two centuries. Much of the original building was still a working hotel. But if you were a local and had the credit, Saturday night was the night at Doc's. You could bet on the best local music, and all your friends would be there, whether you wanted to see them or not.

Jonathan, Tarris and Georgia squeezed their way to the bar. People didn't seem to notice Tarris's "walking" chair, or if they did, they were cool enough not to stare or ask questions. Taos still retained a touch of the Old West. People here left you alone.

"I know what you two want!" the bartender said, pointing at Tarris and Georgia. "But I'm clueless about him. What'll it be, friend?"

"Scotch, house blend is fine. With ice, no water, please," Jonathan said, taking an elbow in the ribs from a large Indian with a three-foot ponytail.

"I'm so sorry," the big Indian said in a deep voice. His skin was the color of rich coffee, and his eyes nearly black. Deep age lines radiated from their corners and deepened when he smiled. "My name is Whitehorse, Jacob Whitehorse. And you?"

"Jonathan Kortel."

"Are you new to Taos?" He eyed him seriously.

"Visiting some friends just outside the city."

"Well, welcome to Taos, Mr. Kortel. I hope you have a good stay." He turned and resumed his conversation with another tall Indian, who looked over the shoulder of Jacob Whitehorse at Jonathan. Jonathan smiled and took his drink from Tarris. Georgia was busy hunting down a table.

"You certainly are lucky, Tarris. She seems very nice," Jonathan said when Georgia waved to them from across the room.

"Yeah, I lucked out on this one. I just hope I can make her happy."

Jonathan and Tarris settled at the table while Georgia summoned a waiter. Jonathan watched the regulars of Doc's go about their business. Families chattered and laughed in the large booths. Men shook hands and bellied up to the bar. Couples cuddled by the fireplace. The two Indians stayed at the bar. Every so often, one or the other would glance in his direction. It began to put Jonathan's netdar up.

"Hey, Tarris. Who are the two big guys at the bar?"

"They're gamblers," Georgia cut in. "They come up from Los

Alamos every other weekend."

"Oh. The one with the ponytail seems nice enough. He introduced himself to me at the bar."

"Yeah," Georgia said, "he can't play blackjack to save his life."

They ordered from the specials. It was real food. Not bioenhanced. Jonathan was looking forward to some local cuisine, and he wished Hector was there to share it. He took a long drink from his Scotch.

By the time their food arrived, Doc's was in full swing. The band had set up, and the dance floor was cleared. It was a small group. The lead guitarist was a rotund little man dressed in vintage cowboy ware. His hat was huge compared to the rest of his body, and his thick glasses were an unusual touch, considering the need for eyewear had gone out with the silicon chip. His vest was embroidered in lariat type that read "Riders of the Purple Sage." The bassist was a tall, pretty older woman whose rugged looks matched her jeans. But the oddest of the crew was the blind piano player. She was dressed in an authentic period dress from the 1800s. It was a dress you'd imagine your great-great-great-great-grandmother wearing to the ice cream social. The food, Jonathan noted, was excellent, with subtle flavors a bioprogrammer would envy.

They finished their meals and waited for the band to start. It opened with "Boot Scootin' Boogie." Jonathan noticed that the two big Indians were gone. He looked over at Tarris, who was looking at Georgia.

"Baby, this is our song," Tarris said, taking her hand.

"Come on, lover," Georgia grinned. "Let's show Taos what you can do." She stood up, took his hand and came around the table.

He backed away, engaged the chair's systems and stood up to meet her face with his. He winked at Jonathan.

Jonathan watched them swing to the vintage 20th-century tune with such ease that it was hard to tell that Tarris even had a disability. He smiled as they passed, scootin' across the old wooden floor.

"May we join you?" a deep voice from behind Jonathan asked.

Jonathan turned to see the two big Indians looking down at him. Their large presence gave him a start, and only Jacob Whitehorse was smiling.

"Sure," Jonathan said, "have a seat. And your name is?" Jonathan extended his hand to the silent Indian, who said nothing and didn't return the offer of the handshake.

"Please excuse my friend," Whitehorse said. "He is very shy around crowds. Jonathan, I can call you Jonathan, can't I?" Whitehorse asked.

Jonathan nodded. The silent one didn't strike him as the shy type.

"Let me be blunt, Jonathan. We know who and what you are." A cold chill ran down Jonathan's spine. "But before you get up, we're not the Agency. You know about the Agency?"

Jonathan nodded.

"Then you should know we're not like them. If you're interested in preserving some semblance to your life, you'll meet us at this address tomorrow morning at ten o'clock." He handed him a card, and they both rose to leave.

"Oh, and Jonathan," Whitehorse added. "If you don't show, we can't be responsible for how your life will turn out." He leaned down, his hulking face in shadow from the stage lights. "Think of Tamara, Jonathan....I know you don't want to lose her." He straightened and followed the silent one out the front door.

Tarris and Georgia stumbled to the table laughing. They had been on their third song when he had pulled her from the dance floor.

"How you doing, buddy, having fun yet?" he asked breathlessly. Then Tarris sat so in sync with his chair's transformation that it appeared as if it were part of him.

"Doing great..." Jonathan lied, still staring at the front door.

"Are you sure?" Tarris pressed, following in the direction of his stare.

"Oh yeah." Jonathan tore his eyes from the door. "You two look like you're having a blast. You really are adept with that chair. It's amazing! Don't you get tired with all the implants?"

"Yeah, I get tired. It's tough on the body to walk in this thing." He patted Georgia's knee. "I mean, it doesn't make me a Fred Astaire, but it gets me around."

"It does more than that," Georgia said, winking.

They all laughed. But Jonathan wasn't listening. The words of Jacob Whitehorse kept resounding in his mind. All he could think of was the meeting tomorrow, and the answers it might bring.

The pueblo... 18

The air was crisp, and the swirling wind twisted the steam from Jonathan's coffee into little tornadoes that disappeared as fast as they rose. He stood on Tarris's back porch looking east to the mountains, now silhouetted in their predawn colors of purple and blue. As a lone hawk rode the quickly heating thermals high above his head, Jonathan wondered what the day might bring. He closed his eyes and thought of Tamara. A crack appeared in the kiva next to him.

"May I join you?" Georgia asked, interrupting the morning quiet.

Jonathan smiled as she came up to his side.

"Beautiful, aren't they?" she asked, referring to the mountains.

"Yes, they are." He took a long sip from his coffee.

"Did you bring that with you?" she asked, gesturing to his cup.

"You don't mind? It's my own special blend."

"No, I'm not a purist. Biofoods are fine, I think."

The sun exploded over the mountaintops, flooding the New Mexican land with bright, overexposed color. Jonathan and Georgia diverted their eyes from its intensity. The wind whipped her hair across his face. He looked into her dark, almost pupilless eyes. She was naturally pretty, and a smile crossed his face when he thought how Tarris had seemed so happy with her.

"What?..." she asked, questioning his look.

"Oh, nothing.... You happy with Tarris?"

"Yes," she said, turning back to the view, "he's a good man."

"Yeah, he is."

"You are too, you know." She stepped between Jonathan and the sunrise, pulled her hair off her face and looked deep into his eyes. "You know, you're not like the rest of humanity. You're different, Jonathan Kortel. You're not even like the others that are like you. You know that now, don't you? You're more powerful than they ever could hope to be..."

"Now that's a damn sunrise!" Tarris exclaimed, rolling onto the porch. Jonathan started to say something, but Georgia stopped him and greeted her lover with a kiss.

"I can see why you're out here," Jonathan said. "This land is," he glanced over to Georgia, "powerful."

"Man, I tell you, you can't beat it," Tarris laughed. "It never ceases to amaze me."

"Hey, I'm gonna go into Taos this morning. Do you all need anything?" Jonathan asked.

"Let me go with you," Tarris cut in. "I'll show you around!"

"No thanks. I need a little 'me time,' you understand. I just want to roam around, maybe go out to the Pueblo."

"Come on, baby," Georgia said to Tarris. "I'll cook us a big breakfast. Let's see what the big-time biochef thinks of our special 'Tres Piedras' omelets." She laughed and flipped up the handles of Tarris's chair.

Jonathan watched her begin to wheel Tarris like he was in an old-fashioned wheelchair. It looked oddly affectionate, like it was their special bonding thing – her pushing and him accepting. Tarris reached up and held her hand as they went into the house.

~

For more than 500 years, Taos Pueblo had been one of the oldest working pueblos in New America. What was once a tourist trap in the latter 20th century had been returned to its original purpose through a change in the elders.

Jonathan drove slowly as he approached the entrance. Two large Indian men in contemporary clothes stopped Jonathan by lowering their military issue Light-Force weapons and letting the ends of the barrels rest on the hood of his car. Their mirrored sunglasses reflected the car and 180 degrees of the scene behind it. One with a red bandanna approached the car's window. He tapped the glass with the end of his weapon.

Jonathan lowered the window. "I'm here to meet with Jacob Whitehorse."

The bandanna Indian didn't respond. He waved to his partner to let Jonathan pass.

Jonathan slowly pulled into the Pueblo. The people in the

plaza moved out of the way, ignoring him as if he and his car didn't exist. The square was large and filled with men, women and children going about their affairs. The whole scene was like stepping back through time. Some people were in native dress, while others wore modern business bioware. Children played on front stoops with their netpad game units, and old men sat together in what little shade the sparse trees supplied. Jonathan crept along, searching for some indication of where he should go, when, suddenly, a tall Indian appeared at the hood of the car. Jonathan slammed the brake system, kicking up a dust cloud. When it settled, Jacob Whitehorse was smiling from the front of the car.

"Welcome, Jonathan," he said. "I'm so glad you chose to come." He opened the door for him and took his keys. A young Indian boy jumped into the driver's seat.

"Don't worry," Whitehorse said. He pointed to a shaded spot under a set of two trees. "He'll just park your car over there."

Jonathan didn't say a word.

"This was a very smart move on your part," Whitehorse continued, putting his large hand on Jonathan's shoulder. "There are many people who want to meet you."

Whitehorse led Jonathan through the maze of Pueblo streets. Ducking under a low archway, he brought him to a small courtyard where about a dozen people were milling around. They were of various ethnicity: some were Indian, some black, others white or Hispanic. The courtyard grew quiet at their appearance, and everyone turned to greet them. Jonathan scanned their faces and could feel compassion, almost as if they were family.

"Ladies and gentlemen," Whitehorse said in his deep voice,

"this is Jonathan Kortel." No one responded, other than to continue smiling. He glanced at Jonathan. "These are your people, Jonathan. Welcome home."

A small Indian girl broke from the crowd and walked right up to within a foot of Jonathan. She didn't say anything for a moment. Then she slowly rose off the ground until she came face to face with him. Hovering in front of him, she kissed him on the cheek. "Welcome to Taos Pueblo, Mr. Kortel," she said in a soft voice. Then she turned in the air, spread her arms and floated back toward the group, giggling all the way.

A woman gently pushed her way forward to catch the little girl in her arms. It was Georgia.

She hesitantly smiled at Jonathan.

The people began to laugh a little, and Whitehorse motioned for Jonathan to go and meet them. He headed straight for Georgia. She set down the little girl, who scurried off behind the group, and met his quizzical eyes through her dark black bangs.

"Look," she said sheepishly, "this isn't what you think."

"And what do I think?" Jonathan said coolly. "Or are you one of those who already knows what I'm thinking?"

"No, no, come on now, don't be that way. These are good people. We're just like you, Jonathan. Well, sort of."

"Does Tarris know?" he pressed.

She turned away. Jonathan grabbed her arm. Quiet descended once again on the courtyard.

"Please don't tell me you were planted for me," he said angrily. Whitehorse looked up from a conversation.

"No, Jonathan," she said, though she would not meet his

glare. "I love Tarris, really..."

Jonathan's look said he didn't buy it. He tightened his grip on her arm. Whitehorse stepped closer.

"Okay, okay! At first, yes, I was a set up. We knew of you and your tie with Tarris. We bet you'd come to him eventually." She tried to wriggle free. He firmed his grip. Whitehorse carefully began to make his way to them.

"Believe me, Jonathan," she quietly pleaded, "it wasn't supposed to turn out the way it did. I told you" – Jonathan pulled her close to his face – "Tarris is very persuasive."

Jonathan's grip was extreme. Georgia winced in agony. Whitehorse was nearly within reach of Jonathan when suddenly he shot 15 feet into the air. Jonathan looked up at the big Indian, who was now floating like a Macy's parade balloon. "This is between me and Georgia!"

"I know, Jonathan," Jacob yelled down, "but she's telling you the truth!"

Georgia was clawing at his grip with her free hand. "Please, Jonathan, I love Tarris with all my heart!" She broke down into tears.

Jonathan released her arm. Shocked at himself, he examined his hand like it had acted on its own. He took in the whole scene: Georgia rubbing her arm, glaring at him in awe and anger, Whitehorse dangling helplessly in the air, the crowd waiting in stunned silence for his next move.

Jonathan was overwhelmed. "I'm so sorry..." he blurted, and ran out of the courtyard.

Whitehorse fell to the ground, kicking and flailing.

"Go, Georgia! Get him!" he commanded, struggling to his feet. "We can't afford to lose him!"

Georgia immediately sprinted after him.

~

Jonathan tried to remember the way back, but the more frantically he searched, the more lost he became. "That's all I need is to join some fucking Indian cult," he swore under his breath. People stared at him as he ran past.

Running down an alley he hoped was the way out, he turned a corner and ran headlong into the chest of the silent Indian.

Jonathan fell back to the ground.

"Shit..." he said, picking himself up. The Indian didn't respond.

"Jonathan!" Georgia called from the end of the alley.

He turned and saw Georgia running toward him, clutching her arm.

"Jonathan! Come on!" She grabbed his hand and yanked him away from the large Indian, who lunged at them and just missed Jonathan's shirt.

Georgia pulled him through an archway and into the open square. "In the car!" she said.

"I don't have the keys!" he answered, sliding to the door.

An old Indian seated across from the car threw the keys at him. "Come back now," he said, revealing a toothless smile.

They jumped in, and Jonathan started the car and gunned it in reverse. Three old women scattered like cats.

"Sorry, sorry!" he said, as if they could actually hear him.

As they approached the gate, the two guards put their left hands to their ears, then looked up at the car.

"Jonathan! Stop!" Georgia screamed. "This isn't some movie!"

Jonathan looked at her and smiled.

The two Indians charged their Light-Force weapons and raised them at the car.

"Jonathan?!..." Georgia scrunched herself down in the seat.

Five feet from hitting the men and the gate, the two Indians were vaulted up and over the car, and the gates flew open, slamming hard against the adobe walls.

Jonathan grinned at Georgia and raised an eyebrow. Georgia looked at him through her dark bangs and smiled that smile.

~

"James, it looks like Mr. Kortel's first meeting with the Rogues did not go so well," said Jimbo's partner. He snapped the field optics shut and returned them to their case.

"Yeah," Jimbo said, tracking the car, "and it looks like our hero gets a new girl, too."

"Don't be so sure. If she is a true Rogue, her loyalty will be wherever Whitehorse wants it. I should know. I trained him."

He struggled to light another cigarette. Jimbo stepped over, stared at the lighter, mentally created a field flux wall just in front of it and blocked the wind.

"Thank you, James. I was just about to do that myself." He blew a perfect ring. "I am hungry. We should see what this city has to offer."

"What about them?" Jimbo asked, indicating the dust trail growing more distant from the Pueblo.

"Oh, we have time. She will work on him, tell him about the Rogues, talk down the Agency...you know, the usual. Jonathan will become enamored with the romantic vision of the Rogues, world peace and all. But if he is as smart as I think, he will catch on to Whitehorse soon enough." He blew another smoke ring and watched the dust cloud rise into the warm midday air.

"Yeah, well, what if he doesn't get enamored?"

"Then we have an easier time selling Mr. Kortel on the Agency."

"You got this all figured out, don't you?"

His partner kept watching the cloud.

"What if he isn't enamored with *us*?" Jimbo asked.

"Then, James, things might get a little ugly." His cigarette left his mouth, snuffed itself out and dropped to the ground. His arms remained folded.

The Rogues... 19

There was no conversation on the trip back to the Interway. Jonathan's mind was thick with confusion. He struggled with his conflicting images of Georgia: the original "Tarris loving" one, and the new "Indian cult" version.

When he finally reached the Interway for the hour-long ride back to Tres Piedras, he broke the silence: "Were you ever going to tell him?"

"That depends," Georgia quietly started. "If you join us, then yes, he'll find out eventually. But if you choose not to, then I don't see the point. Why hurt him. Anyway, if you leave, I'm leaving the Rogues and staying with Tarris."

"You really do love him?" he asked, searching her face for signs of lying.

She hesitated. "Yes, I do. I know it's hard for you to believe, but you have to. I've come to love your friend very much. Whether you turn out to be The Infinite Tel or not, I'm staying with Tarris."

"The Infinite Tel? What the hell is that?"

"You don't know?" she asked, surprised.

"No!" he said, mimicking her surprise. "Come on, Georgia. I'm new to this game. You all are 'hovering' and 'floating' about, giving the hairy eyeball and saving villages. Hell, I'm just over here stopping light waves with my mind!"

Georgia looked at Jonathan in shock.

"Yeah, got you on that one. Whitehorse didn't tell you about that little episode, did he?"

"No," she said somberly.

"Stopped a Light-Force bioweapon beam within two inches of my girl..." he quit in midsentence, suddenly realizing that he had never referred to Tamara that way.

"Girlfriend, Jonathan?" Georgia finished.

"Yeah...girlfriend," he said and turned his attention to back to the Interway.

~

For 20 miles it was quiet.

"So, what's The Infinite Tel?" Jonathan asked, breaking the tension. "What do you all think I am? Some sort of Confucius or Mohammed or Buddha?" He looked over at her. "Or Christ?"

"No, nothing like that. But possibly that important," she answered.

"Oh yeah, I'm the Son of God," he said, and rolled his eyes.

"No, but your impact on man could be as long-lasting."

"You're serious about this stuff, aren't you?"

She nodded.

"Okay then, tell me about...what did you call them...the Rogues?"

Georgia spent the next 30 minutes explaining the splinter group that had broken away from the Agency more than 10 years ago. Some of the most talented Tels had become disillusioned with the direction of the Agency and had left to form an underground group dedicated to world peace. Their efforts had made a difference throughout South America and Asia.

"So how did the disenchanted end up in the Land of Enchantment?" Jonathan asked.

"Jacob Whitehorse."

"He's the head man? Tell me about him. Do Indians have more potential of being telekinetic than most?...You know, with their culture being so tied to the land and all?"

"Well, statistically, Potentials that are at least 70% Native American do exhibit abilities that are at Level 5 or higher. Now, whether that's because they're Native American, I don't know. What I do know is Jacob Whitehorse is a powerful Tel."

"Who came up with the concept of The Infinite Tel?"

"Jacob..." Jonathan said in unison with Georgia. "Right, got it. So what do you all do? Fight oppression, poverty, crime? Go where no man has gone before?" he mocked.

"We go where we're needed. There's a lot of work to be done in the world. If a small village in, say, Bogota needs help after a flood, we move in and give them a little nudge. Help recess the water or move large amounts of debris. You know, things like that. And we never reveal ourselves, ever!"

"That's admirable. I can buy into that," he said. "But where would I fit in?"

"You could help stop conflicts, or even a war. Maybe bring people to a bargaining table." She shifted in the seat to face him. "Think of it! You could reveal the Tel subculture to the rest of the world and possibly help usher in a new age for mankind." She reached over and touched his arm.

"Well, before you anoint me the new messiah, what are we going to do about Tarris?"

"I think it would be best if neither of us said anything until you decide. I don't want to lose him."

"Fair enough." He drove the rest of the way in silence, trying to sort out his next move.

~

"Look what I picked up in Taos!" Jonathan said to Tarris as Georgia stepped out of the car.

"Baby, where's the truck?" Tarris asked.

"It died in Taos."

"Shit. I'll go deal with it tomorrow." Tarris motored back into the house, and Georgia gave Jonathan the thumbs up.

After dinner, Tarris and Jonathan relaxed by the fire. The meal was good, but Jonathan thought the pesto could have used a little programming to punch the flavors. He took a long sip from his Scotch and thought about his conversation with Georgia. If the Rogues really were the telekinetic version of Green Peace, maybe it wouldn't hurt to join them. World peace. Saving lives. Who could argue with that? But revealing the Tel subculture seemed dangerous to him. Not much different, he reasoned, than the government revealing the evidence of aliens on earth.

He laughed into his Scotch.

"Are you all right?" Georgia asked from the kitchen.

"Yeah. My Scotch just went down the wrong way," he lied, wiping his chin.

Tarris had fallen asleep in his chair, and Georgia was peering into the refrigerator. "Darn, the milk is bad, and I wanted to make waffles for us in the morning."

"I'll go get some. There's a biomart in town, isn't there?"

"Biomart? Jonathan, please," she laughed.

"Okay, mart. Is there a mart?"

"Yes, it's just as you enter town, off to the right."

"Ok, I'll be back in a sec."

"Jonathan," she yelled and whispered at the same time. "Be careful."

"Now, don't worry. It's me – faster than a beam of speeding photons."

~

TP Mart was void of customers and, for that matter, counter help. Jonathan walked down the aisles of biodiapers, synthoil and flip-flops.

"Flip-flops," he mused. "I haven't seen these in years." He threw a pair of black ones in his basket. As he approached the checkout station, a small Hispanic man seemed to rise from beneath the counter.

"Sorry," the TP Mart clerk said, "I be cleaning under the sink."

Jonathan paid and left. The parking lot was oddly still. Then again, it was almost one in the morning. He stopped to soak up the New Mexican night sky. Its inky blackness was the perfect backdrop for the billions of stars the universe had on display. A shooting star sliced through the sky.

"I wonder if I'll ever stop one of those?" he pondered out loud.

"You might, if you're smart and do the right thing."

The deep voice of Jacob Whitehorse almost made Jonathan drop his bag. Jonathan spun around. "Damn, Jacob, don't sneak up on me like that."

Jacob and his silent friend slowly walked out of the shadows. "Jonathan, has Georgia talked with you about us?" Jacob asked.

"Yes."

"Well?"

"Well, what? You want an answer like that? I just met you folks today, and it wasn't the best introduction I've ever had."

"Jonathan...we're not fucking around here," Whitehorse said.

"Okay, Jacob, easy. You wouldn't hurt your messiah, would you?" The Scotch was beginning to show itself.

A searing pain cut through Jonathan's skull. He collapsed to his hands and knees and writhed in pain on the warm dirt.

Whitehorse and the silent Indian walked up. "How funny is it now, Mr. Messiah?"

The silent Indian smiled.

"Oh, that's good, that's real good..." Jonathan said. The pain increased. He buried his head between his knees. "Oh my God!" he screamed. He rolled to his side and curled up into a fetal position.

"Should we intervene, sir?" Jimbo asked.

"No," his partner answered. "I know Whitehorse." He adjusted his field optics. "He will take him to the 'threshold' and hold him there to make his point."

"How do you know?"

"It is what I would do."

Jonathan was crying from the pain tearing at his mind. Whitehorse and the silent Indian just stood and watched.

"Jonathan, let us help you develop your skill. We can teach you how to harness it and put it to great use."

"Yeah, like fucking with people's brains, AUGH!" Jonathan curled more tightly as the pain reached the threshold point.

"If need be," Whitehorse said softly.

"Sir, he looks majorly screwed here," Jimbo said.

"Just wait, James. I think we are about to get a 'level test' from Mr. Kortel."

"Please, Jonathan, listen to reason!" Whitehorse demanded.

Jonathan suddenly stopped struggling, and Whitehorse and his companion bent down to check on him.

The silent one felt it first. He fell to one knee. His face went white. Whitehorse began to back away. The silent Indian lifted his head, his face twisted in agony. His mouth moved like he was crying, but there was no sound. Jonathan was still curled on the ground. The silent Indian took his head in both hands, and, to Whitehorse's horror, a small dent appeared on his forehead that slowly expanded.

Blood poured from his nose. He collapsed without making a sound.

A muffled voice came up from the dirt: "Now who's fucking with who, Whitehorse?" Jonathan struggled to his feet.

"Now that's interesting," Jimbo said, not pulling his eyes from his field optics.

"Jonathan!" Whitehorse exclaimed. "I would have never gone that far!"

"No? I don't recall ever reading about Green Peace using pain threshold tricks to stop whaling. What did you do at the Agency, Whitehorse? Really?" Jonathan rubbed his head and staggered toward him.

Whitehorse backed away. "Jonathan, you've killed a man!" he said, changing the subject.

"He's not going to die," Jonathan answered. "Now, he might have one hell of a headache, but a little bioregeneration should do him fine. I'm not sure I'll be able to say the same for you."

Whitehorse grabbed his head and dropped to the ground.

Jonathan watched with contempt, as Whitehorse convulsed in the dirt. He calmly wiped his face with his sleeve.

In the distance, a dog began to howl.

~

"I think that will be quite enough, Jonathan," the senior Tel said. "Well done, well done." He was clapping his hands and smoking a cigarette, Jimbo in tow.

"Who are you?" Jonathan asked, retaining his mental grip

on Whitehorse.

Jimbo cut in, “James McCarris, and this is my partner...”

“The Agency!” Jonathan interrupted, pointing his finger.

The senior Tel took a drag from his cigarette and motioned for Jonathan to release Whitehorse, who had slipped into unconsciousness. Jimbo was checking the silent Indian.

“This one’s alive, but he’s going to need a doctor...and fast,” Jimbo said.

“No, he will be all right.” His partner came over to examine the silent Indian’s forehead. “Not bad, Jonathan. A front temporal compression, without severe damage to the brain or the sepra orbital arteries. Very impressive work.” The senior Tel straightened. “I think I can help this man.” Jimbo and Jonathan watched in amazement as the silent Indian’s forehead returned to its natural shape.

“Lesson one: To damage or repair a victim, a Tel must have a complete, commanding knowledge of human anatomy and medical procedures. And you do not! You were lucky tonight, young man. You did well, but you were a millimeter away from severing the artery. He would have hemorrhaged and been dead in seconds.” He put out his cigarette.

“So, who are you, the good guys?” Jonathan asked.

“That all depends on your point of view,” Jimbo said.

“James is right, Jonathan. It is all a matter of point of view. Take Jacob here.” He strolled over to Whitehorse. “He was my finest student – loyal, powerful and cunning. But he has one weakness. He sees the world as black and white.”

“But isn’t he...aren’t they helping the underdog?” Jonathan asked.

"The underdog?" the senior Tel asked, turning to Jonathan. "Define the underdog. One man's militia for peace is another man's death squad for a government. A saved village today harbors terrorists tomorrow. Overthrow a regime and usher in another dictator. At one time this band of Rogues were some of our best, but now they meddle in the affairs of nations. They do not see the big picture. They are out of their league, and they should return to us. The world, Jonathan, is still a very dangerous place..." he walked back over to Jonathan and got right into his face, "...as you should know."

He walked away and lit another cigarette. The dog still could be faintly heard, his howl carried to them on the cool night wind.

"I do know," Jonathan said softly. The senior Tel's words hit him hard. He had always felt cheated out of his boyhood and truly wondered what it would have been like to have parents. Real parents. Parents who would have loved him and protected him.

"Listen, man," Jimbo said quietly. "There are no good guys or bad guys, just agendas. And you'll have to decide which agenda works for you."

"Jonathan," the senior Tel called out. He was standing about 20 feet away. He had his back to them and was looking up at the stars. "Do you want to make a difference?"

"Well, I don't know what I...HEY!" Jonathan was abruptly lifted 70 feet into the air. "I DON'T LIKE HEIGHTS!"

Jimbo was caught off guard by his partner's theatrics.

"Listen to me, and listen well, Mr. Kortel!" the senior Tel yelled. "We need you and you need us!"

"Alright, Alright! I get the picture!"

"James, think fast," he said, releasing his control over Jonathan.

"HEYYY...!"

Jonathan fell 60 feet before Jimbo mentally caught him. Hands on his hips, he shot a contemptuous look at his partner. Jonathan hung six feet off the ground, suspended face down like a puppet on invisible strings. The senior Tel slowly walked up to him. They were now face to face.

"We are not *fucking* around either, Jonathan." He took a long drag off his cigarette.

"What if I don't want to go with either of you..." Jonathan began, but he was stopped by a sharp pain in his shoulder. He grimaced in agony.

The senior Tel said nothing.

Jimbo looked away.

"What are you doing?!" Jonathan screamed, and panic filled his face. He felt the pain tear through his shoulder as his arm shifted of its own accord under his shirt.

"In plain English," the senior Tel said casually, "I am separating your arm from your shoulder." He leaned in closer. "And I could do a lot worse." Then as quickly as it began, the pain suddenly ceased. "We are not monsters, Jonathan, contrary to what you may think."

Jonathan glared back and began to prep for whatever he could bring forth. He was going to show this bastard what he was made of.

"Do not bother, Jonathan," the senior Tel bluffed. "You are strong, but inconsistent and untrained. I am a Level 8, very consistent, and very well trained."

The bluff worked; Jonathan backed off. The senior Tel gently lowered him to his feet.

"That was a little demonstration in control, on both of our parts." He acted as if he was about to walk away, when suddenly he spun on his heels and came back to within an inch of Jonathan's face. "I could kill you where you stand," he threatened. "You would never feel it, and no one would ever know who did it." He took the last drag off his cigarette and casually set off for the car.

Jimbo walked up to Jonathan with his hands in his pockets. "Think about it, man. He's a little over the top, but he makes a good point." And he made that click sound for emphasis.

~

The compound was quiet when Jonathan got out of the car. It was now three in the morning, and he was exhausted. He leaned against the hood and rubbed his shoulder.

The impact of his meetings with the Agency and the Rogues was soaking in. It was obvious to Jonathan that the Rogues, despite their "help the world" platform, were not what they seemed. Jacob Whitehorse had done a pretty thorough disinformation job on Georgia and probably the rest of the group. Jonathan thought it obvious that the big Indian's agenda was not world peace. To him, Whitehorse seemed borderline psycho, and he probably had his own agenda for the world that focused particularly on his place in it.

At least the Agency presented itself pretty straight up. They didn't hide their agenda; in fact, they reveled in it. And their view of the world did strike a deep chord within him.

The house was still, the living room empty. Jonathan crept to the freezer and got an icy gelpack for his throbbing head. He also washed down a fistful of bioprophin.

"Where've you been?" Georgia asked, appearing in the kitchen archway.

Jonathan turned, the gelpack covering half his face.

Georgia gasped. "What happened?"

"Like you don't know?" Jonathan cut back.

"No!" Georgia said, stepping toward him. She reached up to touch his head, but he pushed her hand away.

"Your fearless leader made a serious impression on me, literally."

"Jacob did this?"

Jonathan shot her a "cut the crap" look.

"What did he do to you?"

Jonathan studied her. From all indications, she truly was clueless to Whitehorse's ruthlessness.

"Well," he said, "let's just say Whitehorse has a different view of the world and the Rogues' role in it." He rubbed the gelpack across his forehead.

From where she stood, Georgia was backlit from the living room light, and Jonathan couldn't help noticing her naked frame through the robe.

"And I met the Agency boys, too," he said, dropping into one of the antique Mexican leather chairs by the big window.

"What were they like?" she asked, curling into the chair's identical twin across from him. The top of her robe fell open and she quickly gathered it about her, never taking her eyes off Jonathan.

"Well," Jonathan said, pretending not to notice, "they're government guys, real pros, and they present a compelling argument for joining the Agency. At least they don't mask their agenda, and they have a pretty realistic view of the world."

Jonathan closed his eyes and draped the gelpack over his face.

"Hey," she said, leaning over the table, "I know about Jacob Whitehorse. We all do. But you have to understand, he and the others like him are powerful men. You got a taste of that tonight. They're passionate about their beliefs. Yes, their methods may be a bit extreme at times, but their motives are genuine. And they truly believe you could be The Infinite Tel."

She settled back into the chair, her dark hair decorating her shoulders. In the light of the small lamp, she seemed prettier than Jonathan had ever seen her. She closed her eyes.

Jonathan didn't know whom to trust, and he wasn't about to buy Georgia's "Jacob Whitehorse is really a good guy" line.

"I know one thing for sure," he said. He pulled the gelpack from his face. "I'm too tired to pick my life's destiny right now. I'm going to bed. Good night, Georgia."

Georgia watched Jonathan as he slowly walked down the dark hallway. She sat quietly, hugging a large pillow, and contemplated Jonathan's plight. If he was The Infinite Tel, then he might choose neither the Rogues nor the Agency. He might choose to go it on his own and live life as he wished. If he really was as powerful as Whitehorse believed, there might be no way of swaying his decision.

But Georgia knew Whitehorse, and how volatile he had become. If Jonathan Kortel could be forced toward the Rogues, Jacob Whitehorse would find a way.

No matter the cost.

Destiny... 20

Hector watched Marco, one of the line chefs, open a new shipment of hydrotank octopi from Australia. He checked out the manifest: Their genetic profiles were in order, but three of their 20 ink sacks had burst in shipping, which lined the crate with the new fluorescent, genetically altered ink. (Cooking the octopus in its own ink was such the rave in Japan.)

"*Caca!*" Marco declared. "This new distributor is an asshole! They packed these octopi like shit. Look at what we got to clean up, and it's eleven thirty!" Marco carefully lifted each one of the hydrotanks out and laid them on the prep table; they glowed green and yellow in his hands.

Hector didn't care.

Hector hadn't heard from Jonathan in four days, and for him not to show on a Monday without calling gave Hector the sense that something was terribly wrong. Four netmessages in as many days had gone unanswered. In the ten years he had known Jonathan, he had never just disappeared. Hector flipped his netphone around in his hand. He stared off into space.

Enrique couldn't miss the worry on his cousin's face.

He stopped chopping and walked over to his relation. "Are you gonna call him again?"

"I don't know. Why, what's the point? If he wanted to call, he would." He slammed his fist on the metal countertop. The kitchen came to a halt.

"Hey!" Enrique barked. "What are you *vatos* looking at, eh?!" and the men of Kitchen Kortel returned to their work.

"It's that fucking dancer," Hector said, still staring. "She's jerking him around, I know it." He finally looked at his cousin. "This is crazy. Jonathan should have called by now. I bet she's twisting his head around. You know how he is when he gets into a chick; he can be led so easily. And those dancers, they're the worst. Believe me, I know!" Hector waved his finger to emphasize his point. "What time is it?"

"It's almost noon. Why?" Enrique asked.

Hector put his netphone down and began to strip off his apron.

"Cousin," Enrique warned, "this is not your affair!"

Hector didn't answer. He threw the apron into the prep sink.

Enrique knew him too well. When Hector got something into his head, it was practically impossible to get it out. Enrique stepped in front of him.

"I just want to see this girl and talk to her," Hector objected. He tried to inch his way past.

Enrique reluctantly stepped aside. "Just watch what you say. Jonathan's a big boy. He can look out for himself, eh?"

Hector grabbed his netphone and charged out of the kitchen. "Claire, I'll be back in a couple of hours," he said to the new hostess, and he stormed toward the front door.

Lost in the thought of getting tough with the dancer, Hector jerked the handle and carried the girl who had hold of the other side right into the restaurant. She stumbled and fell into Hector's large chest.

"I'm terribly sorry, please let me..." Hector started, but he suddenly realized who she was.

Tamara picked up her backpack.

"Aren't you Nicki from the club?" Hector asked, surprised. "I...I...thought you were with Jonathan. What are you doing here?"

"I haven't heard from him in days. That's why I'm here. I thought you all might know where he'd gone."

"Oh," Hector moaned, "this is not good. Not good at all. I thought you two...were..."

"Together?"

"Yes, you were, weren't you?"

"Yes, yes, we were. He hasn't told you, has he?"

"Told me what?!" Hector boomed.

Tamara brushed her hair off her face, and Hector could see the worry in her eyes.

"I'm sorry...Nicki?..." he ventured.

"Actually, Tamara, Tamara Connor." She held out her hand. The big Mexican engulfed it in his own. For the first time he noted her real beauty, and was struck by its intensity.

"Please, come sit down." Hector led Tamara to a small two-top by the kitchen and motioned for Claire. "Would you like something to drink?" he asked.

"Water would be fine, thanks."

Hector sensed a presence about her. A maturity. Something intangible that calmed him. He took a deep breath. "What should Jonathan have told me, Tamara?"

Tamara gave Hector the whole story. She told him about the kit cab accident, the club, the reper and the Light-Force weapon. She also told him about Jonathan's message.

Hector absorbed the tale without a word. He honestly wasn't sure what *to* say. When she finished, he sipped his coffee and eyed her cautiously.

"You don't believe me." She began to get up from the table.

"Now, now...I didn't say that," Hector assured her. "But you have to admit, it's all a little out there."

Tamara took Hector's hand and leaned close to him. "Listen. Jonathan thinks the world of you. You're his family, his only family! That's why I came. I'm not blind. I can tell how you feel about me and what I do. You have to take what I say as true, because it is! I saw it all, Anari saw it all. She was standing right next to him. I wouldn't have come here if I didn't care for him like I do." Her voice began to quiver. "Jonathan and I have something. It's intense. I...look Hector, I have to find him. Where would he go if he needed to get it together, if he needed to really get some answers? Who would he turn to?"

"Well, me, quite frankly. The only other person I could think of would be Tarris. Tarris was like his brother. Hell, he was his brother!"

"Where is he, Hector? Do you know?"

"No," Hector said, rising from the table. "But I do know someone who would...hey?!"

Tamara was already halfway to the door.

~

"Max? Max?" Hector called.

"Good afternoon, Hector. How have you been?" Jonathan's front door unlatched. "And how are you, Miss Connor?"

"I'm fine, Max," Tamara answered, and they entered the loft.

"Max, do you have in your database an address or netaddress for Tarris. You know, his best friend from when he was a kid?"

"Yes," Max said.

"Please download the data into my netpad," Tamara instructed. She checked the address. "New Mexico..."

"Yeah, that's right," Hector cut in. "I remember now. He moved there after the accident."

"What accident?"

"Oh, this guy is a genius, but he took it bad in a biobike crash. It left him a paraplegic. The way Jonathan describes it, he was legally dead, but they brought him back. Too bad the bioregen didn't take all the way....Anyway, he moved to a little town outside of Santa Fe, or something like that....Hey, what happened here?" Hector asked, noticing the condition of the loft.

"I think this is Jonathan getting upset with a message I left."

"Shit, he was pissed," Hector said.

"No, not pissed, I think he was..." Tamara couldn't find the words.

"Hurt, Miss Connor," Max interrupted.

"What?" Tamara asked.

"Jonathan was hurt by the message, Miss Connor," Max corrected.

An uncomfortable silence settled between Tamara and Hector.

"Max," she finally asked, "there hasn't been anything on the net about...you know."

"Jonathan's death?" Max asked.

"Yes..." she answered.

There was a pause. Hector walked over and picked up the broken picture of himself and Jonathan deep-sea fishing.

"No, there has been no information of his death. But his debit chipcard was used at 12 different locations throughout New Mexico."

"Give me the last place he used his card," Hector ordered.

"TP Mart number 23, in Tres Piedras, New Mexico. Will there be anything else?"

"Please, Max," Tamara instructed, "download those locations to my pad."

"Will there be anything else?"

"No Max," she answered. "You've been a great help." She began to leave.

"Miss Connor?" Max asked, stopping them.

"Yeah, Max?" she asked in surprise.

There was another pause.

"Are you and Jonathan in love with each other?"

Tamara was caught totally off guard. It was a simple question and, coming from an artificial intelligence, had an innocent quality about it. It was the kind of question a child might ask a parent that instantly put life into perspective.

Hector turned and looked at Tamara.

For the first time in her life, Tamara felt something she had never had with a man. Comfort. Jonathan just felt right. He fit. Like no other man had ever fit into her life before. "I really don't know what Jonathan feels, Max," she answered. "But yes, Max...I believe I am."

"Thank you, Miss Connor, I'll add that to my database."

Hector smiled at her, and they left the loft.

~

It was almost one o'clock when Jonathan woke up. The house was quiet. Tarris and Georgia were gone. Jonathan entered the kitchen and saw a message flashing on the system panel of the refrigerator. He played the vid. It was Georgia.

"Good afternoon, you." It was odd to see her in a dress, Jonathan thought. "We're going into Taos to get the truck and do a little shopping. There's plenty of food and beers, so help yourself. You know where everything is. I know you had a rough night, so relax. Our casa es su casa. Oh, if you think about it, we feed the strays, and there's some dog food in the kitchen closet. Their bowls are outside." She leaned into the screen, which distorted her face and made her look 20 pounds heavier. "Be careful, Jonathan," she whispered. Then she suddenly pulled back, and the vid ended.

"Great," Jonathan quietly said to himself. "Beer for breakfast. Just what I need, a little hair of the dog."

Jonathan made a sandwich, opened a beer and stepped out onto the deck. The sun behind him filled the San Cristobal Mountains with rich, deep hues. The air was warm, and in the distance, a vintage Harley disrupted the New Mexican quiet with its patented two-cylinder growl.

He ate his sandwich and debated the words of Whitehorse and the Recruiters. If he was as powerful as Whitehorse believed, the Rogues were probably not equipped to train him. And if Whitehorse was as ruthless as he seemed, then Jonathan wanted no part of him. The Agency, on the other hand, had the infrastructure and ability the Rogues lacked. It also seemed that they had a better sense of how the world actually worked and would be better suited to deal with complex global politics. Then, though, there were the rumors of their death squads. It didn't surprise him that the Agency would have this kind of force. Governments for centuries have had elite forces that worked in secret, all in the name of "good," as defined by their particular doctrines. It was the thought of being a part of an organization that controlled whether a person lived or died that unnerved him.

Jonathan picked up his empty beer bottle and peered through the glass at the mountains. "It all depends on how you look at it," he said out loud.

Jonathan closed his eyes and listened to the wind. The sound was rough against his ears. No netphones, no pots or pans banging together, no netpad interfaces, no nightly specials to be programmed. Just wind.

And something licking his fingers.

"Hello there!" he said to the two stray dogs who had wandered up to sniff the new guy. He rubbed behind the ears of the bigger one. "I bet you want your dinners."

Jonathan went into the kitchen and brought back their food bag. The two strays yipped and jumped with anticipation, then attacked their bowls as Jonathan poured them generous portions.

Jonathan returned to his chair on the deck. His life over the last few weeks had changed so much. To discover that you're not as human as you thought would freak anyone. To also discover someone like Tamara and be forced to choose your future at the same time was almost more than he could take. He had come to New Mexico to see an old friend, someone who had always been there for him. Instead, he was introduced to his destiny by two factions of a secret world culture. Both good. Both bad.

What if he was The Infinite Tel?

What if he was destined to usher in a new phase of human development?

What if his future was not his choice?

Jonathan thought of his father and the book, the only item he had to connect him to the life that could have been...with them.

Jonathan was overwhelmed.

No father, no mother, no friend could tell him what to do. He was solo on this one, and what he decided now could possibly change the human landscape forever.

The two dogs came over and put their heads in his lap. Jonathan closed his eyes and listened to the wind.

Rustling in the sage... 21

Jonathan spun his netphone around in his hand. He was afraid to turn it on and discover that the world was looking for him. He knew there would be netmessages from Hector and Tamara. And he knew that eventually he would have to confront his other life.

He clicked it on. Twenty-two messages. Six from Hector. Ten netdirect mails selling everything from the latest hydrobiopaste programs to self-aware refrigerator units that could suggest menu designs or select waiter wardrobe – all without attitude. Three from BioFood Netzine, probably hyping its netvitorial on the fusion of food and biotech.

One from Tamara. He launched it.

"Hey, you," Tamara said in a low and careful voice. "How are you? I hope you're doing what you need to do....If there's anything I can do to make it easier, please...let me know. Ah, hey...look, I went to the loft...and got the message. Sorry, I just needed to see if you were all right. Your message was, well, I don't know what to say. I, I...I know we'll see each other soon. Jonathan, I don't want to lose you....Not now. Look, I'm worried, baby. I want you to be safe. I know you're going through a difficult time, but I know you'll come out of it." There was a long pause. "You're special, Jonathan. I know you know that now. I don't know what's happening to you, but whatever happens, I'll be there for you. Call me...when you're ready. Bye, lover."

The netmessages from Hector followed. He sounded worried. Even more, Jonathan could hear the fear in his voice. Jonathan launched Hector's netID. He was going back online.

"Jonathan!" Hector answered in his all-too-familiar booming voice. "Where the hell are you?"

"Hey, Hector, look, this has been a pretty rough couple of days. I'm not going to be back for a while. There's just a lot I have to sort out."

"I'm sure. Ah, Jonathan, you need to know, Tamara came by the restaurant....She told me everything."

"Everything?"

"Yes, my friend...everything. Are you all right? Do you know what's happening to you?"

"I'm fine, Hector, but to tell you the truth, it's getting a little scary. Look, it's probably not safe to talk on the net. You're going to have to trust me here. I seem to be gaining strength, if that's what you'd call it, every day. It's getting easier and easier to do things that were almost impossible only days ago. But to answer your question, so far, I'm all right."

"Is there anything I can do?"

"Yeah, keep this between you, me and Tamara, okay? I'm not sure how all this is going to end."

"Okay, Jonathan."

"Hector, look...ah, this could get ugly. I mean, there are people..." He stopped himself. "Let's just say there are those who aren't out for my well-being."

"Jonathan, take care and watch yourself, all right?"

"Hector?"

"Yes?"

"It was good partnering with you..."

There was a long silence.

"Shut up, Jonathan." Hector's voice cracked a bit. "Do what you need to do and get your ass back to this kitchen. We have art to make!"

"Okay, Hector. You take care."

"You too, Jonathan." The netline cut out.

Jonathan thought about calling Tamara, but the net was too volatile, and he didn't want to involve her and Nicole any more than he had to. He clicked off the phone and dropped it into his pocket. The two strays were competing for his attention.

His strength had been gaining every day, and his ability to control and focus was becoming more refined. There was always the threat that a passing thought might manifest itself, though. He had to temper his gift, or he would almost never use his hands. The simplest of things were becoming innate to him, and he had to catch himself or he'd expose his true nature. The Recruiter was right: control was vital to a Tel. Without it, life would be chaos. Even dangerous.

Jonathan glanced down at the two dogs. He stopped petting them and mentally lifted them up into the air. As they rose, they whimpered and struggled a little. He began to juggle them slowly 12 feet off the ground. Then he lifted a deck chair to join the two dogs in their aerial acrobatics. The dogs actually seemed to enjoy the spinning and swirling. Jonathan added the outdoor cooker and thought about adding his rental car.

He opened another beer. His netphone signaled.

Startled, because he was off line, Jonathan stopped juggling and let dogs, chair and cooker all hang in the air like some bizarre, living mobile. He connected to the net. Unknown name, unknown number.

"Nice juggling, slick, but pretty amateur for a Tel at your level."

"James?" Jonathan asked in shock.

"Come on, you can call me Jimbo – everyone else does. My partner and I were wondering if last night's little demo scared you a little. You know we didn't want to spook you, but sometimes we've got to improvise, and he's one for the high drama, know what I mean? Anyway, what are you doing right now, besides juggling pets and outdoor furniture?"

"How did you..."

"Launch your phone?"

"Yeah..."

"Jonathan, come on, this is the 2100s. If the Agency wants to connect with you, it will. You'd be surprised how easy it is to launch one of those netphones. Which one is yours again, a MitsuSony? Hell, those pieces of crap couldn't be secured even with a biowall. We'd still get through."

Jonathan searched the area for the two Recruiters. The dogs-and-cooker mobile was still hanging.

"Don't bother looking. We can see you, but you can't see us. Hey, the big dog looks seriously pissed."

Jonathan looked up to find the bigger dog growling, tired of the vertical playtime he had shared with the new guy. Jonathan returned them to earth, and they trotted off to the next handout.

"So," Jimbo started, his voice getting serious. "Are you ready to learn what you can really do?"

"Well, I..."

Jimbo's voice shifted to an authoritarian tone: "Jonathan! It's time to face the music. Whitehorse isn't your answer. You know that. He couldn't teleconnect if his ass depended on it. Listen to your gut! You've got the gift, and you've got it big! Whitehorse knows this, and that's why he wants you. You're a threat to him. He's one mean motherfucker, and he's not going to let you just walk over to our side, if you know what I mean. Come on, let us teach you. You'll be able to do things you never dreamed possible. Believe me, the Agency knows what it's doing, and it doesn't fuck around. And you know what else?"

Jonathan didn't answer.

"You'll finally be with your own kind...and that alone's worth the price of admission."

"I'm listening..."

"Let's just have dinner and talk. No games, no demos and definitely no tricks."

Jonathan rubbed his shoulder.

"Where, Jimbo?"

"Let's meet tonight at The Sage, up on Kit Carson Road, say around seven o'clock?"

"Yeah, that's sounds fine, and hey, Jimbo...just you, not your partner. All right?"

"That's cool, Jonathan. Just me. I'll see you there at seven. And Jonathan, this is a smart move. Trust me on this." Jimbo disconnected.

The netphone hung in front of Jonathan as he leaned back in the chair. The clouds were beginning to build over the mountains, and the wind had picked up again.

As Jonathan finished his beer, his mind wandered back to Hawaii. If he thought hard enough, he could dredge up the fragments of memories from his childhood. The time he started opening his Christmas presents before his mother and father were up. The look on his father's face when he wandered into their bedroom and found them kissing and hugging each other naked. And there were the many trips to the ocean. Hawaii was one of the most beautiful places on earth until the event. Jonathan could still feel the cool water and the power of the surf when he and his father would snorkel the reefs near their home. He could almost taste the salt on his tongue.

The pain rose in his throat, and Jonathan swallowed hard. "It's times like this I could really use you, dad," he said out loud, staring at the netphone that would never connect him to his father in spite of his ten-dollar-a-minute family plan.

There was a rustle in the sage.

About 10 feet from the deck, Jonathan saw a small image appear. Like a holovid from some bad museum exhibit, its translucent surface floated between the sage bushes and played a clip through for about a minute, then repeated itself.

It was his father on the beach.

Jonathan leaned forward, transfixed as he watched his memory play out dimensionally on the New Mexican landscape. The clip shifted, and a new image ran. His father and mother were walking down the path that led from their lab to the main house. They walked and talked, though Jonathan could hear no sound. His mother was dressed in the clothes she always wore to conduct their research: a tight, sleeveless black shirt with khaki knee-length pants worn low on her thin hips. Her chrome belt buckle sported the vintage reclining naked girl like a mud flap from some antique truck. His father wore one of his flower-print bioshirts – with blooms that actually moved as you walked – and shorts that had a dozen small pockets for carrying anything, even though he never did. Both of them had on their white lab coats – just to make them feel like real scientists, they used to say. As they drew near the main house, his mother looked up at Jonathan and winked.

Jonathan slowly began to cry.

"Oh, mother..." he said quietly.

The ground began to shake. Jonathan's beer rattled its way off the chair. A crack appeared in the soil, starting at the deck and ripping toward the image. It widened and swallowed up every sage bush in its path.

Again the ground shook, this time more violently. Another fissure opened up that ran from the deck to the fence at the back of the property. Another split opened and another, until there were 10 fissures radiating from the deck, with Jonathan as the hub.

Jonathan, with his head in his hands, cried out to his dead

parents. “Oh, I miss you, I miss you!” he wailed.

The cooker exploded, sending metal and plastic flying through the air like tiny missiles.

Jonathan jumped to his feet and looked up into the vast expanse of the southwestern sky. “Fuck you, God!” he screamed. “Fuck you!”

The mesquite tree near the deck burst into flames, the needles of fire rising 20 feet into the air.

“Come on, motherfucker,” Jonathan yelled to the sky. “You’ve done this all to me. First you kill my parents, then you make me inhuman! And just as I discover that I will probably never relate to people again, you put in front of me a girl...” Jonathan fell back into the chair sobbing, “...a girl I connect with like no one I’ve ever known. And to top it all off...”

He closed his eyes.

The mesquite tree flamed out.

“...I think I’m in love with her.”

There was another rustle in the sage.

The image had shifted. Now Jonathan watched as his parents sat at their breakfast table, eating what looked like lunch. His mom talks with her mouth full, again with no sound, while his dad reads a netpad. He raises his glass to take a drink, but suddenly they both jerk their heads as if startled by something outside the window above the sink. There’s a flash from outside. His parents lift their arms to cover their faces. The image goes to white.

Jonathan’s netphone signaled again. Unknown name, unknown number.

“Hello?” Jonathan asked tentatively.

"Hi..." a little voice said.

"Nicole."

The netphone was silent.

"Jonathan, are you there?"

An icy feeling ran through his nerves.

"Yes, Jacob, I'm here."

"Jonathan, Nicole is such a pretty little girl..."

"If you hurt her in any way, you motherfu..."

"Don't motherfucker me, young man." Whitehorse's voice was low and stern. "Your display last night was impressive, but you caught me off guard. I can assure you that won't happen again."

"How's your associate, Whitehorse?"

There was a long pause.

"He'll be fine, as soon as they take him off life support."

Jonathan cracked a small smile.

"Jonathan, I am a man who is used to getting what he wants. And I want to have a meeting, just you and me. Tel to Tel. With no telekinetics. And Nicole is my...shall we say, insurance that you'll show?"

"Yes, Whitehorse, I'll show."

"Good. Then meet me at the Pueblo at eleven o'clock tonight. Oh, and Jonathan?"

"Yes, Whitehorse?"

"Don't bring those Agency boys. Do I make myself...clear?"

Jonathan could hear Nicole whimpering in the background. "Yeah, Whitehorse, you're coming in loud and clear."

The line cut off.

The image had disappeared.

~

"Did you hear all that?" the senior Tel asked Jimbo.

Jimbo nodded.

"I told you Whitehorse was a man of means," his partner said, pulling the biomicrotransceiver from his ear.

Through his field optics, Jimbo watched Jonathan get up and walk back into the house. "He's getting stronger almost by the hour," Jimbo said. He refocused on the cracks left in the earth by Jonathan's emotional rage. "That's one hell of a telekinetic display, and what's up with that mental holoprojection manifestation thing? Man, this boy just keeps on surprising us. I've never seen anything like that!"

"Nor have I. All the more reason to convince him, James. And I know you will."

"I'll do my best, sir."

"You will have to, James, because I know Jacob Whitehorse," his partner said, walking up to Jimbo's side. "He will kill that little girl if he does not get Jonathan's loyalty."

"And how do you know that?"

"Because if I were in Whitehorse's place..." the senior Tel turned and looked at Jimbo, "...I would kill her, too."

Showtime... 22

Passing the mirror in the bedroom, Jonathan stopped and checked out what he saw. He saw a man who had changed so much in the last few weeks. This one had to be perfect. There was no room for error – not with Nicole's life on the line. He tightened his gut and held it.

"I'm not the superhero type," he said under his breath.

"I don't know about that," Georgia said from the doorway, her arms folded.

Jonathan turned around as Georgia walked up to him.

"You're more powerful than a locomotive, faster than a speeding bullet, if there were bullets anymore..."

"But I can't leap over tall buildings."

"How do you know? Have you tried yet?"

"The tallest building in Tres Piedras is only two stories."

Georgia laughed.

Jonathan had told Tarris and Georgia about the meetings with Jimbo and Whitehorse, but he hadn't said anything about Nicole. He knew Georgia didn't have any knowledge of Nicole, because when he tested her, she acted as if Whitehorse had been humbled by Jonathan's display. In her eyes, everything was above board, and Whitehorse just wanted to talk.

Humbled my ass, thought Jonathan. Whitehorse had been embarrassed, and he was out to get even. If Jonathan was going to get Nicole back, he might need to recruit the Recruiters.

"You look nice," Georgia said. She brushed off some lint from his sweater and let her hand rest on his shoulder.

Jonathan turned and reached for his netpad on the table across the room. It flew over, but not into his hand.

Georgia handed it to him. "Good luck," she said and kissed him on the cheek.

Surprised, Jonathan looked into her dark eyes. She began to lean closer, her mouth slightly open, but she stopped herself and stepped back, brushing the hair off of her face.

"Thanks," Jonathan said. He pretended not to notice what might have happened.

Georgia, embarrassed, smiled and rushed out of the room.

~

The Sage was quiet, and Jonathan found Jimbo at the bar. Jimbo's tall lanky frame seemed almost too big for the barstool, and his wavy red hair made him look younger than he probably was. He had his back to the door.

"Hello, Jonathan," Jimbo said without turning around.

"James," Jonathan replied cautiously. He climbed onto the barstool next to him.

"Join me?" Jimbo asked, raising his glass.

"Sure."

Jimbo glanced at the bartender, never uttering a word. The bartender looked over suddenly and walked the length of the bar to where they sat.

"Yes, sir, may I help you?" the bartender asked, confused.

"Yes, I'll take an Oban, with ice, no water," Jonathan said and turned his attention to Jimbo, who was still looking straight ahead into the bar mirror.

"Do all you Agency guys wield your ability so freely?" Jonathan asked.

"You ever try getting a bartender's attention in New York?" Jimbo shot back.

There was an awkward silence.

The bartender returned with Jonathan's drink.

More awkward silence.

"You advanced Tels sure like your Scotch," Jimbo finally said.

"Excuse me?"

"You and my partner. You both like Scotch, with ice, no water. It's just funny, that's all." Jimbo slammed back his beer.

"Are you not the same level as your partner?"

"Shit no. He's the highest testing Tel ever. Me? I'm a lowly Level 5. But I think I could get to a Level 6, maybe even seven."

The bartender returned with two plates of food. "A steak for the gentleman," he said, handing one to Jimbo. "And the rainbow trout for his friend."

"Good guess, James," Jonathan said.

"We know a lot about you. It was one of the only things on the menu I'd thought you'd like." Jimbo cut into his steak.

"So tell me, James. What will happen to my life if I go with the Agency?"

"Well," Jimbo began, wiping his chin, "first you'll relocate to D.C. We'll probably get you a nice place, maybe in Georgetown. Then you'll be introduced to the director and his agents, blah, blah, blah.

"But here's the deal, Jonathan. You are one special Tel." He turned for the first time to face him. "We don't know if we can really teach you anything. Hell, do you have any idea what level you are?"

Jonathan shook his head.

"You, my friend, are at least a Level 8, probably a Level 9. You're stronger than my partner. And like I said, he's the hardest working Tel in show business." Jimbo made that click sound and dug into his mashed potatoes.

"Now don't get me wrong, we can get you all professionaled-up," he continued between forkfuls of potatoes. "You know, teach you control, focus, balance and timing. Make it so your talent is like second nature. But this FTL shit, wow, now that's off the charts, mister. You're definitely in another league. Hell, you're on another planet!" He ordered another beer.

"FTL?" Jonathan asked.

"Faster Than Light? Come on, don't give me that 'I didn't know I did that' routine. You created a grav field strong enough to stop a Light-Force bioweapon dead in its main discharge cycle. You're redefining the laws of physics, Jonathan, and that's way beyond all of us." He leaned over to Jonathan. "And you know you did it too, am I right?"

"Yeah..." Jonathan acknowledged slowly.

"Yeah, I'm damn right," Jimbo said, and he took a gulp from his fresh beer.

"Yes, James, but back to my life. What will my life be like from now on?"

Jimbo stuffed another bite of steak into his mouth, wiped his lips, put the napkin on his plate and turned on the barstool to face Jonathan. He grabbed his beer.

"We don't really know," he said seriously. "You're a whole new animal, Jonathan. You could be The Infinite Tel. But at the very least, you're the next phase, the next evolutionary step for us...for humans." Jimbo took a sip of his beer. "Look man, it's like I said before. There are no good guys or bad guys, just agendas. Our agenda is for you to be what you're meant to be. But we don't know what that is yet, and you don't either. We will, though. It takes time, and it takes the resources only the Agency can provide. Do you really think Whitehorse has the capabilities to develop a Tel of your caliber? Get real. The Rogues at best are a bunch of dysfunctional, mid-level Tels led by a bipolar psycho Indian. Now there's an organization I want to be with." Jimbo finished his beer.

"There's something you should know..." Jonathan began.

"Nicole? Already ahead of you, boss. Whitehorse is certifiable, that's for sure. He'll kill Tamara's kid as sure as I drank that beer. You need to play this out smart, Jonathan. Does Tamara know yet?"

"I don't know. She hasn't called me since her last netmessage, and I've checked, but she's off-line."

"That's odd. She must be in transit, and that means she's probably heading here. Does she know about Tarris?"

"No, but my loft's HDI system knows everything, and she has access to him...I mean it."

"Yeah, it's easy to trace you on the net through your biochip-card incep points. If she's a good mother, she's called her kid and hasn't gotten an answer, so she's probably beginning to get worried. But I doubt she's jumped to the conclusion of kidnapping, or that she's tied your situation to not getting an answer at her grandma's."

"Oh my God, I forgot about her...you don't think..."

"I doubt it. Whitehorse is a psycho, but he's not stupid. Quite the contrary, this man knows his shit. He should: my partner taught him everything he knows. You've got to understand, secrecy is way too important to us. The less people involved, the less of a containment issue you have. He probably STMN'd her. She just lost some memory, that's all. But she'll have one hell of a headache." Jimbo laughed under his breath.

"Yeah, how has that worked? The only organization I know that can keep a secret is the Mafia. And you're telling me you've done it for over a hundred years?"

"Oh, it's not that tough, really. It's a combination of disinformation and containment."

"What type of disinformation?"

"Remember all that UFO crap? You know, Area 51, or whatever it was, and all that shit back at the turn of the century? Hell, it almost became a religion. That was us....It was a perfect dis job. Notice how no one ever got a real great photo of anything? And like hundreds of people would see a huge craft, then it would all just die down? Funny, wasn't it? You see, Jonathan, after World War Two, our kind came onto the scene and freaked everyone out. They thought we would be the super race – take man to the stars. But back then, we crashed more than we flew. Remember the flying saucer crash in 1952 or '53 and the 'alien bodies'? Those were kids. The first real strong Tels back then were kids. And that space shuttle blow up...what was the name?"

"You mean Challenger?" Jonathan said, surprised.

"Yeah, that's it. Man, we screwed that up. That event alone set the Agency back 20 years. Remember the Kennedys?"

"Ah come on, the Agency didn't kill the Kennedys, did it?"

"Nah, not all of them. John was mob, but Bobby, so I've heard, was us. Total coincidence with that guy with the two same names....What were they...Turhan something? I can't remember. But I heard we fried Bobby about a second before the other guy shot him. Lucky for Bobby, he probably never felt a thing. I don't know about John Jr., I think that was all him."

"Why Bobby?"

"I was told he was a real ball buster and was going to shut the Agency down. Something about budgets and all. That's when the Agency went into shadow..."

"Shadow?"

"Yeah, it's our slang for how we exist. Back then, very few in government knew about us. Now...*nobody* knows. And the Level 8's keep it that way."

"Mind displacement?"

"You've been reading up. I bet that's Tarris, right?"

"Yeah. He gave me a textbook to read."

"Hah!" Jimbo laughed sarcastically. "It's probably giving you only a millionth of what we're really about. But come with us, and you'll see for yourself. Look, Jonathan, this is a no-brainer here. You can go with the Rogues, but I mean, really, mentally moving logs to free a river in some bug-infested rain forest? You're basically a telekinetic beaver. Now that's exciting, eh? Besides, I doubt Whitehorse wants you to do good around the world. My guess is he's got bigger plans for you. Plans that probably involve changing around some governments." Jimbo motioned as if he were about to let Jonathan in on the world's biggest secret. "Jonathan, you need to know: Whitehorse is very, very dangerous. He'll do whatever it takes." He leaned closer. "Whatever."

Jimbo leaned back on his stool and took a big swig from his beer.

"What about Nicole and Tamara?" Jonathan asked.

"Yeah, well, we wish you hadn't connected with her. We were almost ready to contact you. But, no matter," Jimbo said, climbing off the stool. "We've got to get her back and keep Tamara safe. And that's a commitment from the Agency. Think of it as a show of good faith." Jimbo stuck out his hand.

"Yeah, but Whitehorse said..." Jonathan started.

"We already know what he said, and we won't be there...will we?" Jimbo winked at Jonathan.

As Jonathan saw it, he had no choice. His inexperience left him vulnerable, and the Agency knew how to deal with ruthlessly dangerous men such as Whitehorse. Plus, he didn't want any harm to come to Nicole or Tamara. Jimbo seemed like a good "company man," but Jonathan was still not sure of the true intentions of the Agency.

Jonathan reached for Jimbo's hand, and a static discharge leaped between them before their fingers met.

"Good move, Mr. Kortel, welcome to the Agency," Jimbo said, shaking his hand. He pulled Jonathan closer and looked right into his eyes. "If this is going to work, you need to do it our way....Are we clear on this?"

Jonathan nodded.

"Good," Jimbo said firmly. "Now, let's go get that little girl."

~

The Pueblo was dark. Jonathan's car headlights flooded the entrance, and the two guards were conspicuously absent. The gates were wide open.

Jonathan drove slowly into the plaza area. No one else was in sight. A large bonfire roared in the center of the plaza, and the Pueblo's adobe walls were awash in deep contrasts of orange, yellow and black that danced across the uneven surfaces. As the shadows moved in sync with the flames, it gave the Pueblo a Dali-like feel. It gave Jonathan the creeps.

When Jonathan pulled around the fire, Jacob Whitehorse stepped from the dark shadows into the path of the car.

Nicole was in his arms.

Jonathan engaged the braking system, and the car stopped amid a small dust cloud.

Whitehorse stood his ground. He wasn't smiling this time.

"Well, Whitehorse," Jonathan said as he closed the car door.

"I'm here. Now give me the little girl."

Whitehorse just stood there, silently tracking Jonathan's every move. Nicole looked scared. She reached her hand toward Jonathan.

"We had a deal, Whitehorse." At Jonathan's first step, six Indians emerged from the shadows, each one carrying an M-21 Tactical Light-Force biorifle. They flanked him three and three.

"Yes," Whitehorse said, "we had a deal. But I need your assurance. No telekinetics, and I'll just hold onto little Miss Connor here as security."

Jonathan spun slowly around to size up each Indian.

"Oh, I know you're FTL against one bioweapon, but I seriously doubt you can duplicate that against six. Are we getting the picture here, Jonathan?"

"Okay, Whitehorse, I'm getting the picture. Now let's talk."

Whitehorse walked inside the circle of men. "How was your dinner with James? Did he feed you the company line?"

"I suppose," Jonathan said, not taking his eyes off Whitehorse.

"And you bought into it, didn't you?" Whitehorse accused, circling Jonathan.

"Well, they do have a compelling argument."

"Did he tell you about their 'special units?' About the men and women trained to be assassins, to do covert ops across the world?"

"Well, no, we never..."

"And I'm sure he didn't tell you about the other world 'Agencies' and their men and women, and their death units? I think not!"

Nicole began to squirm.

"And he obviously never said a thing about the deaths that take place when different Agencies with different agendas run up against each other. Well let me tell you something..." Whitehorse stopped circling and stood right in front of him. "...I know a little about death."

Nicole was beginning to cry.

"The Agency that Jimbo so eloquently described to you killed my wife." He was now inches from Jonathan's face. "And the man who ordered her assignment is James's partner."

The light from the fire painted Whitehorse's face in harsh contrasts. Jonathan saw the years of bitter hatred stored in his eyes, and he knew then that Nicole's life was in grave danger. As Whitehorse walked away, Nicole looked back over his shoulder at Jonathan. Tears were running down her cheeks.

"What do you want, Whitehorse? You want me to join you in your quest for world peace? Or is there another agenda here? Tell me!"

Whitehorse quickly turned. Nicole screamed.

"Of course I do!" he yelled. The six Indians charged their bioweapons; their collective whine echoed through the Pueblo.

"You're a Level 10, Jonathan. Don't you see that?! Together, we can bring balance back to the world and correct years of oppression. I can give my people justice from the goddamn white man!" The glow from the fire gave Whitehorse a demonic look. "Jonathan, you can usher in a new beginning for mankind! You're the next step! The Agency knows this. That's why they've been watching you, testing you. Remember the cab accident? That was a test. And guess who administered that test?"

Whitehorse began heading toward Jonathan. "The same man who sent my wife to her death, almost sent Tamara to hers."

He was three feet from him.

"Jonathan," he bellowed. "Open your eyes! The world is not what it seems. These men, these...Recruiters, are nothing more than henchmen for an organization that answers to no one. It's unchecked and unpoliced. It can do whatever it pleases...." He drew less than a foot from Jonathan. "...It can kill whoever it wants, and no one is held responsible."

"Yeah, well you might be right," Jonathan said while Whitehorse walked away from him. "But you're holding a little girl who should really be in the arms of her mother."

Whitehorse shook his head, his back still to him. "Ohhh Jonathan. I was afraid you would say something stupid like that." He slowly turned, and Jonathan saw he wasn't holding Nicole anymore. She was suspended about a foot away from him, kicking her legs and crying uncontrollably. Whitehorse had his hands in his pockets and looked fairly relaxed – for a homicidal psychopath.

Jonathan didn't dare move.

"You know," Whitehorse said in low voice, "I could crush her little brain in seconds." He narrowed his eyes at Jonathan.

"Go to hell, Whitehorse," Jonathan quietly uttered, and Whitehorse jerked forward like he'd been punched in the back. His face registered shock, his mouth flew open, and his arms and legs were outstretched like something was tearing his limbs from his body. He began to rise off the ground, and a gurgling noise was coming from his throat.

At the same instant, Nicole flew away from Whitehorse, over Jonathan's head and out of the circle of Indians. She screamed all the way.

Surprised to see their leader seemingly floating away, the Indians leveled their bioweapons at Jonathan's head. His vision turned to colors, then twinkling, then swirling. A symphony of tones filled his mind.

He went into phase.

Six bioweapons discharging filled the plaza with light like midday in Taos.

Jonathan, his arms outstretched, hovered a foot off the ground. His eyes were opened wide and staring up at Whitehorse. The six Indians were held tight in his imaging field: their bioweapons caught in mid-discharge with motionless beams of light protruding from their guns.

Jimbo and his partner calmly walked into the circle. Nicole was in Jimbo's arms.

The senior Tel walked up to Jonathan.

"You know, Jonathan, you have a dilemma here. If you relax your imaging, the bioweapons will discharge, killing both of us. I can keep Jacob up there for some time. But how long can you hold these weapons in check?"

He took a drag off his cigarette. A drop of blood fell, landing on the top of the senior Tel's shoe. Another drop fell to the dirt.

"You could move yourself out of the circle," he continued. "But there is Law Number 5: a Tel cannot move himself. Gravitational displacement does not work in reverse, but obviously you again are proving our laws and levels are mistaken. You are hovering right now, so you must be able to move yourself! Do it, Jonathan!"

He walked around to face Jonathan. Jimbo slowly backed out of the circle.

"I'm going to stay in the middle until you move yourself out. NOW DO IT!"

Jonathan lowered his head to view the senior Tel.

"You used a contraction," Jonathan said hoarsely, and he rose about seven feet and floated backwards out of the circle.

The senior Tel smiled and followed.

As soon as Jonathan's feet touched the ground, the six bioweapons finished their discharge. Foolishly, Whitehorse's men had lined up directly across from each other, and they weren't faster than light.

Jimbo buried Nicole's head from the sight.

There was no sound. No screams. Just the creation of six small puddles of biomatter where each man had stood.

The senior Tel lit another cigarette.

Jonathan collapsed to the ground. Wiping the blood from his nose, he looked up at Whitehorse, who was still suspended about 20 feet in the air.

"What are you going to do with him?" Jonathan asked.

The senior Tel turned and looked up almost forgetfully at Whitehorse. He walked back into the center of the ring of former Indians, and Whitehorse began a descent that stopped about seven feet off the ground.

"Jacob, can you hear me?" the senior Tel called up to him between drags. "Jacob?" he asked again. He didn't get a verbal response. Instead, the senior Tel suddenly reached for his throat as his cigarette dropped to the ground. Jacob Whitehorse fell to earth, landing on his hands and feet.

Jimbo, who had handed Nicole to Jonathan, began to rush to his partner's aid, but the senior Tel waved him off as he fell to one knee.

There was panic in Jimbo's eyes.

Whitehorse regained his composure while the senior Tel struggled for air. "I've waited a long time for this, Zvara," Whitehorse said, circling the senior Tel.

Jimbo's face betrayed his shock at hearing that name.

"What's the matter?" Jonathan asked. "Don't you know who he is?"

"He told me he was someone else, but Whitehorse just called him Zvara!" Jimbo whispered. "Armando Zvara's kind of an urban myth in the Agency. We were told he was dead. Damn, this is too much."

Jonathan and Jimbo watched as the two Level 8's completely focused on each other and began round one of their telekinetic heavyweight bout. But in this ring, the stakes were much higher.

Jonathan tried to intervene but was too weak from displacing six bioweapons.

"Don't try, Jonathan. You're in no condition to help Zvara."

"Is there anything we can do?" Jonathan asked.

"No, their field strengths will be too strong, at least for me."

"Can you call in reinforcements?"

Jimbo looked tersely at Jonathan. "We're not the damn army. This looks like it's between Whitehorse and Cas...I mean, Zvara."

Whitehorse stepped closer. Zvara looked up at him, his eyes

partially rolled back from the lack of oxygen. Suddenly, Whitehorse was thrown to the ground as if he had been kicked in the chest. He rolled to his side coughing and spitting blood. The dust gently settled around him.

Zvara was now on his feet. "Jacob," he coughed, wiping the sweat from his brow. "Do you really think you can take me on?"

Zvara doubled over, grabbing at his stomach. He groaned in agony and dropped to his knees. He vomited in the dirt.

"Shit," Jimbo whispered, "this doesn't look good. We need an exit plan – and fast."

"Why isn't Zvara winning?" Jonathan whispered back. Nicole turned her head and clung tightly to Jonathan's neck. He had never held her before, and a strangely protective instinct welled inside him.

"I don't know. He should be kicking Whitehorse's ass right about now. Come on!" Jimbo began pushing them toward the car.

"Where are you going, James?" Whitehorse asked, his attention drawn to their movement. "Don't you want to see your partner here die...oh, ohhh my GOD!!" Whitehorse screamed in midsentence and stumbled backwards, reaching for his face.

Armando Zvara was coughing as he rose to his feet. He wiped the bile from his mouth.

"And I have waited a long time for this, Jacob," Zvara said, stumbling toward him.

Jimbo grabbed Jonathan's shoulder: "Hold on." They stood next to the car and expectantly waited for Zvara to demonstrate why he was the highest testing Tel ever.

Whitehorse seemed frozen, his hands clutching his face. Thick, red blood oozed between his fingers.

"I should have..." Zvara started, but he stopped and raised his head as if to peer into the New Mexican night sky.

A shooting star passed overhead.

Whitehorse lowered his hands. His dark eyes reflected the orange radiance of the fire, and his blood was smeared in streaks across his face. The big Indian was now in warrior mode.

Zvara's arms were outstretched from his shoulders, and he began to rise off the ground. Whitehorse glared as Zvara slowly rose 10 feet and rotated horizontally onto his back. Whitehorse was about to crucify the killer of his wife on a cross only his mind could see.

The color had drained from Jimbo's face.

"It's over," he said quietly. "Let's get the hell out of here."

Jonathan handed Nicole to Jimbo and climbed into the pilot's seat. Jimbo took the passenger side and held her tightly against his chest. Whitehorse paid no attention.

They sped toward the main gate, and Jimbo turned in his seat to look back into the plaza. Through the dust raised in their wake, he could see Whitehorse laughing at his partner, who hung Christ-like in the air.

Whitehorse had positioned him over the fire.

Escape... 23

It was four in the morning when Jimbo, Jonathan and Nicole finally entered Tarris's compound. The ride back had been quiet. Neither man wanted to relive the events of the night. Jimbo broke the silence for barely 20 minutes to tell Jonathan about the Agency legend, Zvara.

As a child entering the Agency, Armando Zvara had shown great promise, possibly the potential to ascend to the unthinkable status of Level 9. He grew in strength as he grew in age. Taking on the tough assignments, he demonstrated an uncanny ability to adapt and reconfigure his grav field to match, or better, whatever or whoever was in his way.

He became the ultimate weapon.

It was only a matter of time before the Agency put its prodigy to work. Zvara was dispatched throughout the world, correcting issues and delivering the Agency's own special brand of justice. All in the name of good.

Zvara rose through the ranks and created for himself a status that teetered on the edge of myth. He became the youngest Director the Agency ever had and soon gained control of the world's most secret organization. No one challenged him. No one, that is, until a big Indian from the desert southwest began finishing assignments before the assigned Tels could.

Jacob Whitehorse thought he'd shake things up at the Agency. Armando Zvara was intrigued with this *rogue* Tel.

Their partnership became the stuff of legend. They dominated the Tel world for nearly a decade, but then the collaboration crumbled. Zvara made a fatal mistake with the big Indian from the desert. He fell in love with his wife.

The affair lasted nearly three years. But when Zvara demanded that she choose between him and Whitehorse, he failed to foresee the dire consequences of her choice. Wrought with jealousy and blinded by power, Zvara directed Whitehorse to a dangerous assignment. Only Zvara knew how dangerous it really was. But the result was not the death of Whitehorse.

It was of his wife.

The loss of his soulmate changed Whitehorse. He began questioning Agency policy, refusing directives, and challenging Zvara's power. He turned his back on the Agency and went underground, creating an alternative group for Tels who were fed up with the Agency's agenda. He named this new group after the nickname Zvara had given him so many years ago.

For his part, Zvara was chastised for such reckless use of power. He was stripped of his title and demoted to the Recruiter Division of the Agency. In the wake of the incident, the world's most powerful organization also adopted a new form of management for itself. It would never be headed by one person again.

Jimbo pulled the rental up to the house and flooded the front porch with light. The door swung open, and Tamara and Georgia stepped out with Tarris rolling behind them. Tamara ran toward Jimbo, who was holding Nicole.

"Oh, my God!" she said, shocked to see her child in the middle of New Mexico. "What are you doing with Nicki?!"

"It's a long story, baby, but thank this guy here," Jonathan said, motioning to Jimbo. "He got her out of danger."

Tamara gathered Nicole into her arms and kissed her on the forehead. She looked over to Jonathan. "Oh, baby..." She hugged and kissed him, then suddenly stopped.

"Grannie..." she said with fear in her voice.

"Go ahead and call her Tamara," Jimbo said. "But I'll bet she's okay – a little in pain probably – but okay."

Tamara instantly pulled out her netphone. Georgia, arms folded, stood silently. Jonathan looked over at her.

"What happened?" Tarris demanded.

"I'll tell you what," Jonathan answered, eyes still on Georgia. "Right now, I'd give anything to be just a simple, powerless man. You can have this telekinesis crap."

"We thought you'd be back hours ago," Tarris said.

"Well, sir," Jimbo cut in. "We had a little business to take care of."

"Oh, I'm sorry everyone," Jonathan said. "This is James McCarris. He's with the Agency."

"Ma'am," Jimbo said, shaking Georgia's hand.

"Oh, thank you, James," Tamara said and snapped her netphone shut. "Grannie's okay. She doesn't remember a thing." She stepped over and hugged him. Nicole giggled for the first time.

"Yes, ma'am. It was our obligation to Jonathan to get your daughter back. She's a real pretty little girl." Jimbo's Southern drawl was thicker than usual, and he tickled Nicole under her chin. "Your grandmother will be all right, little one." He looked down at his transwatch. "Jonathan, we need to get out of this state as soon as we can. Tarris, do you know when the first flights start taking off from Albuquerque?"

"Ummm, the earliest I've ever seen is a five o'clock. I think it's a Nations Air into Daley or O'Hare. I can't remember which."

"No problem, I'll confirm that. Okay, Jonathan, get packing," Jimbo said, going professional. "And Tarris, do you have any weapons, bio or conventional?"

Tarris smiled and stood up with his chair. "Follow me, Mr. McCarris."

Jimbo pulled out his netphone, amazed by Tarris's walking chair, and followed him back behind one of the metal buildings.

Georgia stopped Jonathan as he headed toward the house with Tamara. "So, you're going with the Agency?"

"Hey, baby," Jonathan said, "give me a moment, please." Tamara read his look. She took Nicole's hand and continued into the house.

The light of dawn was beginning to fill the sky as Georgia and Jonathan stood alone in the compound's courtyard.

"Look, Georgia," he finally said. "I don't know what Whitehorse has said to you, but that man is out-of-control crazy. What I saw last night confirmed to me that the Rogues are way too under the netdar for me. And you should really think twice about staying with them. At least get rid of Whitehorse. Like I said, he's evil on a stick."

"We've had discussions about just that, but we're split as a group. I told you before, if you went with the Agency, I would leave the Rogues and stay with Tarris." She looked down, then toward the house. "Tamara seems like a nice girl....It's...just..."

"Just what, Georgia?"

Her dark hair blew across her face, and he stepped closer.

"Since I've met you...I..." She turned away. Jonathan pulled her around to face him. "Look," he said quietly, "I feel it, too. You and I are Tels. We probably have more in common with each other than Tamara and I, or even you and Tarris." He stopped and looked into her eyes. "Don't get me wrong..." He hesitated. "Another time or place, yeah, I'd be after you in a heartbeat. But not now."

He ran a finger down the side of her face, pulling her hair aside. "I would love to kiss you right now," he continued. "But that would be wrong. Way wrong."

Jonathan touched her on the lips with his finger, and a static discharge passed between them. He turned and walked into the house.

~

Tarris led Jimbo to the second building from the house, maneuvering almost effortlessly around rocks and sage bushes. The flimsy metal building was Tarris's workshop, where he built the modifications to his chair. The room was large and contained work tables, computers, biofabrication equipment and an 8-foot flat, liquid crystal TVid screen. Tarris moved one of the work tables aside to expose a large metal floor locker with an integrated systems lock. He transformed downward into a standard chair and began the sequence for unlocking the case. The system hummed and whined until the lock tripped. The lid slowly raised, and Tarris smiled at Jimbo.

Jimbo was viewing an impressive array of weaponry. A 20th-century M-16 lay on top of the pile, with the rest a mix of bio hand-held weapons and three Hitachi/Wesson Light-Force biorifles.

"Wow, now you're talking." Jimbo said, kneeling to examine the various weapons. "Tarris, you old survivalist. I'm glad you call me friend."

"You just never know," Tarris said proudly.

"No, you don't, and today we're gonna need most of these. Do you mind?" Jimbo asked, pointing to the antique M-16. He picked it up reverently, like he was handling a delicate glass sculpture. "Yeah..." He lifted the gun to his shoulder. "Now this is what I'm talking about. This here's a weapon."

"Damn near perfect shape, too." Tarris said. "But for my money, give me a Light-Force any day." He reached in and brought out a Beretta Light-Force Hand-Held. The contrast between its chrome and flat-grey surfaces made the weapon appear almost toylike, but anyone who had witnessed its bioshifting results knew that it was anything but. He stuffed it into his coat pocket.

Jimbo set the M-16 down and lifted out the three biorifles. "One for each of us," he said. He pocketed a Beretta for good measure.

~

Jonathan busily packed. He told Tamara about the Rogues, the Agency and the ordeal at the Pueblo. Tamara quietly listened as she washed up Nicole. Tamara was dressed in her mannish way: work boots, baggy rip-stop pants with four large pockets down each leg and a vinyl T-shirt. Jonathan packed the last case and watched her with Nicole. He had not seen her much as a mother, and the contrast to how he had seen her in Liquid Courage was, well...beautiful, he thought.

Tamara could feel his stare and turned around, brushing her curls off her face. "What?...Why are you smiling?"

"I'm sorry. I rambled on about myself, and you're listening so patiently, and it hits me. What you're doing. It's so real. I've just never really seen you...you know...in action."

"In action?"

"As a mother. It's okay, I find it quite wonderful, actually. You seem to be a natural. So...happy."

Tamara smiled and resumed washing Nicole.

~

Tarris closed the lid and reinitialized the locking sequence. Jimbo had picked up the biorifles and was heading for the door.

"Where's your partner?" Tarris asked.

Jimbo's hand froze on the doorknob, his back to Tarris. "When we left, he was still fighting Whitehorse in the middle of the plaza."

"And?" Tarris pressed.

"I doubt he won," Jimbo said gravely and opened the door. He trotted over to Jonathan's rental car.

"Hold on," Tarris said. "I wouldn't take that piece of shit. Come over here." He started "walking" toward the third metal building. When he reached it, he put his hand in his pocket, and the large front door began to open, revealing an antique 2035 Hummer with full off-road setup and desert military paint job.

Jimbo smiled for the first time that night.

"Now this will get us to Albuquerque," Tarris said proudly, "any way we want." He pushed the controller in his pocket again, and the Hummer turned over, producing the odd multipitched hum of a dozen different retrofitted aftermarket engine parts grinding together. The lights came on and flooded the area with bright yellow and white lights.

The Hummer rolled out of the building and right up to Jimbo, who was standing with the bioweapons in his arms. "Sweet..." he said.

Jonathan, Tamara, Nicole and Georgia emerged from the house.

"Tarris, are you sure this thing will get us there?" Georgia asked over the noise of the engine.

"Baby, this will get you anywhere. Stow the gear and let's get going. We haven't much time."

Tarris climbed into the pilot's seat, with Georgia in shotgun.

Tamara and Nicole sat in the middle of the rear seat with Jonathan and Jimbo flanking them, biorifles ready on the floor. Georgia checked her weapon's system pad, then turned back to Jonathan.

"Ever discharged one of these?"

"Honestly, no," he answered. "But I'm a quick learner."

"I'll show you," Tamara said. She lifted the Hitachi/Wesson off the floor, flipped it around and began the precheck on the system pad. The whine stopped everyone cold.

"Tamara!" Tarris yelled. "What are you doing?"

"Relax, everyone, it's not loading. It's charging. See?" She flipped it again, with the system pad facing out. "This yellow light is standby, not load. And besides, this isn't the right pitch. The loading sequence is just a little higher, listen."

She pressed a pad sequence and the weapon began loading, its whine just slightly higher. She quickly shut it down to standby and spun it around in one hand so that the butt end faced Jonathan. Everyone in the Hummer collectively turned and looked at her. "Hey," she said, "picked it up in Nevada." She winked at Jonathan. Nicole giggled.

~

They charged out of the mountains riding an empty Interway as the sun was cresting over the mountaintops, sending golden rays streaking across the peaks. The tension in the Hummer was thick. Whitehorse was a seriously resourceful man, and they all assumed he would try to stop them before they got out of New Mexico.

Jimbo was working his netphone. "...Bill, don't give me any crap, we're in a situation here," he barked. "...I know that most of the team is in the Middle East....I know that, too....Put Berger on." There was a long pause. "Berger, why the hell didn't you tell me my partner was Zvara?...Oh, right, like that's gonna help the situation....Ah, I don't know....No, he waved us off. Besides, you know my level parameters....I doubt it, sir....Yes, sir...Yes, sir...Thank you, sir, that will help a lot." He clicked off his netphone and looked out the window.

They all bounced in sync as the Hummer sped toward Albuquerque.

~

"That's odd," Jimbo said, finally breaking the silence.

"What's that?" Georgia asked.

"I would have bet you that Whitehorse would have showed by now. We're almost to the airport."

"I think you spoke too soon, Jimbo," Tarris said. He pointed to the rear vidscreen. About 200 yards back, a pair of car lights approached them at a high rate of speed.

"Showtime..." Jimbo said, still looking out the window.

The car kept gaining. Tarris pushed the antique to its limits, but even with his retrofittings, the Hummer could only do 120 mph max, and he was already pushing it on the flat stretches.

"Everyone ready?" Jimbo asked.

They all nodded. Jonathan looked at Tamara and handed her back the biorifle. "Here, looks like you know how to use it better than I do. Give me your hand-held."

Tamara took the Hitachi/Wesson and handed Jonathan the Beretta. "Give me the window," she said and they crawled over each other in the cramped cabin. She settled in, reviewed the system pad and propped the Hitachi/Wesson between her legs. "Cocked and locked."

Jimbo and Tarris laughed.

Jonathan was now next to Nicole. She looked up, and he

brushed the hair off her face. When he glanced up, he caught Georgia staring at him.

"Here they come!" Tarris said.

"Be sharp, everyone!" Jimbo ordered.

The car pulled right up to their bumper, held for a moment, then jerked to the side lane and flew past, chewing up the road ahead of them.

"I don't get this," Jimbo said, frustrated. "Where's Whitehorse?"

"This doesn't feel right," Tarris agreed.

"Maybe," Georgia said, "he got what he needed when he dealt with your partner."

Jimbo shot her a look.

~

"Welcome to Georgia O'Keefe International airport, please state your airline, flight number and departure or arrival time," the simvoice said through the netradio of the Hummer.

"Nations Air, 1213, departure, six thirty," Tarris answered.

"Thank you. Please follow the signs to terminal 3, Gate 17. Have a nice flight."

Tarris pulled up to the curb, and the Hummer released some steam from under the hood. They hid the weapons under the mats and climbed out. One baggage handler grabbed their gear as Jimbo handed another his netpad.

"Four through to Chi town," the first said. "Now isn't she precious." He tickled Nicole in the belly; she grinned and buried her face in Tamara's neck.

"Just give me your eyes right here, everyone," the second handler said. He raised his handheld WAA scanner and processed their retinas. "Thank you, you're all checked through to Daley/Chicago. Have a safe flight."

Jimbo took the handler's netpad and entered in his tip.

"Thank you, sir!" he said with a tip of his hat.

"Well, buddy," Tarris said to Jonathan, "not quite the relaxing time off you were looking for, eh?"

Jonathan put down his carry-on and walked over to his friend. "Nah, I guess not." Jonathan gazed awkwardly at his shoes like he couldn't think of the right thing to say. "Thanks for everything, Tarris," he finally settled on. "You be safe...and take care of that lady."

"Listen, Jonny, we may not see each other for a long time, so good luck, little brother. I hope you find what you're looking for." Tarris glanced at Tamara and Nicole, then back to Jonathan and smiled.

Jonathan grabbed his friend and hugged him. They shook hands, and Tarris "walked" to the Hummer and climbed in.

Georgia stood there quietly with her arms folded.

Jonathan motioned to Tamara and Jimbo to go on. "I'll catch up with you at security, okay?"

Jimbo nodded and led Tamara through the huge sliding glass doors into the terminal.

"You take care of him, you understand me," Jonathan said.

Georgia didn't answer. She walked up and took his hands. A plane passed overhead as she came up to his ear. "My love goes with you, Jonathan. Please be careful." She kissed him on the cheek, turned and crawled up into the Hummer. She lowered the window.

"Go save the world for us, will you, little buddy!" Tarris laughed from the pilot's seat.

Georgia silently mouthed "goodbye." And smiled that smile.

Dear God... 24

The huge Airbus was crowded with ski tourists and business types. Because of their last-minute reservations, Jonathan, Jimbo and Tamara were assigned seats in the back of the plane on the first level near the workout gym. Jonathan stowed his bag while Jimbo took his seat in front of Nicole and Tamara. Nicole stretched her arms and reached for Jonathan. He picked her up and placed her in his lap. Tamara smiled.

"I think she likes me," he declared.

"I think you're cool," Nicole said in her little voice.

Tamara began to laugh. Jonathan, surprised, was infected by it and broke out laughing for the first time in several days. The release felt good.

An elderly lady across the aisle with her head buried in a vidbook shot them a look.

Jimbo clicked his netphone off and turned around to face Jonathan. "Okay, we're all set. There'll be a car waiting for us when we land in Chicago to take you to your apartments...or wherever you need to go....Hey, what's so funny?"

"Nothing, James. You had to be there," Jonathan said. He and Tamara froze for a second, exchanged looks, and burst out laughing again.

Nicole smiled at Jimbo. "I think you're cool, too."

"Ladies and gentlemen, this is your first officer Mike Mathews, and sitting next to me in the captain's chair is Jackson Stoval. We've been cleared for vert takeoff and we'd like to ask the flight attendants to finish preparing the cabins for an early departure from New Mexico. You folks in the gym: get your last mile in, we'll be lifting off in approximately 10 minutes."

Jonathan leaned back into the seat and finally began to relax while the flight attendants scurried up and down the aisles, prepping the different cabins for takeoff.

He reached over and gently squeezed Tamara's hand. She squeezed back.

The lights dimmed as the holojectors lowered from their various ports in the cabin and began the preflight holovid. Thirty life-size, holojected flight attendants began explaining the safety procedures and emergency escape routes. A lone flight attendant came up the aisle, spot-checking different passengers. Her face eerily merged with the holoattendants when she walked through each holojection.

She stopped at Jonathan's seat. "What a darling little girl. You two must be very proud." She continued down the aisle, and Tamara squeezed his hand tighter.

"Ladies and gentlemen, this is your first officer again. We've been cleared for vert takeoff, and we'd like to ask the flight attendants to please take their jump seats."

The lights dimmed further, and the plane's turbines started up. Their rhythmic hum built to an apogee as the plane was moved backwards out onto the tarmac. Jerking to a halt, the muffled sounds of the ground crew's disengagements traveled down the fuselage, each station uncoupling from the huge aircraft from front to back. There was a moment of quiet where the sense of activity, either in the plane or on the tarmac, disappeared. Then the turbines roared to life. The plane vibrated, shuddered and began to lift vertically into the early morning sky.

It hovered briefly at 300 feet to receive air space clearance from O'Keefe tower; its engines droned deeply, fighting the winds pouring down off the mountains. Then the plane rotated on its center axis, pointed its nose up slightly and began the transition from vertical to horizontal flight. Without spilling a single first-class drink, it slowly edged forward, headed toward the mountaintops and the airspace of the Midwest.

"Ladies and gentlemen, we've completed our transition sequence and begun our flight to Chicago's Richard J. Daley Airport. Our computer puts us in on time, even though we've had a head start out of Albuquerque, we've got a head wind which should eat up any extra time we gained. We'll be climbing over the mountains and might get a little chop, so I'm going to ask that the flight attendants please remain in their jump seats until it's safe to move about the cabins. Thank you."

Four large turbines shifted from the low tone of vertical takeoff to the high-pitched whine of horizontal flight. The plane's angle of attack increased, and Jonathan clicked his seat out of takeoff position. He leaned back into its body fitting fabric – not as nice as the first-class's biofitting seats. They would mold to the passenger's frame, but as far as Jonathan was concerned, anything that would help him sleep was perfect.

He closed his eyes.

The TVid screens in the headrests glowed up, and NNN came on.

"Good morning. Yesterday in the former Hawaiian Islands, scientists believe that they've detected a shift in the..."

Tamara reached over and touched Jonathan's arm. He kept watching and patted her hand at his shoulder.

"Don't worry, baby. I'm not going to get all emotional on you. I've been watching this stuff for years now. I learned to tune it out a long time ago."

The plane buffeted a bit as it neared the mountains. Both Jimbo's and Jonathan's TVid screens suddenly went blue, then a flight attendant appeared on the screen.

"Mr. McCarris? Mr. Kortel?" she asked in a serious tone. "You both have an emergency netcall. Shall I put it through?"

They nodded, surprised. The flight attendant was replaced with a commercial about the latest biodiaper. Jimbo turned around and looked seriously at Jonathan through the gap in the seats. The netphones in their arm rests buzzed, and they slowly picked them up in unison.

"Relaxed, gentlemen?" asked Jacob Whitehorse.

Jimbo's hand began to tremble. Jonathan's heart began to race.

"It's too bad you all left so early last night. Armando and I talked over old times and had a few laughs. Didn't we, old friend?"

There was a long pause.

"James?..." Zvara's voice was weak and broken.

Shocked, Jimbo could barely speak. "Are...are you all right, sir?"

"Forget about me, James, your job is to get Jonathan..."

"Enough!" Whitehorse interrupted. "Jonathan, you really should have come with me. I'm so surprised..."

"Whitehorse!" Jonathan pleaded. "You're out of control. I'm not worth the deaths that have happened already. Don't kill Zvara, please. I'm not the Infinite whatever you call it, believe me. Jimbo says I'm probably just a Level 8, but that's it! Please don't kill anymore. I'm not worth it!"

"Oh, but you are, Jonathan. James isn't telling you the truth, are you, James?"

Jimbo was silent.

"I thought so. James, did you tell him about the results of the GDRD test, or the Field level tests, or the Grav Reflux data?"

Jimbo still didn't respond.

"The Agency," Whitehorse said in disgust. "They're no better than we are." He paused. "I've waited a long time for you, Jonathan. You may not know it now, but you have the potential for great things. To take our kind beyond anything we have ever imagined. I believe you are The Infinite Tel, and I know the Agency does, too. I'll give you one more opportunity. Come with me, and we'll change the world!"

A quiet hiss from the net connection filled their ears.

"Jonathan?"

"No, Whitehorse...I won't."

Whitehorse sighed. "Look at that little darling Nicole for me, will you?"

Jonathan complied, unsure what Whitehorse was up to.

"Now, take a look at your beautiful girlfriend."

Jonathan did, although he felt a gnawing unease.

"Look at those lovely blond curls that fall so delicately over her face. And her lips...they're so full. And her eyes, look into her eyes, Jonathan. What do you see?"

Tamara sensed his gaze. She turned from the window and met his stare. She smiled softly.

"I...I see *love*, Whitehorse."

"Then enjoy that love, Jonathan Kortel, because it will be the last thing you will ever see!" The netline cut out.

Jimbo jumped to his feet so fast he hit his head on the storage bin. He spun around to face Jonathan.

"Sir, you must take your seat," the flight attendant scolded from the TVid screen. "We're still climbing over the mountains!"

"Jonathan!" There was absolute panic in Jimbo's voice. "Jonathan!" People around them began to turn and take notice.

"James, easy, easy, we're on our way. Whitehorse can't..."

Jonathan stopped dead in midsentence, suddenly realizing what he was saying.

"Dear God..." Jonathan said to himself. "He wouldn't."

"The hell he wouldn't," Jimbo replied.

Tamara's eyes widened. She had figured out what they where talking about. "No!...Oh no! Not my baby!" She scooped up Nicole and held her to her chest.

"Sir, please!" the flight attendant yelled from the TVid screen. "If you don't sit down, I'll have someone physically restrain you. Now take your seat immediately!"

Jimbo spun back around to face the screen. "Lady, if you don't get me the captain right fucking now, there won't be a seat left to take!"

Her face turned white, and the screen went blank. The cabin became oddly quiet.

Then it hit.

Jimbo was just stepping into the aisle when the Tactical Short Range Bioweapon tore through the plane's fuselage. The TSRB was an efficient, shoulder-launched surface-to-air missile capable of bringing down anything from a unmanned drone to a Nations Airbus and its 520 tons of metals, electronics and plastics. Not to mention its 652 manifest head count of human cargo. The TSRB engaged its target not by exploding, but by releasing a biomatrix warhead at the point of impact. In this case, the point of impact was just behind the first-class cabin, near the number one lavatory.

At 7:03:03 a.m. Mountain Daylight Time, Nations Air Flight 1213 heavy, ascending out of Albuquerque, New Mexico, to 60,000 feet would have declared an air emergency. But the captain, along with his crew, the two levels of first-class, the forward galleys, and the numbers one and two lavatories were gone.

The front quarter of the plane had been sheared off.

The warhead's biomatrix was glowing bright green as it traveled around the bulkhead from the point of impact. It was only a matter of seconds before it would consume the entire frame and tear the aircraft apart, raining bits of plane and human across the arid landscape.

To Jonathan, everything appeared a grotesque slow-motion ballet. Metal, plastic and pieces of first-class passengers flew through the cabin, riding the 400-mph wave of bitter cold air that rushed into the now-open cabin.

The haunting death screams of the remaining 500-odd passengers and crew faded from his hearing. The wall of air punched him in the face, slamming him back against his seat. Simultaneously, he watched in horror as Jimbo was lifted and flung down the aisle, followed closely by a lower part of an arm that still held the pretakeoff cocktail reserved for first-class passengers.

Jonathan slowly turned to Tamara. Her face was contorted as bits of plane flew between them carried by the savage rush of air. She wasn't holding Nicole anymore.

An overwhelming heat took over his body. He burned from the inside out with such intensity it made him want to tear his skin from his body like an old shirt. His vision violently shifted to vivid, swirling colors that exploded across his field of view. It shifted to white. A pure, smooth, blinding white. The music followed, but this time it didn't fill only his mind.

It filled his soul.

Like a million angels singing, the chorus reached its crescendo. The music consumed his entire being.

And subsumed it into what seemed like eternity.

~

Jonathan's vision returned, and what he saw was beyond his comprehension. The cabin, the passengers, the debris – the whole plane itself – were frozen as if the horrific moment had been captured in a photo. A hideously lit and gruesomely staged image. Jonathan had opened his eyes to a nightmare no one should see. The plane was tilted down and to the right, caught in Jonathan's telekinetic gravitational suspension field, 10,234 feet above the earth.

He stood and hit his head on a woman's purse. Its contents spilled in a spray pattern that hung in the air. The woman herself was caught in midair above the seats in a bizarre gymnasticlike position just a few rows ahead of her purse.

He turned to check Tamara. She was caught in a silent scream, her tears motionless like little crystals, her hair pulled straight out by a wind he could no longer feel. Behind Tamara, in the arms of a large businessman, he saw Nicole. She had flown six rows before she stopped, her face almost touching the man's stomach. One of her little arms was bent behind her and her leg was caught in mid-kick. He was looking down, as if preparing to wrap his big arms around her.

Jonathan slowly turned back to the aisle, afraid of what he would see. About twelve rows back, Jimbo was suspended upside down, his left arm touching the floor and his feet almost touching the upper bulkhead. Shock was written on his face. He was entangled with a flight attendant whose nose was a spray of blood from his

400-mph elbow. The force of the impact had lifted her out of her shoes.

Jonathan began to traverse his way up the aisle, heading for the front of the plane. He ducked in and out of wreckage, gingerly stepping over people and contorting his way through, trying not to disturb any part of the motionless carnage. The air was freezing in the huge gaping maw that had been the first quarter of the plane. Jonathan inched his way to the edge of the torn fuselage. He looked down through the tangle of wires and fiber optic cables, down through the wispy clouds to the mountaintops a mile below.

He jerked back with fear, stumbling into a passenger in the front row of remaining seats. Her feet and ankles had been consumed by the biomatrix. Startled, he jumped off her and fell into the aisle. The whole row was in various states of debiolization.

Jonathan scrambled to his feet and noticed for the first time how the biomatrix worked. It first consumed everything in its immediate strike zone, then fingered out through the electronics of the massive aircraft. Its bright green glow had traveled along cables and wires like needles shooting toward the back of the plane.

Jonathan began making his way back to his seat. He entered the back cabin, but the closer he came to his row, the stranger he felt. He noticed someone in his seat, or, more accurately, suspended slightly above his seat in a half-sitting, half-standing position.

It was himself.

Jonathan tried to hurry down the aisle but, like a dream, his way kept getting blocked by debris he couldn't seem to clear fast enough. He stumbled to his seat and looked down at himself. He was almost standing up – his head and eyes rolled back, his arms outstretched from his sides. A small amount of blood was coming out his nose and being pushed back across his cheek by the phantom wind. Jonathan reached down and touched the top of his head. It was hot, almost too hot to touch. He felt suddenly qualmish and threw up into the aisle. The shock of the scene began to sink in. Wiping his chin, he couldn't take his eyes off of himself.

The plane violently jerked to the left and knocked him to the floor. From his hands and knees, he saw blood start pouring from the nose of himself in the seat. His own nose hurt. He put his hand to his face and came away with blood on his fingers. He stood up, his legs unsteady. The blood rushed from his head. Faintly, he grabbed for the edge of a seat to steady himself.

Again his vision shifted, and the choir of angels resumed their chorus. This time, though, it seemed to come from outside the plane.

From the clouds themselves.

It's a miracle... 25

"How do you feel?" Tamara asked Jimbo.

"I'll be okay. My elbow is sore, and I think I cracked a rib. I can't really tell without my equipment, and I don't feel like digging through the belly of this plane right now to find it. You think he's going to be all right?" he asked, gesturing toward Jonathan, who was wrapped in a blanket, asleep in the shadow of the plane's gigantic wing on a cushion pulled from one of the sleeper cabins.

The massive Airbus rested on its belly in the middle of a valley on the eastern slope of the Sangre de Cristos. It lay in the warm sun like a huge silver snake that had been decapitated. The cockpit and first-class cabin had been cleanly sheared off by the TSRB's impact. At the severed front, brightly colored fiber optic biocables and hydraulic tubing dangled in the wind like techno entrails on a giant metal carcass. Hundreds of people milled about. Some were helping older passengers, while others just sat in shock. Families huddled together and tended to their children; individuals collected into small groups. The flight attendants who had survived were organizing people as best they could or calming those who were panicking. Given the enormity of the event, most people were rather calm, considering they had just been through what all collectively agreed was a miracle.

Five doctors who had been on board were tending to the injured and helping identify the dead. One of them approached Jimbo, who was sitting on the ground cradling his broken rib.

"How you doing, son?"

"I'm all right, but how's our friend there doing, doc?" Jimbo asked, pointing to Jonathan.

"I don't know. He appears to be in some kind of coma. I can't really tell without my BMP. He seems generally okay. No broken bones. He had some blood loss from his nose hemorrhaging, but besides being unconscious, he's fine."

"Hey, doc, could you use some standard netpads and some scanner equipment?"

"Hell yes. You a doctor?"

"No, but if you go through the cargo area, look for three silver cases and bring them here. They'll have what you need to help these people out."

The doctor called over one of his colleagues, and they ran to the front of the plane.

"Tamara, help me up please." Jimbo said.

She gave him her hand, and they walked over to Jonathan. Nicole was sitting next to him.

"He's not woke up yet, Mommy."

"Don't worry, baby, he will. I promise." She bent down and stroked his forehead.

"I still can't believe it," Jimbo said. "He's beyond what we ever thought humans could achieve." He lifted his face to the wing looming over them. "This is unbelievable. He moved this plane out of the air, down at least a mile to the ground, and held a grav field so vast...it's...unthinka..." Overwhelmed, Jimbo reached for Tamara as the consequence of Jonathan's telekinetic power sunk in.

"James, are you all right?" Tamara asked. She jumped to her feet to steady him.

"Yeah, it's all just a bit much, I guess. Whitehorse was right. He is the next step for our kind. He could be the next evolutionary path."

Both looked down at him.

"You really love him, don't you?" he questioned.

She smiled. "With all my heart, James. And you know what's funny? I really can't tell you why. But I know I do...I *feel* it."

"Can you handle this, Tamara?" He waved at the airplane. "This is some powerful shit here."

"I'm a tough girl, James, I can handle it."

"That's not the question. Most non-Tels eventually leave their Tel lovers because...well, you know. It's just too different. They can't relate. You understand? And Jonathan's a new human, for God's sake. This is all new ground; we're into uncharted territory here."

"She can handle it," Jonathan said roughly. He sat up and coughed.

"Hey, you, we thought we'd lost you," Tamara said, kneeling

down beside him.

"What happened. Did we crash?"

Tamara looked up at Jimbo.

"What, what's going on?..." Jonathan said. "Oh, you got to be kidding me. Did I do this?" He leaned back onto the cushion.

Jimbo knelt down. "Yeah," he said, patting his shoulder. "I'm afraid you did this all by yourself."

Jonathan moaned. "I thought it was a dream."

"Tell me about it. Tell me about this *dream*," Jimbo pressed.

"Obviously it wasn't, because I remember all of it – the passing through the clouds, the landing. But there was a part that was really weird, I mean weirder than this weird." He briefly glanced at the plane. "It was right after I went into phase. I thought I came out of it, but everything – the plane, the people – everything was suspended, except me...or least part of me. I mean, there were two of me, one sitting in the seat and me, walking through the plane...up in the air." He pointed to the sky. "Everything was held in my grav field displacement. Then I, the one walking through the plane, went into phase again and...oh, I can't explain it. My head hurts." He curled into a ball under the blanket.

"Baby, it's okay. We believe you," Tamara consoled. "I mean after this, I'll believe anything."

Nicole patted him through the blanket.

Jonathan slowly pulled the blanket off his face. "Hey, how many are, you know..."

"Dead?" Jimbo asked.

Jonathan nodded.

"The count seems to be right around 150. That's all of first-class, the flight crew and some people who were caught early in the biomatrix." He motioned to 13 bodies covered in blankets by the tail of the plane. Jimbo leaned closer. "You saved over 500 lives, Jonathan. Keep that in your mind when the reality of this situation gets to be too much for you. It's one of the only things that's keeping me from breaking down right here." Jimbo's voice cracked, and his eyes welled with tears.

"Oh, James," Tamara said, putting her arm around him.

Jonathan grabbed Jimbo's arm. "Hey, man," Jonathan said. "This was a rough thing to go through. I know what you're feeling. We all do." He looked to the mountains. "You wouldn't believe what I saw up there..."

"Are these them, young man?" the doctor asked, walking up with the three silver cases under his arms.

"What?...Oh, great," Jimbo said, composing himself. He stood to greet them. "Just set them down right here."

Jimbo knelt beside them and went through the unlocking sequence on their system pads. The cases hissed, and their lids rose in sync with each other.

The doctor looked down into the array of proprietary biotechnology. In all his years in medicine, he had never seen this type of equipment before. "Now, what do you do exactly?"

Jimbo hesitated. "I work in government, sir. Let's just leave it at that, shall we?"

Jimbo carefully fished through the different devices, pulling out five small netpads, half the size of standard ones, and two Kyosera hand-held netlink medscanners. Each piece was nestled in its own cocoon of biofiber foam. When Jimbo lifted out a piece of equipment, the living foam reset back to the default shape of a circle or square. When he placed an item back, the foam's memory would reconform to the specific parameters of the equipment's shape.

"Here you go, sir," Jimbo said. "These should help with your diagnosis and treatments."

The doctor looked over the different devices. He hesitated. "Son, ah...these are a little out of my league."

Jimbo looked to Jonathan and raised an eyebrow.

"No problem. Come on, I'll work with you and get you familiar with them." He grabbed a netphone from the case, pocketed it and walked off with the doctor. The three silver cases slowly closed, hissing together as they locked down.

~

Jonathan sat up and surveyed the area. "How long have we been down?" he asked.

"About an hour," Tamara replied.

"It won't be long before help arrives. A big plane like this doesn't just drop off the netdar without O'Keefe, the NAA, NORAD and God knows who else tracking it. And I'm sure they won't believe what they'll find out here."

"Most of the passengers are saying it was a miracle. That God intervened."

Jonathan rubbed his head. "Well, this god has a splitting headache. Help me up, please, baby?" Tamara helped Jonathan to his feet. Nicole hugged his leg.

A booming voice came from behind them. "Where's that little girl I caught?" The large businessman who had caught Nicole came walking up. He laughed as Nicole hid behind Jonathan's leg. "How's she doing?"

"As well as can be expected," Tamara said.

"I see you're up and around," he said, looking at Jonathan. "Name's Marshall, Calvin Marshall." He extended his hand.

"Jonathan. I guess you've already met Tamara."

"Yes, and Nicole, too."

"I can't thank you enough for saving her life," Tamara said.

"Aw, it was no problem. Like I said earlier, when I came to, she was lying there in my lap, and we were already on the ground, for heaven sakes. It's the darndest thing I've ever seen. Gives me the willies just thinking about it. Well, I just wanted to see how she's doing. You all have a beautiful child there."

He left to join a large group of people collecting their baggage from the plane's cargo hold.

Tamara laughed a little under her breath.

Jonathan shook his head. "This 'you've got a beautiful kid' routine is getting just a little weird."

Nicole never let go of his leg.

~

Jimbo left the doctors on their own and returned. He clicked his netphone off as he approached. "The Agency says they're going to send a private plane out for us. It'll meet us at O'Keefe." He gingerly rubbed his broken rib. "There are probably 500 netphones on this flight, and each one of them has called somebody about the 'miracle' landing. The news of this crash is all over the net. Hell, I think half these people are on their netphones right now doing interviews."

"Yeah, they're all going for their fifteen minutes," Jonathan agreed.

"No doubt," Jimbo said. "And they've dispatched a damn army to rescue us. They'll probably be here within the hour. What's funny is there aren't any reports of the missile. Nothing on the newsnet about this plane being hit. They're all saying it was a catastrophic structural failure. I know we have masking technology for missiles and planes, but that's real 'black' stuff. How Whitehorse got hold of that kind of weaponry is beyond me."

Jonathan walked over to the three equipment cases that sat innocently in the bright New Mexican sun. Their smooth silver skins were void of any visible seams, and their simple design gave no hint to the powerful technology stored inside them. Jimbo quietly stepped up behind him.

"All this for me?" Jonathan asked, still looking down at the cases.

"Oh yeah," Jimbo replied, clearly uncomfortable with the question. "For you, only our best."

Both Tels stood silently as the wind swirled dust around their feet. "Jonathan," Jimbo finally said, "what Whitehorse told you up there was partially true, and I'm sorry." He hesitated. "Zvara and I did hold back some data results, but not because we were trying to trick you or something. It's...just..."

"Just what, James?"

"Look, man, right now you're developing at an alarming rate. I won't get into details here, but you need to know that you're probably leaving Level 8. Hell, I know you've left that level." He waved his arms around at the plane. "I mean, come on – landing a

400-ton airplane, stopping a Light-Force....Oh, yeah, we see this kind of stuff all the time at the Agency. Seriously, Jonathan, you're scaring me a little here. I don't know where you're going to level off. I wish your field hadn't been so huge up there. Otherwise, my equipment could have taken readings during your phase. But you held *everything* in field. I'm surprised you didn't bring down a damn satellite along with this plane."

Jonathan broke into a smile.

"Don't get any smart-ass ideas, mister. You're strong, but you're not *that* strong. I'm drawing the line. And don't even think about one of the space stations."

"James, do you really think..."

"Listen, Jonathan," Jimbo said, stepping closer. "I like you. I like Tamara. Hell, I even like Nicole, and I'm not into kids. But there's something else you need to know." He leaned in and looked Jonathan right in the eyes. "If you do go...you know, 'critical' on me, I have my orders."

"Critical?" Jonathan questioned seriously.

"Yeah. Some Tels who develop too fast for their bodies to handle go what we call 'critical.' During their phases, they can literally fry. Or implode. I've even read of some who exploded. You, my friend, get hot when you phase. Real hot..."

"I know. When I was outside myself, I touched the top of my head...my other head, and it was burning up."

"That's what I'm talking about. It's like a fever. Except this is the mother of all fevers."

"Why doesn't it cause injury, like brain damage?"

"That's something we don't know too much about. There

haven't been many cases, and certainly nothing like you. It's like I told your girlfriend, we're in uncharted territory here. Until we get you back and get our teams on you, I'm flying by the seat of my pants." He looked up at the big engine looming overhead and shook his head.

"So, James," Jonathan asked gravely. "What *are* your orders?"

Jimbo hesitated and turned away. "It all depends. If you look like you're going to hurt yourself, I'm tranq'n you. If you look like you're going to hurt someone else...someone innocent, I'm going to tranq you then, too."

"And what if my power gets out of hand, like dangerously beyond my own control?" Jonathan pressed. "What then?"

Jimbo sighed and knelt by the biggest of the three cases. He worked its system pad, and the lid slowly opened. Moving aside a shelf, he reached in and pulled out a small gunlike device. Its chrome surface reflected the midday sun, and Jonathan noticed two tiny buttons: one red and one green.

"Then," Jimbo said, standing up, "I use this."

"And what is that?" Jonathan asked tentatively.

"A TGD-1200 Field Matter Disrupter. Custom-made, one of a kind." Jimbo spun it around in his hand.

"In layman's terms?"

Jimbo hesitated. "A death ray."

There was a long silence. The wind began to pick up.

"If I have to use this," Jimbo whispered, going serious on him, "you'll probably be begging me to."

He returned the TGD-1200 to its compartment in the big

silver case. The biofoam shifted to match its shape and swallowed it like gray quicksand. Jimbo stood, and they silently watched the lid slowly close. It made a hissing sound, indicating it was locked down and secured.

The wind began to blow harder around them. Jimbo walked away to join Tamara and Nicole, who had retrieved their baggage and were now sitting on the cushion playing one of Tarris's netgames together. Wearing the biosensory headgear that had made Tarris so famous, Tamara and Nicole laughed as they raced each other in the virtual Net Grand Prix.

Jonathan hadn't moved.

His attention was held captive by the bright silver case. Jimbo's words echoed in his mind while he stood quietly in the valley of the mountains named for the Blood of Christ.

Crossing... 26

The lights gradually came up. Jonathan leaned back into his favorite chair; its biofabric cradled his telekinetically exhausted body. It was almost midnight, and he was glad to be home in the loft. In the last five days, he had gotten 18 hours of sleep, and he had taxed his telekinetic prowess to its limits. Having tossed men about like garbage, put another in a coma, stopped not one, but six Light-Force bioweapons, grav-fluxed his own body out of a deadly situation, halted a biomatrix warhead, and brought down a 520-ton airliner from 11,000 feet (saving over 500 lives), Jonathan Kortel did what most people do after a tough week.

He poured himself a drink.

Putting the glass to his forehead, he let its cool moisture spread over his tired brow. His mind was off-line.

What he had hoped would be an enlightening visit to an old

and dear friend turned out to be quite literally a living nightmare. He closed his eyes and recalled the events of the last week. How ironic, he bemusedly observed, to have almost died so horrifically in the land of enchantment.

The Scotch burned his throat with every swallow.

The sheer stress of his telekinetic phases had strained his body to its limits. The extreme heat he experienced during each phase had left his muscles aching, while the nasal hemorrhage had made his throat dry and sore. He hadn't shaved or showered, and his skin had taken on a pasty appearance, like he had been ill for a month. Worse, his head ached continuously like a migraine caught in some torturously vicious repeat loop. In short, Jonathan Kortel felt like shit, and he was seriously considering taking Tamara and Nicole and dropping out of sight for about 30 years.

He drifted into sleep.

~

"Jonathan."

The loft's system waited.

"Jonathan, excuse me, but you have a netcall."

He coughed. "Yeah...Max...what time is it?"

"It's three thirty in the morning, sir, and you have a netcall from Miss Connor."

"Oh, put it through please...and no visual."

"Jonathan, I can't sleep..."

"Nicole, honey," Jonathan said, surprised, "where's your mommy?"

"She's asleep with Teddy Boo, but I had a bad dream."

"Honey, it'll be okay. You're safe now. Be a good girl and go crawl in bed with your mommy and Teddy Roo..."

"Teddy Boo..."

"Yeah, Boo, Teddy Boo...just crawl back to bed and snuggle with your mommy. Sweet dreams, you, okay?"

"Okay, night night." The line cut out.

"I wish I was Teddy Boo," Jonathan said. He sat in the dark of the living room, gazing out the large windows at the Chicago skyline and the lake beyond. Lights twinkled through the city heat that radiated from the concrete 30 stories below. It all looked so foreign. What had been familiar only days ago now seemed distant, almost alienlike, as if he had landed on another planet whose populace had nothing in common with him. If the events of the last week had taught him anything, it was that he was not like anyone else. He wasn't even like any other Tel. But what he was, or what he would become, was as elusive to him as the good night's rest he so desperately desired.

He began to fall asleep, again.

~

"Jonathan."

There was a pause as the system waited.

"Jonathan, excuse me, but you have a netcall..."

"Yeah...Max...what time is it this time?"

"It's six thirty in the morning, sir, and you have a netcall from a James McCarris."

"Yeah...okay. Put it through."

"Jonathan, I hope I'm not...man, whoa, you look like crap..." Jimbo said from the six-foot TVid screen.

"Thanks, Jimbo. I was hoping for a little rest here. Why are you calling so early?"

"Well, a couple of things. One, I'm packing up and heading for Washington. I gotta debrief, do my reports and get things prepped for you. Two, our sources tell us that Whitehorse has gone underground, which doesn't surprise me. The Rogues can scatter pretty easily and reassemble whenever and wherever they want. But having Whitehorse missing means it isn't safe for you....Hey, are you falling asleep?"

"No, no..." Jonathan said sleepily. "Please, I'm listening."

"And third..." Jimbo hesitated.

"What?" Jonathan demanded.

"Have you tried Tarris or Georgia lately?"

"All I've tried is to get some sleep. Why, what's up?"

"I don't know. I've called, thinking Georgia might know where Whitehorse is, but there's no answer, and they haven't returned any of my netmessages. Isn't that a little odd?"

"Not really. Tarris is one for keeping to himself. It wouldn't surprise me if he didn't connect, especially after a week like we've had."

"Yeah, I know, but it's me...my number. I would think they would try and connect, especially after an incident like the plane, wouldn't you?"

"Tarris is a weird guy. Don't get me wrong, I love him like a brother, but I bet Georgia probably has broached the Rogue subject with him. And that, more than likely, didn't go down too well. Plus, he's reclusive. I mean, look at that compound where they live. And we know he's not a big fan of the government. James...you are the government, after all. Nah, I wouldn't get too worried yet. I'm not."

Jonathan let his eyes close again.

"Maybe you're right." The lid hissed shut on the last of his equipment cases. "I'll give them a try later. It's just that my seventh sense is picking something up on them. You know what I mean?...Jonathan? Jonathan!"

"Yeah, boss...I'm here," he said, jerking back from half-sleep.

"Can I ask you a personal question?"

"Sure, why not."

"What are you going to do with Tamara?" he quietly asked.

"What do you mean?"

"Well, you know she really cares for you. I mean, I think she's pretty much in love with you."

"Yeah, I know. So?"

"I've never heard you say that."

Jonathan kept his eyes closed and sunk deeper into the chair.

"Listen," Jimbo said, "if I've struck a nerve here..."

"No, no, it's not that. It's just...how can I put this?" Jonathan rubbed the sleep from his eyes. "Only a couple of weeks ago, I was normal. I had a business, a life, friends, a couple of girls I was seeing and..."

"And what?" Jimbo folded a shirt.

"And I was...human." Jonathan opened his eyes.

An awkward silence fell over their conversation. Jimbo stopped packing his clothes, faced the lens and moved to the middle of the apartment that had been the base of operations for him and Zvara. Jonathan, struggling for words, stared out the loft's big windows at the sun cresting over the top of the skyline.

"Then..." Jonathan said finally, "...I met Tamara..."

Jimbo folded his arms.

"...and I stopped a Light-Force weapon," he continued, his voice cracking a little.

Jimbo's TVid image didn't change.

Jonathan stared at the sunrise.

"Hey, James?" he asked, still staring.

"Yeah, man, what is it?"

Jonathan hesitated and then looked directly into the TVid screen. "What's happening to me?" A lump came up in his throat.

Jimbo moved closer to the lens. "You're 'crossing' man...that's all," His face filled the screen.

Jonathan leaned forward toward the TVid. "Crossing?"

"Yeah, it's the moment when a Potential finally realizes what they are...*really* realizes. I've seen it happen a hundred times. That's one reason why I'm here – to help you get through this."

"Yeah, but this is different. I'm different."

"You wouldn't believe how many times I've heard that. But you know something?"

"What?"

"This time, you're right. You are different, Jonathan. You're the most different thing...person...whatever, to hit this planet since...since..." Jimbo was caught in his own analogy.

"Since what, James?"

"Since...I don't know...Christ himself, probably." Jimbo was looking down, his arms still folded tightly across his chest.

Jonathan closed his eyes and leaned back into the chair; its memory quickly reshaped to accept his body.

"Hey, look, I'm not saying you're the Second Coming. I'm

just saying that your presence could have a great impact on mankind. I mean, Jonathan...wake up. You're doing things that we thought could never be done."

Clearly uncomfortable with the subject, Jimbo swept his hair back off his forehead. He sat down on the edge of the bed. "Jonathan, this is one of the most difficult times a Tel faces. The crossing is considered to be almost a sacred time. It's not like we don robes and chant, but you're entering a brotherhood of sorts. There are very few of us, really. When you consider the total population, we're just a drop in the bucket. But, you, my friend..." Jimbo walked back toward the lens, filling the screen. "...you are the most important drop ever."

Jonathan kept his eyes closed.

"Hey, how do you feel?" Jimbo asked sincerely.

"Like shit."

"You've been through a lot in the last couple of days. But don't let this crossing stuff get to you too much. Now get some rest, okay? I'll call you when I get into Washington." Jimbo returned to his packing.

"Oh, hey," he said, coming back before the call could end. "You never answered my question."

Jonathan's eyes remained closed. "I know, Jimbo. Talk to you later."

The TVid screen cutout.

Jonathan opened his eyes and looked around. The early morning sun was beginning to flood the living room. His service had cleaned the loft, and only the emptiness left by the destroyed items gave any clue to the telekinetic fit he had thrown. Many of the most precious objects that had defined his life were gone. One of the pieces that had survived was a folk art crucifix he had purchased on a visit to Hector and his family in what was now called Old Mexico.

He raised his arm, and the cross flew across the living room and into his waiting hand. He studied its rough wooden surface. His fingers glided gently across the hand-carved Christ. His head was tilted to one side, and his expression was sad. The artisan had carved away the minimal amount to perfectly capture the moment of the Savior's death.

Jonathan contemplated its meaning.

"I'm no Christ..." he said. His eyes slowly closed, and as he slipped back into sleep, the cross slid out of his hand and dropped gently to the floor.

Point of difference... 27

Georgia bit into the carrot, which snapped hard in her mouth. She watched the stray dogs wolf down their evening dinner and glanced over to the TVid screen, debating whether she should call or not. She had never seen Tarris so angry. It was almost like he had become another man.

Since Jonathan had decided to go with the Agency, Georgia intended to keep her promise of leaving the Rogues, but not without coming clean with Tarris. On the way back from O'Keefe International, she had told him everything about her association with the Rogues. Needless to say, it hadn't gone over as well as she had hoped.

~

Tarris was enraged. No matter how hard Georgia tried to

explain her feelings for him, all he heard was that she had been a plant and that their relationship had been a fabrication for Jacob Whitehorse's agenda.

Driving back to Tres Piedras like a madman, he twice almost crashed the Hummer, and his silence hung in the cabin like a rotting carcass. Roaring into the compound, Tarris skidded up to the front door of the main house and demanded that she get out. Then he drove around to the back of his workshop and began loading up the Hummer.

He also called her a whore.

Georgia was in the bedroom by the time Tarris came "walking" in. He stormed through the house gathering things into a large canvas bag. Walking into the bedroom, he ignored her and headed straight to the dresser, yanking open the top drawer so hard that it flew out of his hands and crashed to the floor. He dug through its contents until he found what he needed. Tarris, who had been clean since the accident, was going to take a ride.

Georgia watched in fear as he scooped up the small plastic bag of biodrug, stuffed it in his coat pocket and stormed out. Clambering up into the Hummer, he glared at her as she stood at the front door. He spat on the ground and drove off just as the sun dipped below the mountains that loaned their name to the town.

~

Georgia took a bite off the carrot and looked again at the TVid screen. Jonathan's netnumber was on the monitor, ready to log in. Tarris had been gone almost three hours. She took another bite, hesitated, and pressed the send button.

His image came on the screen. “Morning, Georgia, what’s up?”

“I’m sorry, Jonathan, I didn’t mean to wake you...”

“That’s okay, it seems to be the in thing to do today. What time is it?”

“It’s seven thirty here, so it’s eight thirty where you are. Were you sleeping?”

“Yeah....So what’s the matter? You look worried. I know James has been trying to get ahold of you. Are you all right?”

Georgia, folding her arms, teared up and looked away from the screen.

“Georgia?” Jonathan sat up. “What’s the matter?”

Georgia waved off the question without a response.

“Hey, come on, talk to me.” Jonathan had slid to the edge of the ottoman, which made his image fill the screen.

Georgia looked back. Tears were running down her face. “I told Tarris about my involvement with the Rogues,” she said between sniffles.

“I figured you would. Did you tell him...everything?”

“Yes...”

“And he went biothermal, didn’t he?”

Georgia nodded and burst into tears. A vase holding a fresh bouquet of desert flowers exploded behind her.

“Easy there, girl,” Jonathan soothed. “Cry anymore and you could destroy that shack you live in. Believe me, I speak from experience.”

Georgia grinned through her tears.

“Now, what’s going on?”

“Tarris just went crazy. He wouldn’t listen to me. He really feels like our relationship was just a ruse to get you to come out. And then he packed up and stormed out of here, to God knows where. And...he..."

"He what?"

"He called me a whore and spit at me."

Jonathan scooted closer. Georgia turned around and looked at the remains of the vase.

"It was a risk you had to take. Ignorance is bliss, as they say, but I think you can never go wrong with honesty. He would have eventually found out, and it's best he heard it from you, not someone else."

Georgia had calmed down and was quietly listening.

"Besides, he does have a point. I mean, I know that you grew to care for him, but would you have ever gotten together if the situation was different?...You know, more of a natural beginning and not mapped out by Whitehorse?"

Georgia nervously averted her eyes.

"If I know Tarris, he's probably run off to a hole somewhere to get his head straight, and he'll be back....What's wrong now?"

Georgia pensively folded her arms and moved into the corner of the room.

"Georgia?..." Jonathan pressed.

"He...he took something else."

Jonathan knew what that "something else" was.

"How much did he take?"

"Not much. I didn't even know he had any. I'm worried, Jonathan. You know how he gets when he's riding. He's so unpredictable...."

"Hey, did you take the weapons out of the truck?"

"No..." Georgia said slowly. "Oh, God, this isn't good."

"No, it's not. You don't think he would try to go after Whitehorse, do you?"

"I don't see how. He wouldn't know where to look after the plane crash. And I assume that was you?"

Jonathan sheepishly nodded.

"God, Jonathan, you're unbelievable. It's all over the net. The TVid news shows are calling it a miracle, an act of...are you okay?"

"I don't really want to talk about it right now, if you don't mind."

Georgia nodded knowingly. "Like I was saying, after news of the plane, most of the Rogues wondered if it had been Whitehorse. But we're still not sure how..."

"Biowarhead. Jimbo thinks it was delivered on some kind of masked missile...real Black Op stuff. Do you know how Whitehorse could have gotten hold of that kind of weaponry?"

"Whitehorse made a lot of friends when he was in the Agency, and I think he's maintained many of those relationships since he started the Rogues. Most were in the military."

"That explains a lot right there."

"This is going to split the Rogues up. Whitehorse had become way too militant for most of the members, and I think there was going to be some action taken against him. But now it doesn't matter. He's disappeared, and nobody knows where he's gone."

"James's sources say he's gone into hiding, whatever that means. You wouldn't know where that is, would you?"

"I can't think of any place right now. There were a few who

were pretty loyal to his cause. But they've disappeared too. They could be anywhere. If I hear of anything, I'll call you or Jimbo."

"Yeah, that would be good. I don't like having this crazy, psycho Indian on the loose. I feel like I should be looking over my shoulder all the damn time."

"Jonathan, if you can bring down a plane, you can handle Whitehorse."

"I wish it were that easy."

"You know something else?" Georgia stared blankly at the TVid. "There's a part of me that's relieved...that I told him."

Jonathan's image blipped a little from the satellite connection. When it cleared, he was smiling.

"What?" she asked.

"Oh, nothing..."

"What, Jonathan."

"Well...it's nothing..."

"Come on. Don't play games with me."

"It's just...you know, sometimes you look so....No, wait, I can't...I've got to go, so call me if you hear from Tarris, or if you hear anything about Whitehorse, okay? You take care." Jonathan quickly cut the line.

Georgia took the last bite out of the carrot and slowly smiled.

~

It had been almost a week since Jonathan had returned. A week of preparation, reflection and the occasional dodge of overzealous reporters trying to make their careers with the plane "crash" of the century. On his list of things to get done, one task stood out above them all as the one he was least looking forward to.

Jonathan cautiously opened the door to the restaurant, knowing that his unexpected appearance would set the kitchen off like a bomb.

A new hostess greeted him. "Welcome to Kortel's, table for one, sir?" she asked.

"Sure...table for one, thanks," he said, testing out the new girl. Her clothes said she was a professional, with a contemporary edge. She led him to a two-top near the front. The waiters almost gave away his scam, but he silenced them with a finger to his lips.

"Here you are, sir. Will this be all right?"

"No, I was hoping for something in the back, something a little more removed."

"Ah, no problem, let me see..." She led him through the busy restaurant to a secluded table near the bar.

"Would this be okay, sir?"

"Actually," he said, continuing his scam, "I was wondering if you could set me up in the hallway...by the bathrooms? I'm very private you know." He acted paranoid, constantly looking about.

"Ah...yes, well...whatever the gentleman would like. I'll have one of the busboys set up a table. Just give me a moment....Would you like to sit at the bar?" She gestured for him to sit.

"Oh, I can't! It's too exposed, much too exposed...I'll just stand right here if that's okay with you," he said, playing it up for all it was worth.

"Very good, sir. I'll be right back to set up your table." She put the netpad to her chest and turned on her heels right into a small group of wait staff gathered behind her. They all broke out laughing.

"Whatever you're laughing at...it's not very funny!" she sternly scolded them. They all struggled to control themselves. "What? What's going on?"

"Hey, everyone, she's right!" Jonathan said firmly. The staff jumped to attention. "If a customer wants to dine alone...in private, then at Kortel's we certainly don't laugh at him. We make it happen. Right...ah, what's your name?"

"Kimball, and you are?..." she said, turning to face him.

"Jonathan, Jonathan Kortel." He extended his hand and stifled a laugh.

"Oh, sir, I'm so sorry. I didn't know. They said you might not be back for several weeks." She whipped around and lunged at the staff. They recoiled, laughing, and some snapped their bar rags at her.

"Okay you all, back to work!" Hector's booming voice announced, and the staff scattered like cats back to their stations.

"Jonathan!" He grabbed him by the shoulders. "We thought you'd be gone awhile." He leaned in, his voice going soft. "How are you?"

"I'm fine, Hector, but who is the new hostess? Man, where did you get her?" He watched her walk back to the front of the restaurant.

"Ah, yes. That lovely thing is Enrique's cousin, Kimball. She's not a bad hostess, I might add."

"Hell, we'll get repeat from the businessmen alone with her. Forget the food."

Hector looked over his partner closely. "Jonathan," he confided in a low tone, "you look tired, my friend, even a little sick.

Are you all right?"

"I'm all right, really. But it's been a long week. It wasn't the trip I was hoping for. Say, Hector," he put his arm around him, "I came in because I wanted to talk with you. Can Enrique or Marco close up tonight?"

"Sure, Marco can. Let me clean up, and we'll go."

"Great. Let's go to the Blind Monkey for a drink."

Jonathan entered the kitchen to a round of high-fives from the men who turned his bioprogramming into reality. The air was saturated with the pungent smells of cilantro and curry. And as he walked around laughing, talking and spot-checking the cuisine, melancholia descended upon him that took him by surprise. In the eyes of the men who had been so much of his life for the last five years, he saw something that he had never really taken the time to notice before.

Love.

They shared a love that men have for one another when they come through a difficult time together, when they share an accomplishment and look back proudly at what they have done. Such was the feeling Jonathan shared with the men of Kitchen Kortel. At the same time, though, he felt like a stranger in his own house. He looked at the crew he had come to call family and felt the same way he had in the loft when he had looked out over the city: an overwhelming sense that his life, the life he had shared with these men, the life he had created with Hector, and the life he could have had with Tamara, was coming to an end.

Jimbo was right.

He was "crossing," and there was nothing to stop it. It was

as inevitable as death, and Jonathan was beginning to accept the harsh reality of who he was. Or, more accurately, what he wasn't. Because to Jonathan, that was the point of difference.

In his mind, he wasn't human anymore.

~

"Look what the cat dragged in!" Deaka announced.

"Hey, Deaka," Jonathan said.

"A little early for you two. Are you guys drinking or are you gracing us with eating?"

She slid her netpad down the front of her jeans. Deaka had always given them a little grief, but she couldn't deny that she was slightly envious. Here were two of the hottest young Turks in the city's restaurant scene, and they chose her bar to hang. Deaka, though she never would admit it, also was flattered.

"Nah, we're just drinking, Deaka," Hector answered, and they walked past her and into the bar.

The Blind Monkey was slow, and it was easy to find a seat. While Jonathan and Hector pulled in their stools, the bartender was already pouring their favorite drinks.

Hector licked the salt from the rim of his glass and turned to face Jonathan.

"So, my friend, what is on your mind, eh?"

Jonathan took a long, slow sip of Scotch.

"Hector," he started, "have you ever had an epiphany?"

"Well, if you consider my first divorce, yes. Why?"

"My friend, I have had one hell of an epiphany."

"Is it Tamara? She seems like a sweet girl but..."

"No, it's not her. It's something else....Something that's a little hard to describe." Seeking comfort in his Scotch, Jonathan took another long drink. "I'm not really sure where to begin," he said wiping his mouth.

For the next hour, Hector sat in silence as Jonathan told him everything, from his childhood to the incident with the plane. At times it was hard for Jonathan to talk, especially about the crossing and its life-changing ramifications.

Hector intently listened. The concept was remarkable, and the revelation that a hidden society of new humans had been evolving for the last 150 years was almost too much to believe.

He ordered a double shot when Jonathan finished. The bartender placed the tequila on the bar.

"Well?" Jonathan asked.

"It's all...so..." Hector stammered.

"Unbelievable?"

"Well, quite frankly, yes! I didn't believe Tamara when she told me. I mean, you have to admit this all sounds like some bad sci-fi vid."

Jonathan read the skepticism in Hector's voice. Jimbo had warned him not to say anything. Non-Tels won't believe or accept the news, he had told him. Especially relatives and close friends. "You don't believe me, do you?"

Hector shrugged.

Jimbo also said not to give any demos.

Jonathan looked to the back of the bar where the bottles of liquor sat stacked in neat rows. He waited for the bartender to turn his back, then raised his left hand in front of Hector's face. A bottle of vodka flew into it; Hector almost jumped off his stool. Jonathan released the bottle, and it floated back to its place on the shelf.

Hector slammed his tequila.

"Now, are you getting the picture?" Jonathan asked with a smile.

"Jonathan, this is a miracle!" He crossed himself and looked to the ceiling.

"Hey, whoa, it's not a miracle. It's a combination of gravity displacement, genetics, evolution and mind control. Along with a few hundred other factors that I'm going to learn about at the Agency. You see, we're..."

"We're?" Hector interrupted.

"Sorry...we're called Tels. It's short for telekinetics. What I was going to say was that we're like lighting rods. We're conduits to channel gravity and alter its properties, though I'm not sure how yet. Hopefully, the Agency is going to teach me."

Jonathan noticed that his close friend had inched back on his stool, and he could sense that Hector was wrestling with his feelings for Jonathan the old friend and his fear of Jonathan the telekinetic. He could also sense something else. It was the last of Jimbo's warnings: the alienation of friends and family. He was probably going to lose Hector as a friend.

Hector was staring blankly into the mirror behind the bar.

"Are you scared of me, Hector?"

"No, no...it's just that this is all so...so...weird. One day you're my partner and friend....The next, you're...you're..."

"I'm what, Hector?"

Hector almost had to force himself to look at Jonathan. He took a deep breath before continuing. "You're not like us...I'm mean you are, but you're not. Know what I mean?" He stared straight ahead into the mirror again.

"Believe me," Jonathan said, "I know what you mean. I've been wrestling with this for the last couple of weeks now, and it's still pretty weird for me, too. Look, Hector," Jonathan pulled his stool closer, "I don't want to give up what we have here. This is a great partnership. I couldn't ask for a better organic chef than Hector Ruez – or a better friend. But I know what I am now, and I've got to see where this will take me. I've been given a great gift, and I owe it to myself to discover my potential."

Hector couldn't face his friend.

"Hector, it's me, *Jonathan*. I'm still the same. I haven't changed that much..."

"But you *will*."

"Hector!" Jonathan said as he grabbed the big Mexican by the shoulder and spun him on his stool. "I'm not going to let our friendship just...just slip away because I'm different. I'm not really sure if I'm going to stay with the Agency. Yes, I want to see what they have to offer, and yes, I'm going to use their help to keep Tamara and Nicole safe. But I'm not going to disappear behind some virt wall that develops because I'm a Tel and you're not!" Jonathan's voice had risen to the point that some of the people around the bar began to take notice.

Hector studied Jonathan's face. "Jonathan," he said finally, "I haven't come this far with you just to abandon a friendship that's endured the things we've had to deal with. If you need to go and discover who you are or what you are, then I'll be behind you all the way. And so will the kitchen. We're not going away just cause you're gone for awhile. We have your programs on file. Hell, we haven't even gotten to half of them yet. The restaurant is called Kortel's, not Ruez's, and there's a reason for that."

Jonathan heard what Hector was saying, but he knew that Jimbo was right. Their relationship would never be the same again.

"When are you going?" Hector asked.

"Soon. There's something I have to take care of before I go..."

"Jonathan?..." Hector began.

Jonathan knew what was coming.

"...What about Tamara?...What are you going to do about her?"

He didn't answer, instead checking his netwatch. "I've got to go, Hector, I'll see you tomorrow." He stepped off the stool and walked toward the front of the Blind Monkey.

"Do you love her?" Hector called after him.

Jonathan stopped but didn't look back. "Good night, Hector." He headed for the exit.

Guess I do... 28

Anari checked her netpad for the current tally on her tables. She had the Den and its clients choreographed to her own unique rhythm. These poor marks wouldn't know that they had been part of her show until they checked their chipcard netstatements the next morning. By then, Anari would be surfing the next wave of horny businessmen, whose expectations for Liquid Courage were as high as their multinational corporate spending limits.

Anari was in the zone, and it wasn't even midnight.

As she hustled the six-top full of Canadian medtronic salesmen, she saw two tall, older marks walk in and stand impatiently, like they were waiting for their luggage at O'Hare.

Perfect, she thought, *first-timers*.

"Would you gentlemen like a booth tonight?" she screamed over the vicious sounds of RageOn, a black market sampling from the Russian underground.

The two marks nodded. Anari led them through the smoky darkness to a secluded booth set back from the main stage. Their tailored biofabric suits were the finest Rome could produce, and as the two men sat, the suits reset to the tailor's preprogrammed settings, purging any wrinkles and giving the fabric a crisp, new appearance.

These boys smelled of money, and Anari was out to break her own record. "And what would you gentlemen like this evening, for drinks and the ladiesss?" She hung on the "S" like a snake.

"I would like a vodka martini, dirty...*very* dirty," the taller one answered as he stared at Anari.

The other mark was caught up with the dancer on the main stage. He didn't look over.

"Make that two..." the taller one added, and he ran his finger down her arm.

"Yes, I think I know just the martini for you, sir."

Anari turned to go. Without warning, the taller one grabbed her arm, which startled her because the clientele in the Den were usually prescreened, and any display of aggression toward the wait staff, even as little as grabbing an arm, was strictly forbidden.

"Sir?!" Anari demanded.

The taller one smiled a smile that had been cultivated through years of official practice and pulled Anari into the table. He reached across her chest, slightly grazing her nipples, and took her netpad from her belt. Without letting go, he entered a gratuity that not only set a new record for Anari, but raised the bar beyond what she would achieve for probably the next 20 years.

Anari looked down at the amount and almost wet her latex.

"Sir! Thank you, sir!" He let go and let out a laugh that competed with RageOn for air time.

Power Dicks, she thought. Men who got off roughing up women, then making it all right in their minds by buying back their actions with guilt money. She hadn't seen guys like this in a long time, but that was fine with her: what you had to put up with usually didn't justify the reward. These two had set a new standard, though. Anari was ready to play.

"Two dirty martinis coming right up."

She headed for the bar, quickly calculating her total for the evening. When she got to the drink station, she tapped her best friend on the shoulder and nodded toward the booth with the two older marks.

Tamara cut off the Japanese netjournalist she had been hustling for over an hour and spun her barstool in the direction of Anari's nod.

"Power Dicks," Anari said into her ear. It was all she needed to say. Tamara knew these types and could play with the best of them. This single mom had been around a few times, and a couple of insecure high-threads with a passion for demeaning women didn't phase her at all.

New Mexico was a week behind her, and it had taken Anari that long to convince her to get back to work. Yes, she had been through some rough shit, Anari had lectured. And yes, it had been life changing. But sitting around her apartment wasn't going to pay the bills. Or get Jonathan to call back.

Tamara pulled the front of her dress down a little and walked her best "fuck me" walk over to their booth. Both men watched her approach with the cool of players who had been in the game for quite a while. Tamara slid next to the tall one, while never letting her attention fall from the other.

"You gentlemen look like you could use a little company. Do you mind if I join you?" she cooed, wrapping herself around the taller one's arm.

He smiled and nodded and looked at his friend, who leaned on the table and grinned.

Anari arrived and presented their martinis along with Tamara's drink, which she had left at the bar, compliments of Nippon NetNews. She winked at Tamara and left the booth.

"I propose a toast," Tamara declared.

"To what?" the taller one asked.

"To living large and loving long." She raised her glass. "My name is Nicki, what's yours?" She extended her hand to him.

He leaned back into the booth and shifted his attention to the girl on the main stage. He sipped his martini, holding the glass like this was one of a thousand cocktail parties he had attended. "Oh, now...Nicki...that's such an appropriate stage name. I should have guessed." He laughed under his breath, not looking at her, and pulled the olive off its swizzle stick. His white teeth glowed in the black light of the Den.

Puzzled, Tamara began to take a drink. The other Power Dick hadn't said a word; in fact, she now noticed, he hadn't even touched his martini yet.

"Oh, I'm so sorry, let me introduce myself," the talkative one said, holding his glass out and casually looking at it like he was inspecting for flaws. "My name is Jacob Whitehorse."

Tamara's drink never made it to her lips. The glass slipped

from her hand, but Whitehorse caught it with his mind. As the drink hung suspended in front of her, he grabbed her body and held it tightly, like a vice.

He was still inspecting his drink.

Caught in Whitehorse's telekinetic grip, she sat there unable to move. He allowed her to blink and breathe, but nothing else. To her, it was as if every major muscle group had been paralyzed. Her nerves, on the other hand, were fully functional. If she had been able, Tamara would have been trembling.

Whitehorse leaned close, and she could see his years chiseled deeply into his skin.

"Tamara," he said, looking straight into her eyes, "you look so pretty tonight. I can see why Jonathan is attracted to you." He ran his fingertips down the edge of her face, lightly parting her hair with his index finger.

"You know," he continued, "our Mr. Kortel has made a poor decision – not only for himself, but for you as well."

He sat back and leisurely finished his martini.

"I'm so sorry to bring you into this, but Jonathan leaves me no choice, really. You see, your boyfriend is quite extraordinary. He's the next step, you know. I'd venture to say he's not really that human anymore." Whitehorse put down his empty glass. "What's it like," he said, running his finger down her jawline, "to make love to someone who isn't human?" He leaned in so close that she could smell the gin on his breath, and his demeanor instantly changed. "Do you really think, Tamara, that a Tel like him will stay with a *whore* like you?"

He sunk back into the booth and again watched the dancer

on the main stage. Tamara could see him with her peripheral vision. He sensed her attention and slowly grinned.

"The Agency will change him. Mark my words, young lady. The Jonathan Kortel you know won't exist a year from now. The Agency is not a family show, regardless of what they tell you. They'll change him so subtly you won't know it's happening until it's too late."

Whitehorse reached into his coat pocket and pulled out a small Light-Force handgun. Smaller than the one the reper had used. Probably the smallest bioweapon Tamara had ever seen.

"We're going to leave the club now, Tamara, and when I release you, I want you to act perfectly normal. You're a good actress. I'm sure you've done it all your life."

Tamara felt her muscles relax, like a painless cramp had instantly disappeared.

"My dear, you're trembling," he said.

"Please, Mr. Whitehorse..."

"I said act normal, and that means shutting up!"

Tamara felt a pressure on her throat as if an invisible hand was beginning to choke her. She gagged from the pain.

"Now get up and lead us out of here. And don't worry about the other employees. We'll take care of them, believe me." Whitehorse charged the weapon.

All of them slowly rose from the booth and started toward the exit. In the dark, smoky environment of the Den, their actions hardly appeared out of place, except Anari didn't have her car this evening, and her ride was now walking out of the club.

"Hey, Nicki," she said, catching up to them. "Are you just showing these gentlemen to the..."

Anari stopped in midsentence when Whitehorse's partner turned and looked at her. A blank expression washed over her face, and she stood motionless while her drink tray crashed to the carpet.

As they walked out into the main club, Tamara looked back and saw Anari collapse to the floor. The Den's gigantic door slowly closed on the scene.

"Don't worry about your friend," Whitehorse said. "You should be worrying about yourself." He jabbed the Light-Force hard into her ribs.

Liquid Courage was cranking, due in part to the free publicity it had gained from the wild rumors of a paranormal who had saved a dancer's life, even though no one could confirm or deny the event. They slowly pushed their way through the crowd of parafreaks and Liquid regulars, and Whitehorse became increasingly more agitated.

"How can you work among this waste of humanity?" he whispered into Tamara's ear.

They walked past the main bar toward the entrance to the club. Suddenly, Whitehorse jerked Tamara to a halt. His grip on her arm tightened so much she grimaced from the pain. Whitehorse turned to his silent partner and motioned to the entrance with his head. His partner smiled. Tamara, being a foot shorter than the two Indians, couldn't see what they were looking at.

"This is more perfect than I could have planned," Whitehorse said. He smiled at Tamara. "Your boyfriend is here."

Jonathan stood at the entrance talking to Joshua. The crowd around the bar thinned and left Whitehorse, his partner and Tamara exposed.

Whitehorse pressed the Light-Force even tighter against

Tamara's back. "Let's all smile when Jonathan looks over, shall we?" he announced. His partner laughed a little under his breath.

Jonathan ended his conversation with Joshua and began to walk toward the Den. He took in the circus of Liquid Courage and wondered if he would ever get used to it. He hadn't returned Tamara's net calls, partly because he had been busy preparing to go to Washington and partly because he didn't know what to do next. Jimbo's words kept playing in his head, and strangely, they made sense. But he had never met a girl who affected him like Tamara, and no matter how hard he tried to rationalize it, his heart kept getting in the way.

His eyes swept the club to the main bar where he saw Whitehorse, his partner and Tamara. They were smiling at him in a freakish sort of way. Jonathan froze and locked eyes with Whitehorse. Both of his fists instinctively clenched as he prepared to phase. Whitehorse slowly shook his head and stroked Tamara's hair. Jonathan backed down, and Whitehorse dropped his smile. He noticed that Whitehorse's right hand had never left Tamara's back. He stepped toward them, but Whitehorse jammed the Light-Force against her spine, jerking her forward. She shook her head at Jonathan. He stopped again. A drunken frat kid bumped into him and kept walking.

Whitehorse leaned down to Tamara. "Is there anywhere in this godforsaken place where we can talk privately?"

"Yes," she answered, "but it's back through the Den."

"All right, let's go." Whitehorse motioned for Jonathan to move toward the Den. He moved past, and Whitehorse and Tamara fell in behind him. The silent Indian trailed.

The Den had a long line of marks waiting to get in.

"I'm going to need some incentive to get us back in," Tamara said. "You have any Liquid cash?"

Whitehorse answered by pushing the tip of the Light-Force between two of her ribs. They bypassed the line and confronted the vampiresque doorman.

"Nicki," the doorman sneered. "You're back so soon, but you'll have to wait just like the rest."

Tamara grabbed the vamp's balls through his thin nylon pants and squeezed, her thumb pressing hard against his scrotum.

The doorman jumped and sneered at Tamara. "Ohhh," he moaned. "I didn't know you wanted to play."

Tamara squeezed even harder. "I want into the Den, Kastor, and I want in right fucking now!"

"Well, dear, you'll have to...AUGH!"

Tamara's thumbnail began to draw blood. "If I had wanted to play, Kastor, I would have ripped these off of you."

The door slowly started to open.

"Well *done*, Miss Connor," Whitehorse said, and they entered the Den.

~

Anari was propped on a barstool with an icegel at her head. She saw Tamara first and started to approach, but Tamara stopped her with a raised eyebrow. Whitehorse, Jonathan and the silent Indian filed in close behind. Jonathan glanced over as they walked through the Den; his look said it all.

Anari, streetie that she was, read the moment instantly. She hopped off the stool and headed for the main offices of Liquid Courage.

Tamara led them past the Den's main stage toward the kitchen, but before she reached the back hallway, she stopped at a set of glass doors whose thick curtains deadened the sounds coming from the Den. She swiped her chipcard, and the doors clicked open. They stepped out onto a large balcony 40 stories above the pavement. The wind whipped at their legs.

Whitehorse pushed Tamara into the center of the balcony and followed with the Light-Force still leveled at her. He grabbed her arm and walked her over the edge of the balcony, which was surrounded by a waist-high wall.

"Lovely view," he said, casually tilting his head to see the street below. Tamara betrayed no emotion at all.

Jonathan emerged, a Light-Force trained against his back by Whitehorse's partner.

"Now, Jonathan, before you get any brilliant ideas about being faster than these weapons, let me remind you that the butt of this Light-Force is directly touching your dear girlfriend's back. You might be FTL, but you're not that fast. She'll be biomatter faster that you can create a field flux to stop it. And, by the way, I've already developed a grav field around the two of us."

A huge clay planter in the far corner of the balcony flew at Whitehorse so fast that it hit his grav field in a blur. Tamara ducked involuntarily, but Whitehorse calmly stood his ground, never flinching. It bounced off the grav field and over the edge of the balcony, where it stopped in midair and hung waiting to fall.

"That's the spirit, Jonathan!" Whitehorse laughed. "But we can't forget the innocent people of Chicago. That would cause quite a mess when it impacted the sidewalk."

The huge planter floated back over their heads and settled into its corner across the deck. Whitehorse watched it all the way and then turned his attention back to Jonathan.

"Look, Whitehorse," Jonathan pleaded, "this is between you and me, not her. Let her go, and you can take me wherever you want. You want to go back to New Mexico, fine. Africa? Fine. I don't care. Just let her go!"

"Always the chivalrous one, aren't we, Jonathan? What high drama! No, I think I need to hold on to your pretty little whore here for just a little longer."

Whitehorse stepped around Tamara and raised the Light-Force to the side of her head. He jammed it so hard that Tamara's head was shoved at a right angle. She winced at the pain.

Suddenly the balcony door flew open. Anari charged out with a military issue Walther PPKLF. She hit a combat stance with both hands cupping the Light-Force, its light tip pointed directly at the head of the silent Indian.

He spun around to use Jonathan as a shield. Jonathan felt the Light-Force dig into his back.

"Don't be a hero, Kortel," the Indian whispered and pushed the Light-Force deeper into his kidneys.

"Drop your weapon you motherfucker," Anari screamed at Whitehorse, "or I turn Cochise here into biomatter!"

A deep rumbling drowned out the noise of the city, and the building began to shake. The tower's structural skeleton creaked and cracked as it fought against the earthquake that affected only one square block of Chicago real estate. Everyone on the balcony was thrown about like rag dolls; everyone except Jonathan, who was in phase, floating just slightly off the floor.

He was staring directly at Whitehorse.

Anari hardly lost her balance or her bead on the head of the silent Indian. He stumbled and fell to one side of Jonathan. A bright flash of light caught everyone off guard. The earthquake stopped.

Whitehorse regained his footing and his grip on Tamara as Jonathan touched down into the puddle of biomatter that had been Whitehorse's partner.

Anari shifted her attention and her sights onto Whitehorse. "Drop...your...fucking...gun. Now!" she yelled.

Whitehorse glared fiercely at Anari. His face had the look of death as he trained his hauntingly dark eyes at her.

"I don't think so, bitch," he said viciously.

Anari was lifted off the balcony so fast she didn't have time to discharge her weapon. Her body was a blur as she headed for Wacker Drive. Her scream faded and was replaced by the howl of the wind off of Lake Michigan.

Tamara gasped as she watched her dearest friend thrown to her death like a football. Jonathan tried to grab her as she went over the edge, but he was coming out of phase and didn't have enough reaction speed to match Whitehorse.

"An eye for an eye, eh, Jonathan?" Whitehorse chuckled.

Tamara was sobbing into her hands.

~

James McCarris had a hunch, and like all good Southern boys, he bet on his hunches. And Jimbo was betting that Whitehorse would come after Tamara.

When he pulled to the top level of the parking garage next to the tower where Liquid Courage occupied the 43rd floor, he was hoping that his hunch was wrong. But as he stepped from his car, he heard what seemed to be the screeching of a brake system in need of new synthfluid. It wasn't coming from the street, though. It was coming from above. He looked up the side of the tower and saw the wriggling figure of a small woman hurtling toward the parking garage pavement.

He went into phase.

Pushing his Tel level to its limits, he caught her at the 21st floor and slowed her free-fall to a crawl. She stopped struggling and leaned back in a sitting position for the rest of the way down. She barely bent her knees when she touched the cement.

"Hey, are you all right?" Jimbo asked, running over to where she had landed.

Anari stood in the harsh mercury vapor light, her arms folded tightly across her chest. Her lower jaw jittered in sync with her shaking.

"Hey, hey...it's okay now," he said, consoling the pretty little Asian girl.

She still couldn't reply and shook even more.

"You're safe now. I'm not going to hurt you. Let me introduce myself," he said putting his hand to her shoulder. "My name is James, James McCarris."

Anari instantly stopped shaking and pulled back, pointing at him. "Jimbo!" she exclaimed.

"How the hell do you know that?" he asked, dumfounded.

"Come on," Anari yelled, grabbing his arm. "They're still

up there!"

She jerked him along as they ran toward the parking garage elevators. Jimbo wiped some blood from under his nose and smiled as he ran with her. His hunch had paid off.

~

Jonathan, still coming out of phase, couldn't help Anari as she plunged to her death. He pulled himself away from the scene and faced Whitehorse, who had returned the Light-Force weapon to Tamara's temple. "I'm going to kill you, Whitehorse," he said, wiping the blood from his nose, "if it's the last thing I do on this earth!"

"Well, cowboy, it might be," Whitehorse replied. He mentally lifted Tamara up and over the edge of the balcony, dangling her 430 feet above Chicago.

Drained from the telekinetic earthquake he had induced, Jonathan struggled into phase. He weakly punched at Whitehorse, knocking him slightly to one side. Whitehorse grav fluxed a narrow field directly into Jonathan's chest, slamming him hard against the deck. His blood splattered across his hands as his head impacted the wood surface.

"Don't even *think* about phasing against me," Whitehorse uttered. He let Tamara drop 5 feet.

Tamara jerked to a halt like she had landed on an invisible table; her arms and legs flailed helplessly as her hair blew violently about her face. "OH GOD, JONATHAN," she screamed from her telekinetic purgatory. "PLEASE DON'T LET ME DIE!"

Her tears fell into the abyss.

Jonathan stumbled to the wall and reached desperately for her.

"BABY, I WON'T LET YOU DIE!"

He looked back at Whitehorse, who stood there smiling as his ponytail whipped in the wind. His Light-Force pointed directly at Jonathan.

"Little telekinetic dilemma?" Whitehorse mocked.

Jonathan's attention vacillated between Tamara and Whitehorse, desperately searching for an opportunity to strike.

"I'd say so!" Whitehorse gloated. "Sure, I lowered my grav field to be able to discharge this weapon, but..." He raised his hand and pointed at Tamara. "...I also control the fate of your lovely girlfriend.

"So here's the test, Jonathan. I'm going to fire at you with this Light-Force, a weapon I know you can stop, but I'm also going to release your girlfriend 40 stories to her death. You can't save her and yourself. Once you're in phase for one, you can't prevent the other. Save her and you die, or save yourself, and she dies."

He raised the weapon. "Jonathan...the choice is yours."

Jonathan's vision instantly went to white, but he couldn't distinguish whether the cause was the Light-Force or his own entry into phase.

The nanosecond of flash filled an eternity.

Jonathan's vision returned, pure white giving way to blurry shapes of varying contrasts. The scene on the balcony came back into focus, and he could see the beam from the Light-Force weapon suspended about 10 inches from the muzzle. Whitehorse was frozen in the pose he held before Jonathan had gone into phase. His ponytail was sticking straight out from the side of his head, and his mouth was caught on the last word he had said.

Jonathan slowly turned to look at Tamara. All he could see

was the Chicago skyline.

"NOOOO!!!"

He lunged at the balcony wall and looked down on the fate of his lover. There, five stories below, was Tamara facing down, her arms and legs spread-eagled like a skydiver. She was slowly rising back toward the balcony.

"I can't let a Level 10 lose his girlfriend to a Level 8," Jimbo said. He pulled a toothpick from his mouth. "I would *never* hear the end of it."

"JIMBO!" Jonathan yelled. He turned to find the Tel and Anari walking toward him from the balcony door.

Jimbo pointed to Whitehorse. "Don't forget your flux field, Mr. I'mthemostpowerfulTelever," he said, half grinning. "That Light-Force is still in a state of discharge!"

Jonathan again focused his attention on Whitehorse, who was still suspended in his flux field.

Tamara appeared above the balcony wall and gently settled onto the deck. Too shocked to speak, she rushed toward Jonathan with her arms outspread.

"Easy, chicky" Anari cautioned, "he still has that Indian in...in..."

"...a Level 10 Grav Field Flux Suspension," Jimbo helpfully finished with a smile.

Anari eyed the Southerner and returned his smile.

"Can you hold him much longer?" Jimbo asked.

"Just for a minute or more," Jonathan said. Blood was dripping from his nostrils. "Anari, do you still have that Light-Force?"

"Absofuckinglutely!" She pulled the weapon from the crotch

of her pants.

"Put it on him while I get into position." Jonathan stepped to the side of Whitehorse's hand that held the Light-Force. "Cover your eyes, everyone, this might be bright."

He released Whitehorse. The Light-Force finished its discharge. The beam flashed out over the city and harmlessly dissipated. Jonathan snatched the weapon from Whitehorse's hand and jammed it into his ribs.

"I know *you're* not FTL, Whitehorse..." Jonathan whispered into his ear. "...so don't even *think* of going telekinetic on me."

The sun was beginning to break over Lake Michigan. Whitehorse turned and looked at Jonathan through its rays and, for a second, Jonathan thought that the big Indian from the Southwest was going to give in. Whitehorse's face seemed spotlighted as the sun crept between the buildings.

He smiled evil as his answer. "You don't have the balls, white man."

Jonathan felt a sharp pain drill down into his mind from Whitehorse's telekinetic invasion.

The flash from the Light-Force filled the balcony faster than the sun could rise.

~

Everyone except Jonathan had been caught off guard by the discharge, and they rubbed their eyes in a desperate attempt to soothe their retinas. He surveyed his temporarily blinded friends and lowered the weapon.

"You all okay over there?" he asked.

“Oh yeah, we’ll all being doing great,” Jimbo said, blindly waving in what he thought was Jonathan’s direction, “in about a fricking hour!”

Jonathan didn’t say a word as he reflectively watched a beam of light slowly pass over the puddle of biomatter that, only a moment earlier, had been Jacob Whitehorse.

“Guess I do...” he answered to the puddle, and he raised his face to the morning sun as it crested over the city.

Containment... 29

The elevator was viscid with silence as they rode down to the parking garage floor. Jimbo was conspicuously beside Anari, who, in turn, was leaning on the Southerner for physical, if not mental, support. Jonathan held Tamara and gently kissed the top of her head. She had her eyes closed and was hugging him tightly across his chest.

Tamara's emotions were surprisingly calm, but her mind was racing. In the last week, she had had her child kidnapped, her best friend and herself almost killed, and had been through enough life experiences to fill at least 20 lives.

All because of the man she was now hugging.

She wrestled with the reality that the one she had fallen in love with might be more than she could handle, and Jimbo's comments about the statistical inevitability of their relationship ending because she was not a Tel cut deeply into her heart. All her life, she had never played by the rules. She had always done it her way. *Why should I start now,* she thought. She squeezed him even tighter.

At the 23rd floor the doors slid open, and a cleaning woman began to enter. Stopping, she looked over each one of them, raised her eyebrows and gingerly stepped back out of the elevator. The doors slowly closed.

~

When the elevator finally reached the parking level, they all piled out and began walking toward their cars.

All except Anari. "Ah, I need a ride here."

"Oh, sweetie, I'm so sorry," Tamara said. "Come on, I'll take you home."

"Hey," Jimbo offered, "I can take you home....If that's okay?"

Anari smiled at him.

Jimbo put his arm around her and whispered into her ear, "I have to talk to Jonathan for a second. I'm on the top level. It's a silver MicrosoftFord."

Anari began walking up the ramp to the upper level, then turned back and graced everyone with a shit-eating grin.

"Excuse me, Tamara," Jimbo said in a serious tone that made her uneasy. "I need to talk to Jonathan for a bit."

"It's all right, baby," Jonathan reassured her. "I'll meet you back at the loft." He kissed her on the cheek. She looked over to Jimbo, then back to Jonathan and tilted her head with that "is everything okay?" kind of look. He smiled and gestured toward her car. She turned and slowly walked away, not letting her fingers fall away from his hand until the last second.

Both men watched Tamara get into her car and drive down the ramp. They waited as another car drove past.

"You know, Jonathan, you *crossed* up there," Jimbo said, turning to face him.

Jonathan didn't answer or meet his gaze.

"I guess I won't be needing this any more."

Jimbo handed him the tattered Melville novel. Jonathan pondered the only tangible evidence that he had ever had a father and quietly pocketed the small book. For a moment, both Tels remained silent.

"You know," Jimbo said somberly, "I have a serious containment issue here."

"I know," Jonathan answered, still looking away.

"I'm going to have to bring in a Level 8 to handle all the erasing," Jimbo warned.

"Everyone?" Jonathan asked.

Jimbo flicked his toothpick. "Everyone."

Jonathan finally looked at him. "If you want me to come to the Agency, you don't do Tamara and Nicole."

Jimbo didn't say a word. He just smiled and headed for the upper level ramp.

"Do you understand, me?" Jonathan called out.

"Good night, Jonathan, and get some rest...." Jimbo kept walking. "...You're going to need it."

At peace... 30

Jonathan felt himself falling.

He jerked back from the dream. Opening his eyes, the pitch black of the bedroom was disorienting, and his clothes were drenched in sweat. He rolled over to find empty indentations in the pillows. "Oh no..." he quietly said to himself. "Max, where is Tamara?"

"Miss Connor is on the main balcony, sir."

"Whewww," he whispered, and he looked over to the clock. 11:28 p.m.

~

Jonathan walked down the stairs into the loft's unlit living room and saw Tamara silhouetted through the sheer curtains, which were billowing in the warm night wind. She was leaning on the balcony railing, looking out over the city.

"I don't think I can go out onto another balcony for a long time," he said, smiling at her from the large glass door.

She didn't respond.

"Hey, you, what's the matter?" he asked. He walked up and leaned on the railing next to her.

Tamara still remained silent.

He put his arms around her, and her curly hair flicked at his face. They stood there and listened to the hum of the city.

"Look, baby," he softly began, "I'm sorry. Real sorry. I...I just reacted..."

"...shhh," she said, putting her finger to his lips. "James explained it all to me. Don't worry, I understand. You didn't have any control over the choice. The instinct to save yourself overpowers any other drive. Like James said. You're strong, Jonathan Kortel, but not that strong...*yet*."

"Yeah, but I should have..."

"...saved yourself first, then dealt with me." She stroked the side of his face. "No, it's not that Jonathan....It's just that you've nev..."

Jonathan put his finger to her lips. "...shhh," he said, pulling her tightly into his arms. "I love you so much, Tamara. I...I just had to let go of a lot of things first."

As they kissed, he felt a cold feeling pass over his heart, and he was suddenly gripped by the realization of what this moment might be.

The last thing that she would remember of him.

Tamara pulled back to see her lover's eyes. "You know I can't stay. I've got Nicki tonight."

Jonathan was dying inside. He wanted to tell her...to *warn* her.

It took all of his willpower not to break down and reveal Jimbo's plan. But he didn't. He just nodded and remained silent.

He knew that Jimbo was right.

The beginning... 31

The Blind Monkey was busy for 10:30 in the morning.

Jonathan waited for the next available booth.

Sammy, the morning host, motioned for him to take one of the six-tops by the window. Sliding into the booth, he looked out at the corner where he had first realized what he was. The kit cab test had been ruthless, he thought, but it did set the stage for his true development.

He thought of Zvara.

The girl in the booth in front of him turned around. "Excuse me," she asked, "but can I have your ketchup?"

"Sure..." Jonathan said, not paying attention. He was still preoccupied with thoughts of the senior Tel and all that had happened over the last few weeks.

"Thanks," she said.

The voice was familiar. A tingle shot through Jonathan's

nervous system.

He looked up.

It was Tamara.

Jonathan's heart collapsed with the cold realization that Jimbo had already started. His throat tightened, and tears began to form at the edges of his eyes. Nausea started to build in his stomach, and he clenched his jaw.

He had lost his parents.

He had lost his childhood.

He had lost his humanity.

And now, he had lost his love.

She turned back and looked at him. "Have we met?"

Every nerve cell and every ounce of his strength strained against his desire to tell her what they had had. What they had shared. What they had been.

"No..." he barely uttered.

She smiled, and her eyes disappeared into little slits. His mind instantly went back to the club. To the Den. To the first time he had seen her smile.

"Funny, you seem so familiar. Well, thanks." She turned her back to him.

A small tear rolled down Jonathan's cheek as a small head rose from behind the edge of Tamara's booth. Little Nicole looked at him and giggled.

Jonathan wanted to tear his heart from his chest, and at his level, he could have easily done it. He ran from the booth, out of the Blind Monkey and onto the busy sidewalk. His mind, his body and his soul ached beyond his capacity to control. He wanted to vomit.

Wildly looking about, he focused his rage on a netphone booth, which instantly exploded. People screamed and scattered around him as plexiglass and metal rained on the crowded sidewalk. He turned his attention to a biomeal cart, and it blew up, sending plastic, condiments and biopaste spattering violently against storefronts and cars.

He was consumed by his loss.

Jonathan ran down the sidewalk, tears and mucus dripping from his face. Everything in his wake either shattered or exploded. His heart pounded erratically his chest.

In his anguish, Jonathan turned into an alley, leaving the crowded sidewalk in chaos from his telekinetic rage. He pushed and kicked at piles of trash, almost slipping on an bright yellow rain slicker that had spilled from a large wet box. Suddenly in the corner of the alley, a translucent image appeared. It floated eerily between an old rusted recycle can and a broken TVid screen.

Jonathan froze in midstep.

It was another memory fragment of his parents. They were standing in their Hawaiian backyard, the beach and ocean visible through the palm trees. They faced forward as if they were looking directly at him. His father was dressed in his favorite Hawaiian shirt, and his mother had on her lab coat and the belt that she loved so much.

Startled, Jonathan gasped and fell back into the wet box of old clothes. He watched his mother, with his father's arm around her, blow him a kiss. He buried his head in his hands and began to sob. Then the image shifted. His mother was saying something to him.

"We love you," she silently mouthed.

A gentle rain began to fall.

Jonathan looked up and let the cool drops hit his face. *My life is just beginning,* he thought.

But as the world's most powerful telekinetic leaned forward and looked back at his parents and the past with which he had finally made peace, a strange calm fell over him.

He thought of his future.

Jonathan Kortel had finally crossed. And he wasn't afraid anymore of his destiny.

THE END

ABOUT THE AUTHOR

Born and raised outside of Chicago, Illinois, this is Mr. Black's first work of science fiction. Today, he lives and works in Dallas, Texas, where he manages his own graphic design firm. He is currently working on the next book in the *The Tel* series.